Death-Touched

MORE BY RHIANNON HELD

THE SILVER SERIES
Silver
Tarnished
Reflected
Wolfsbane

STAND ALONE
Hound and Key
Mirror Bound

Death-Touched

Rhiannon Held

To Corry, Erin, Shanna, and Susan
Who haven't had a dedication yet, and
whose unwavering support deserves it.
Even if we don't have a name.

1

It was a beautiful room for a wedding, Silver decided, even if that wedding had been intended merely as a platform for diplomacy. With that diplomacy refused, that platform empty, the event still lurched onward with its original unwieldy proportions. But with nothing else for it, should she not focus on the beauty of it? For a heartbeat or two, she let her perceptions slip away from what she'd taught herself to see of the world of her mate and her pack. What she saw was not real—or it was not what others had decided together was real—but sunlight stars glittered from every high tree branch around them and showered her with sparkled kisses of fractured colors.

Then she concentrated again. No trees, no ancient grove. A room, filled with hundreds of Were; but the sunlight stars, those remained, albeit as light thrown by small hanging stones. Susan and Silver's soon-to-be stepdaughter, Felicia, had done a wonderful job of decorating. Seven days ago, the Russian alpha had announced he would not be sending his promised envoys to the event specifically planned as an excuse to host them. A week was a nicely calculated period long enough to allow them the illusion of a choice to cancel—if they did not mind seeming to run their hunt based on his howls, in front of their entire pack. So they'd gone forward, but to put the original effort into the details of it, decorations and food, that had been Susan's and Felicia's choice.

Death, slumped with his muzzle on his paws beside her, seemed even darker in protest of the light, blackness vibrating with its intensity in the canine silhouette at the corner of her eye. "So sweet and perfect. Like one of the humans' children's stories." Death used his favorite voice and gave it a mocking note. Silver ignored him. If he was truly uncomfortable, he'd leave.

Her mate, Dare, approached, smiling thinly at her. His wild self paced at his side, steely gray head a little bowed with the weight of their responsibility, their shared worries. It was an advantage Silver had, she supposed, to see wild selves and tame at the same time, and so read moods on the self others could not see. It often balanced poorly against all the other things of her mate's world she could not see, however.

"I'm beginning to wonder if perhaps we should find some excuse to keep everyone here after the usual wedding feasts," Dare said. "Since Russia won't talk, to give us the chance to convince him we have less than no interest in using you as a religious symbol to threaten his borders, he'll be trying something else soon enough."

Silver looked out over the sea of Were from every one of their subpacks and matched the frustrated quality of his smile. "It's a nice idea in theory—" And it was, practically all of their

pack pulled into the safety of numbers, and all those staying behind on alert. But everyone had lives of their own, put on hold
to travel here from their homes across the far-flung Roanoke
pack territory. "But think of the mediation we'd need to do, giv-
en the additional time spent stepping on each other's tails."

Dare snorted and smoothed fingers through his hair. "Too
true. If only Tatiana's sources could tell us something more
about what her former alpha's next move will be."

He'd spoiled the crisp line of the white streak in the dark
at his temple, and Silver reached up to fix it to match the one
on the other side. Their Russian—hostage? defector? somewhere between—had given them much more than they could
have hoped for in terms of background knowledge of Russia's
strength, but information on future plans was obviously much
harder to come by. "If only we knew the right bait to dangle to
prompt it, so it would be in the open and we could simply *deal*
with it. This guessing and prediction is exhausting."

He kissed her forehead, leaned back with a frown in his
eyes. "Silver, I do want you to enjoy your own wedding at least
a little—"

"Only if you promise to as well. Shall we make a pact not
to think on Russia until tomorrow morning?" Neither of them
would keep to it, but they could pretend. She kissed him on
the lips, just a peck. Anything else was for later. "I have a pretty
dress…" She dropped his hand so her good hand would be free
to smooth the skirt. They'd even given her a pocket on one side
to slip her bad hand into. "And they put stars in here." She gestured up and around the room.

"That they did." Dare lowered his head to nip at the side
of her neck, and then tensed in response to whatever he'd seen
over her shoulder. "What—?"

A group of voices rumbled up and then spilled over by the front entrance, and people drifted closer in curiosity. Death's ears pricked up. "Finally." Silver had no doubt Death had been longing for any sort of mischief all day, but she couldn't read from his pleased anticipation if this was likely to be something more serious.

Her cousin's voice lifted above the rest, and Silver frowned. She'd have expected that, as her beta, John would be the one to defuse disagreement, not create it, but his voice was clearly angry. "Now? Now you show up, Hugh? Where were you six years ago?"

"That's none of your business." A male stranger's voice, more calm, but no softer. "The Roanokes may throw me out as they wish, but you have no right to deny me entry."

Silver slipped her hand into the crook of Dare's arm, to ground herself. She needed all her powers of concentration now. She *knew* that voice. Who was it? Dare frowned at her, and she spread her hand wide, still on his arm. "Wait. I…"

"'Who?' is not the question to ask," Death said. "You know who. The question is, how do you feel about him?" For a moment, his borrowed voice held the weight of all the years that Were must have been dead. Death had no voice of his own, had to use instead those of Were already gone.

And Silver did know who. She stumbled a step when she started moving because she caught Dare off-guard and he dragged her back at first. She didn't need the man's scent to verify what she knew, not really, but she kept the word in her voice locked away until she'd drawn close enough to smell him anyway.

A name had power, his name in her voice especially so. "Father?"

Those who had gathered moved aside, except for her cousin, who hovered, protective. And Dare, who kept his arm very steady, as if he expected her to cling. She wished she knew if she wanted to cling. Death had been right—as he almost always was, insufferable cat—she didn't know how she felt.

Her father didn't move. "Silver." He sounded so collected. Silver wished he'd *do* something, so she could react. He looked like she remembered, and not. She'd been so young when he left to wander onward. She'd seen him last with a child's eyes, even had there not been a bloody swath of memories she had locked away between then and now. In those memories, a monster had killed her brother and her pack, had poisoned her blood so she could not see the world properly, could not use her arm. The monster was dead, but the memories could still pull her into madness.

Her memories of her father were clean, if ephemeral, but nothing could be untainted by how she'd changed after the monster.

She remembered him as big, and reassuring. He was of a height with her cousin, now, a little shorter than her mate, and to adult eyes he did seem centered. But centered with his weight forward, ready to move. Always a wanderer, as some Were were.

"He couldn't be bothered to show up when his own son died," John snapped, crossing over to Dare. Silver supposed he assumed she was too emotionally tangled up to be counted on to throw her own father out. "There's being a wanderer, and there's being a cat's bastard."

"And I'm here to speak to my own daughter now, if you'd stop getting in my way, *Nephew*." Despite the heavy, almost insulting, emphasis, her father's wild self stood quietly, no snarl, no lowered ears, no raised hackles.

It hit Silver like a blow to her voice: her wild self was dead, she couldn't remember what it had looked like, but would it not have had something of the wild selves of her parents? Her mother was dead as well, but her father's wild self was right here for her to see. Its mostly gray fur whitened outward from a center bar of dusty brown that crowned its spine and striped down the top of its muzzle. Had Silver's wild self looked anything like that?

But the death of her wild self was buried deep in the center of all the things she could by no account allow herself to remember, or risk losing herself completely. Silver whined softly without meaning to. Death snorted. "Is he even worth this much trouble?"

Her father's head dropped. "I didn't come to upset anyone." He turned away.

"Wait." Silver's mind tried to follow other useless trails—his blue eyes, strong line to his jaw, were those anything like her brother's had once been?—but she focused on his words here and now, and things snapped into focus. "You used the right name." Usually, those who'd known her before tried to use the name that belonged to the woman she was no longer, and that hurt. But her father...hadn't. He was trying, at least, and if he was trying, he deserved to stay.

She pulled away from Dare, and her father turned back. She got as far as standing before him when she ran out of reaction and fell back into confusion again. He looked her over, and even though his eyes crinkled with concern over what he found, she let him. It was only fair given how she must have been staring at him a few moments ago. He reached out and smoothed a lock of her white hair off her shoulder.

"If you say she looks like her mother, I think your nephew

is going to call you a liar," Dare said, dry. The humor held a note of calculation, to Silver's ears, but most around them laughed, and relaxed a little. John still frowned, but her father smiled and it lit up his face.

"She looks like herself," he said, and embraced her. Silver brought her good arm up a beat later. She'd had two arms when she'd hugged him last, though she was not entirely sure she remembered the action, only the comfort. "And a little tiny bit like the cute five-year-old I last saw for any length of time. You've grown up beautiful, puppy."

He tipped his head close to her ear, barely breathing the words to keep them between the pair of them, with so many werewolf ears pricked around them. "And Lady, I wish I could have come here only to tell you that. But there's something I have to talk to you about as soon as possible, privately. If privacy is remotely possible around here."

Silver pulled back to search her father's face properly. Whatever it was, she doubted she would like it. Perhaps it was something to do with a half-sibling of hers. She'd always wondered if she had one. She murmured a low syllable of acknowledgment, thoughts already ranging away. How was privacy to be procured?

Where the food was being prepared, perhaps. That was a room of its own, with fewer eyes to watch and note a conference taking place. Silver dispatched her cousin to a resumption of the beta's duties with a tip of her chin, took a grip on her mate's arm once more, and directed their steps toward that room. He followed her lead without a need for her to voice her thoughts, and her father drifted in their wake.

They could hardly move very quickly without drawing attention, however. And contradicting his stated urgency, her father paused to search the crowd with his gaze. "Will you introduce me to your human? I've heard a lot about her." If she was the one he searched for, Silver was unsurprised his gaze had not alighted yet. Susan was the only human within a room packed full of Were, but all those scents were far too tangled to pick hers out. He would have done better to search for John, as he had fetched up by his wife after leaving their group at the door.

"She's not ours." Silver said it automatically, then smoothed away her frown. Of course everyone knew about the Roanokes' human. She and Dare had known that for years now, but it wasn't often that an outsider was around to remind her of that fact. She traded a look with Dare, and he seemed more resigned than she felt.

"Some might call her your responsibility," Death said. He used the voice of the Were man Susan had killed defending them both. Defending *Silver*, especially. He kept pace with her as they joined Susan, in the same way her father's wild self trotted at his heels. Though in truth, Death never walked behind her. His stride barely admitted to "with" her. "You invited her into the Were world."

And Susan had chosen to set her feet to that path, eyes open. The three of them caught up with her where she was leaning over the laid-out food, automatically straightening, banishing disorganization. She looked beautiful today herself, for all that she'd dressed to deflect attention as she organized. She seemed to find such satisfaction in that role. Her dress flattered and balanced her hips, and her short brown hair seemed to stay right where she'd told it to, soft around her face.

Silver touched Susan's shoulder and nodded to her father. Susan didn't wait for any introductions. "So you're Silver's father. Hugh, my husband said?" She tipped a nod to John, hovering nearby, then offered her hand to shake, a gesture both

Were and humans used here, but Silver could see from her father's surprised reaction that she calculated the pressure to Were standards. She smelled slightly hostile for some reason.

"And you're Susan." Silver's father smiled, pleasant enough. "You're not what I expected."

Susan lifted her eyebrows at him, and brushed her gaze past his, purposely threatening the measuring of dominance that full eye contact held. Silver hid a smile. She enjoyed seeing Susan put people in their places. "You're not either. You don't look at all like the kind of man who abandons his children."

Death laughed, and Silver was silent for a beat, shocked. That wasn't a repetition of John's sentiments; it sounded like an opinion of Susan's own. She took a firm grip on Susan's arm. "He didn't abandon us."

John stepped up to press himself against his wife's back, so Silver moved to give him room. The movement took her closer to her father, and she smelled that his patience with the hostility was wearing thin. She searched for the right words to explain to Susan. "Parents are not necessarily mates. My mother always knew my father was a wanderer."

"So he just gets a pass?" Susan twisted to look at her husband's face, and frowned when she found embarrassment there. "Even when Silver's mother died and he didn't come back?"

Rather than answer, Silver's father looked straight at John, who coughed. "Some Were *are* wanderers. He called, when my aunt died. To make sure the pack was going to take care of Silver and her brother properly. But that's not the point." His words grew faster as he tried to cram in his justification. "The point is that he didn't call, or show up, or even appear to notice when his only son—"

Silver's father made a violent slashing gesture, cutting John off, scent muddying with layers of anger and guilt. "Mistakes in the past cannot be undone. I can't go back and do something different now."

"We are all shaped by our pasts," Silver said quellingly. She didn't know her side in this matter, but she did know she no longer wanted to discuss it at the present time. She focused her attention on her father. He was the author of this distraction in the first place, haring off after Susan. "You wanted to speak to us?"

"Yes, of course," he murmured and dropped his head.

"See how well he listens to his alpha," Death murmured in the same cadence, though he would never bow his head so to anyone. Roamers were not technically under Roanoke authority, except when they chose to attend an event such as this. So she was his alpha, for the space of a few hours. Silver's balance moved under her feet—was this how Dare felt, outranking his parents? The sensation must grow more bearable with familiarity. To outrun it for the moment, she strode away from mate and parent both. She reached the small room for the food far enough ahead for a breath or two of private space before they joined her.

A couple young Were looked up from among the odds and ends of food left from portioning out what had been prepared beforehand, and the greater quantities stockpiled against later need. No great scent from anything heating just at the moment. The young people took the hint from her frown, a jerk of Dare's head, and made themselves scarce.

Dare set his shoulder against the doorway, making his wish for this business to be conducted quickly clear enough. The rest of his manner remained polite, however. "What is it you wished to tell us?"

Silver's father took her hands, bad and good, though she would rather not have allowed him the former. He had to feel the way the weight hung from his grip, but he didn't comment. "I don't want to cry hunter of the wind, but everyone has heard about how Russia came sniffing around, how you had to take one of his spies hostage. I know a couple of Alaskans who came down for the wedding. We're…drinking buddies, I suppose you could say. They're in human more than some, to fish during the season and earn money to help keep the pack going. Then one day they're all laughing it up because this new Russian friend of theirs promised to pay them handsomely for information on the wedding they were going to…and on the Roanokes' human. Because he's planning a prank on the uptight Roanoke pack Were: grab her and hilarity ensues."

"Cat's bastards," Dare muttered under his breath. He jerked immediately for the main room, but Silver freed her good hand and moved to stop him. They'd left Susan standing right next to her husband, and there might still be more to hear from her father. The movement alone was enough to forestall Dare, leaving Silver with her bad hand still in her father's clasp. "What did they think the Russian was going to do after he had her?" Dare asked. "Thank her for her time and let her go?"

Her father's lips thinned. "I don't know. I wasn't invited to meet the guy, though I tried. They didn't want me offering some choice tidbit and making them split the payout. I couldn't get any more details. I judged it better to imply it was a Russian prank on *them*, rather than pushing for anything more."

"Well, we said we wanted to know Russia's next move. I know Tatiana heard something at first about Silver being a target, maybe it was a garbled version of this. It certainly makes much more sense than expecting that an alpha would ever be undefended to that degree." Dare glowered into middle distance. "Of course, given the fact that Russians involved the Alaskans, this could also be a feint, meant to get back to us and keep us focused on the wrong direction." A growl slipped free. "Lady."

"I doubt Russia knows who my father is, much less who his buddies are, to predict the information following any such path to us," Silver said. The Alaska pack attracted stubbornly independent Were who thought sheer contrariness was a virtue, and most of them hardly spent more than a few days at the full in human. They'd hardly be chatting with anyone in the Roanoke pack, in normal circumstances.

Still, Silver watched Death covertly, to see his opinion on matters. He sat tall, clearly much better pleased than before her father had arrived, nose to the scent of trouble. Catching her at the examination, he eased down, mocking her with his relaxation.

Frustrated, Silver retrieved her bad hand from her father and settled it in its pocket again. "I also trust our people sufficiently that if we say, protect Susan in particular, I'd believe them capable of not removing their attention from all other threats. We'll have to ask Susan to stay inside, but she has so much to organize, I don't think she'd have wanted to leave anyway."

"Fair enough. I'll make sure we have a designated guard for each entrance..." Dare's planning trailed internal, then he shook himself out of it, tossed her a smile of fellow feeling for her frustration, and hurried off.

Silver wasted a few moments mapping possibilities to find something *she* could do to help Susan, but came up dry. Hovering over her friend would hardly be useful, however satisfying.

She supposed instead she should follow her promise and pretend once more this was a wedding for her and her mate, not for politics. She tipped her head for her father to follow her in Dare's wake. "Come, I'll do proper introductions for you."

Back amongst the crowd, Portland was the first to approach, not bothering to hide her curiosity. The lush black waves of her hair were fastened back today, keeping them out of the way of the sturdy baby wrapped and dozing peacefully against her front. His shock of similarly dark hair stood up mostly in one big tuft. Everyone loved babies, and his mother loved indulging their attention.

"Father, this is Portland. One of our sub-alphas. And..." The name came more easily to Silver than usual, as she remembered the tininess of his yawn and spread fingers when first she met him. "Nicholas."

Silver's father beamed and stepped over to hold up his hand in silent request. Portland nodded, and he petted Nicholas's hair. It fluffed back up the moment he took his fingers away. "Hugh." His smile spread wider into a full grin. "Can't wait to see a grandbaby of my own."

Silver thought of wincing, but a laugh bubbled up instead. With all the wandering and dead brothers and sons between them, to be awkward over something so normal, like any Were parent and child, was somehow reassuring. Yes, it was the poison that had made her infertile, but she had a daughter in all the ways that mattered. "I'll introduce you to Felicia, then." Dare's daughter had been making such strides in maturity of late, proto-adulthood helping her shed the tangled weight of anger and resentment Dare's in-laws had raised her with, keeping her from him for most of her childhood. Silver rather suspected she could empathize about fraught paternal relationships.

"Silver..." Her father ran fingers roughly through his hair, let his hands fall awkwardly to his sides for lack of anything else to do with them. "I'm keenly aware of my absence from your life, don't feel you have to waste any more time at your own wedding on me." He slowed his steps, and Silver slowed to a stop with him rather than widen the distance as he seemed to think he deserved.

"What else would I be doing with my time? Dwelling on worry about the Russians?" Or holding alpha audiences. Silver looked out at the sea of pack members she shared with Dare, purposely didn't let her gaze alight because she'd remember that problem or this, central in the life of each Were. A word of encouragement she'd meant to gift, a frown of censure she'd meant to inflict. Never enough time in the day for all of that, and she'd promised Dare to enjoy this day in whatever small ways they could find. Pretty dress, remembered childhood love. "Better to catch up with my father while I worry."

"I know it's hypocritical of me to ask, seeing as I added to it, but of all the days, isn't your wedding the one where you are *required* to set aside that kind of worry?" Her father's spark of humor was returning, never deeply buried. She could see how that was a fundamental part of him: roam onward, and let problems fall out as they would, to be dealt with in the moment, not before.

It was not how one held an alphaship, sadly. "Someone must. I won't leave it all for Dare."

"If your pack has any sense at all, someone—dare I hope my nephew, as beta, perhaps?—will talk him out of it too. Let it rest on the numerous shoulders below. That's the exchange of rank, after all, protection for protection." Her father petted her hair aside so he could set a strong hand against her upper back without it slipping. He dropped it to the small, finding a touch to quiet the awkwardness of his hands finally.

"Though they also expect a roaring party every so often," Silver muttered, offering him a smile though she rather thought she'd fallen a little short of the lightness of his humor with hers. "What else is an alpha's wedding good for? Much less a wedding of *two* alphas."

Her father's brows rose. She'd definitely missed the mark on humor, then. Damn. "Didn't you want to get married? Is that a political calculation too? I'm not the one to sing its praises, I know, but from all I hear, it's a fairly enjoyable state."

Death laughed, where he'd settled himself near her feet, different location, same watchful patience. The sound needed no words to accompany it: the roamer, holding forth on matrimony, indeed.

"I love my mate; never doubt it." Silver sought him in the crowd, couldn't find him just at the moment, but felt as if her voice resonated with his proximity all the same. "I did want this—do want this—but the more we planned, the more I wondered. We have been mates for many years now. A wedding doesn't make that more true."

Death's swift rise to his feet jerked her attention to him. He drew all darkness into his black to reflect it back in a seriousness that told her his words were no mere mockery now, but worth truly hearing. "If you feel a thing inside yourself, does voicing it in a vow or prayer make it more true?"

Of course it did. A voice was one's *substance*, created by the Lady Herself. To feel a thing was not necessarily ephemeral but certainly diffuse. To voice it—

Silver closed her eyes for a moment. "Yes. I want this. He knows my love, I know his, but it should be *voiced*, in the Lady's sight." When she opened them again, her father looked bemused, as she supposed well he might, having stood by while she and Death worked things out between themselves. "Come. Enough talk of Russians—and indeed, Lady's vows. Come meet Dare's daughter."

"Yes, hurry up, meet everyone, then get the ceremony over with." Death paced away, leading them both. "Your daylight stars await." Exasperation colored his tone, but shadows fled from his every step, until none remained in the entire room.

Silver let happiness fill her up until she could not help but smile, and pretended not to notice his wedding gift.

2

In hindsight, it seemed so obvious to Andrew. Susan was possibly the most vulnerable person in their pack—not because of her comparative physical weakness, as that was a factor for others as well. No, she was vulnerable because she was a pack member at an intellectual level, not a voice-tied instinctive one, and thus not watched out for with those same instincts.

He caught up to her apportioning serving spoons at the buffet table. She took one look at this face and tucked her extras out of the way at the back of the table and squared her shoulders, as if ready to wade straight from catering logistics into a fist fight. "What's the crisis? Is Silver doing okay, dealing with her father? Anything I can do?"

Andrew couldn't help it, he had to hug her, a quick squeeze before he stepped back. He didn't care if those who didn't know her well didn't have the instincts, they'd damn well do it consciously because their alpha ordered them to. "Hugh brought word that the Russians have been asking around about you, and might try to kidnap you."

"Oh, we're doing a reprise of the 'this human is the weak link in the chain' number with the latest pack, are we?" Susan bared her teeth, one of several gestures she'd picked up from the Were. "And in here, no less." She spread her hands wide. "When I am *embedded* in Were. Come the fuck on. Well, let them try."

Andrew dropped his chin in a nod of respect for her bravery. "Just make sure you stay embedded. Silver didn't think you'd mind, but still, I apologize if it gets inconvenient. I'll be posting plenty of guards at the exits here."

Susan retrieved her spoons. "I'll be careful. I will need to go into work on Monday, but we can cross that bridge when we come to it." Her lips thinned suddenly and Andrew was close enough to catch the first flicker of fear in her scent. "I assume you'll be talking to John next—would you tell him I'll leave Edmond to him? I assume Russians have the same children-are-sacred thing the rest of you have—"

She paused, but Andrew had to grapple with the question in silence for a beat. Of course—even humans wouldn't—but of course they *would*, he vaguely paid attention to the news like any Were—and then Susan must have read his silence for her answer, because she was continuing. "But I wouldn't want him around me if something does go down. To get caught in the crossfire, as it were."

"We will all watch out for your son, if you'll feel better not having him with you." Andrew emphasized his reassurance with a firm squeeze of Susan's shoulder. And Lady grant that he and Silver could settle the Russian problem once and for all, soon, so Susan would never again feel she needed to make that kind of calculation.

Susan nodded, then frowned and strode onward to her next task. Andrew did the same, in another direction. As Andrew wove through the crowd, dropping words in a few key ears to make sure the message to watch out spread widely, designating guards and their responsibilities, he had to admit Silver had been right. He didn't *like* the logistical nightmare of it, but in another way, it was a *relief.* It was something to do.

When he caught himself tempted to walk another circuit of the exits, checking on the guards he'd put in place barely ten minutes before, he forced himself to slow and then stop, washing up at the edge of the crowd. There were still all the other parts of this wedding to get through, all with an alpha's poise, so that if this was a feint, Russia wouldn't have won by nudging the alphas into visible panic in front of their pack. Better to take a few moments, gazing out into the hall, and make sure his calm was in place.

It might seem strange to rent a space from a national park, bastion of the government that would be determined to radio-collar each of them in wolf, the better to eventually shoot them if any livestock was killed. But the building was huge and versatile, not only fit for fundraising banquets as well as public education days, but set among deep trees. Their green beyond the banks of windows was abstract, but their scent was not, stealing in through the doors propped open for airflow and easily beating out the minimal metal and finished wood of the building's walls to cup all the Were in at least a little wild.

On top of that, the crystals strung in the windows were inspired. They snagged the summer sunlight and set it dancing in rainbows on the floor of the hall. And there was Silver, squired by her father, catching a few rainbows of her own as she stepped lightly among the crowd. Andrew let the Russians recede for a few moments as he focused all of his attention on Silver, as she deserved. She was so beautiful today, fine white hair almost floating off her shoulders and shimmering in the light, and the dark blue flowing fabric of her dress clinging to bust and waist and then swirling down from hips to knees. Even her dead arm, where she'd been injected with silver nitrate, looked just fine, tucked into her pocket.

Churning in the crowd across the room caught his attention, and he was already halfway over before he parsed the raised voices enough to recognize them. Laurence, one of the sub-alphas, and one of his pack members from the Richmond pack, Bryce. "Look, we all got our orders from Roanoke Dare already, there's no need for you to interfere," the latter was saying as Andrew reached the edge of the clear space around the two formed when everyone drew back.

"I am not interfering, I am making sure I know enough specifics about what he told you to make sure I *don't* interfere." Laurence was so busy getting in Bryce's face, he didn't seem to notice Andrew or indeed any of his audience. "Outside. You and I need to talk about this." He shoved Bryce toward the nearest side door—the one Andrew had directed him to guard, in fact.

Andrew followed on their heels, catching the door before it could swing shut. Laurence didn't appear to notice him now either as he followed Bryce off the large, concrete step to the sweep of the gravel path leading up to it. Andrew eased the door shut so it didn't slam behind him, and watched them from the slight rise of the step. He'd let this play out a little longer, see how Laurence would deal with this sort of problem.

Laurence was a slight man, so when he stepped into Bryce again, Bryce loomed over him, crossed arms emphasizing the width of his shoulders. Andrew was leaner than most Were men himself, but at least he had the height to balance it. Laurence always seemed braced for bullying about his size that rarely materialized.

"Orders from the Roanoke don't mean you don't have to show me basic respect," Laurence snapped. "What's your problem?"

"You're the one who's always snarling over nothing." Bryce looked away pointedly, but didn't relax his arms. "Say what you want about Rory, at least he had basic *confidence*."

Now Laurence really did snarl. "How dare you throw that name in my face! He was not worthy to be alpha." He neatly swept Bryce's legs, and Bryce, clearly braced instead for a punch, slammed into the ground on his ass. "You will give me the respect I'm due!"

Andrew crossed his own arms and didn't interfere. Whatever Laurence might have done to raise Bryce's hackles, taunting him with Rory wasn't just disrespectful, it was cruel. When Rory had been Roanoke, before Andrew and Silver had deposed him, Laurence had been his beta and taken far more than his fair share of abuse. Laurence knew intimately what an abysmal alpha Rory had been.

Bryce held up his hands in mocking surrender. "It would be a whole lot easier to give it to you if you didn't flinch from a *name*. What are you afraid of, that Rory's going to be hiding in your closet to jump out at you?"

That was the moment when things turned. Or maybe it wasn't, and Andrew had simply missed the signs in Laurence some moment since they'd stepped outside. But now Laurence snapped Bryce's head back with a kick under his chin. And then Bryce was supine and Laurence, panting with rage, leaned down to him, jerked him onto his side by his shoulder, so he could kick again and again—nose, jaw, belly, groin. So fast. Bryce curled up as best he could, but couldn't protect himself. By the time the second kick landed, Andrew had shaken off his shock and was moving, but Laurence dodged and got in half a dozen more before Andrew got him in a tight enough headlock he had to stop.

"No," Andrew growled at Laurence with all the strength of his own rage life had taught him to keep in check. Up close, Laurence stank—not of rage of his own, but of fear, a raging subterranean torrent of it that drove the gears of apparent anger up above that ground him to pieces between them. "You do not *hurt* any member of your pack in this way, Richmond."

The fight drained out of Laurence's body, leaving him sagging against Andrew as he babbled apologies. "I'm sorry—I didn't mean—I went too far—"

Andrew let him go, but held himself ready, lest Laurence try to get in another few blows. Laurence flinched from him instead, cringing as if certain he was now due for far worse than he'd just dealt. It sickened Andrew to see it, and realize how deep-seated the source of that flinch must be.

But he had to deal with the visible wounds first. Andrew knelt beside Bryce, checking him from top to bottom, wiping away the blood from his broken nose and split lip—though those had already healed—to see if anything was too serious for normal werewolf healing to take care of in a few minutes. His nose would have to be reset, and Andrew suspected a couple broken ribs. Bryce's breathing was ragged with the pain, but he remained otherwise silent through the process.

Andrew looked up to Laurence when he was done, and

Laurence cringed anew. "You're stepping down. Silver and I won't have sub-alphas who act like that. I'll inform your beta." He made the words firm, not angry, but there was no softening the impact of their content.

Laurence's eyes widened. "No—please! You're proving them right—I'll be better, I promise. I will never hurt one of my pack members again—"

"For Lady's sake, this isn't about your pride, Laurence," Andrew snapped. "It's about what's best for your people." And for Laurence himself as well, he was beginning to suspect. Andrew should have noticed how insecure Laurence was in his power *long* before it got to his point. "A sub-alpha needs to display good judgment about when violence is necessary."

"I told you I smelled blood. And you said the wedding would be boring!" Two young men had come around on an informal dirt trail that looped around the back side of the building, and had paused to spectate and comment amongst themselves. Kneeling next to fresh blood, Andrew had smelled no hint of their approach.

When they noticed Andrew's attention jerk to them, they dipped into something approximating respectful bows. The Alaskans, Hugh's drinking buddies, he supposed. He vaguely recognized their faces from the last time he'd visited Alaska, but their names escaped him. He presumed they'd arrived at the same time as Hugh, but had decided to run around in the trees until the very last minute. So much the better, if they were the type to laugh over "prank" kidnappings and find violence spiced up boring events.

"Go away," Andrew growled, and the Alaskans went, disappearing back along the dirt trail the way they'd come. At least they had that much sense. He returned his attention to Bryce. "All right, let's get you cleaned up." The man groaned softly, but made it to his feet with Andrew's boost.

"Roanoke Dare—" Laurence started, but he was interrupted by the crunch of car tires on gravel up the access road from the main parking lot at the front.

Andrew judged Bryce wouldn't fall, so he separated himself from the man, braced to meet violence if necessary. He knew of no one from Roanoke who hadn't yet arrived, so if this was one of the Russians—but the young woman had her windows down, taking advantage of the nice weather, and a breeze delivered him her human scent.

And that was an entirely different problem. Bryce was covered in blood from no clear source, difficult to pass off as originating from a nosebleed when he had toe-prints down his shirt. They didn't need anyone helpfully calling the police to investigate an assault. "Deal with her," he told Laurence, for lack of anyone else handy, and grabbed Bryce's arm again to turn them toward the building, away from the car. Bryce walked without wincing, with Andrew's support under his elbow, so the ribs were probably healed and he was working on bruises.

Behind them, the car's engine turned off and the door opened, but the woman didn't exclaim, so he must have turned Bryce in time. "Hey, I'm with the catering company. Can I park back here, do you know?" she asked.

They'd already explained to the catering company once a few hours ago that they didn't want any servers, that had been a mistake, but apparently this particular one hadn't been notified. An easy enough miscommunication for Laurence to explain, so Andrew left him to it.

Andrew opened the door then caught it with his toe to shove it the rest of the way, emphatic enough to jar the attached doorstop down to leave his hands free. Silence spread outward before them, one invisible quality undoubtedly following on the heels of another, the smell of the blood. A new split-second decision: announce Laurence's disgrace widely, or let it spread unofficially on the wings of gossip to give him the option of changing his mind in an official statement later? Framed that way, the answer was obvious, since the latter would give him the chance to both discuss with Silver and sound Laurence out with her, to see if there was any chance of addressing his problem with something less than a permanent demotion.

After guiding Bryce to the side, out of line of sight through the door, Andrew searched out Silver, and gave her a grimace to let her know she didn't need to hurry over. She returned a look of mingled exasperation and worry, which he suspected meant that she'd heard an account of the first part of the incident already and added that to Bryce's visible state now to draw her own conclusions.

John arrived first, Edmond against his hip, Laurence's beta—former beta—not far behind. With her golden tan, she always put him in mind of a lion more than anything canine. The few times he'd spoken to her, she'd always seemed grounded, which was what he needed. He kept his voice low so as not to carry outside to human ears. "John, I'm going to go make sure Laurence got rid of the human. Help Richmond get Bryce cleaned up, would you?"

He tried to pass Bryce off to Richmond, though he'd now recovered sufficiently that he gathered himself with injured dignity between the two of them, and brushed off her touch.

For her part, Richmond stared at Andrew, her whole face a silent question. Bryce muttered something under his breath, probably an obscenity in reference to Laurence, and Andrew made sure not to hear it properly.

"For now. Give it at least until tomorrow, then we'll let you know our final decision," he told Richmond. And everyone else politely not watching in the crowd filling the hall. At least he and Silver had a day's grace—everyone understood that the Roanokes' time alone tonight was to be protected. The wedding feasts—well, meals in this century—would continue for another several days, so the couple deserved at least one night alone.

Richmond nodded, body language firming up, and she set a guiding hand against Bryce's back to urge him toward the kitchen. "I told you to stop fucking needling him," she growled low to him, clearly not meant to be overheard as Andrew's words had been, but carrying in the packed space all the same.

Which only verified what Andrew had observed. Bryce should have been respectful, Laurence shouldn't have overreacted so badly to the disrespect, and Andrew and Silver shouldn't have let Laurence have the sub-alphaship in the first place. John shot Andrew a look of shared frustration before setting Edmond down to follow the others. The six-year-old laughed with excitement and bounded off as if his legs had springs, straight for the door. To investigate the origin of the blood trail, perhaps. Cubs, honestly. Clearly expecting to be swooped up and prevented from reaching adventure, Edmond put on a burst of speed as he crossed the threshold and leaped from the concrete step—

Only to crash into the knees of the human woman standing there, talking to Laurence. He fell back onto his butt, looked up at her, and burst into tears. She tucked her phone away into her pocket and carefully lifted him up. "Sorry, kid. You've got to look before you leap. Where're your parents?"

"Just inside," Andrew told her. The human looked up at him, curiosity clear in her scent. She was short, more on Laurence's scale than anyone else inside. Her fine, black hair, corralled into a professional ponytail, spoke clearly of Asian ancestry her features only hinted at. She was dressed like thousands of anonymous servers he'd encountered before, white blouse and black slacks, but something about her, perhaps the lack of the air of boredom that often accompanied such anonymity, gave her a spark of interest. Just their luck, to end up with a properly observant human when it could cause real trouble.

Perhaps unconsciously prompted by that curiosity, the human unnecessarily escorted Edmond up onto the step. Andrew caught her glancing inside over his shoulder, but he knew by now there was nothing out of the ordinary to see, so he didn't glance guiltily in the same direction. Just a big party. No wolves, no bloody assault victims.

"Edmond, you've got to stay inside, all right? Go find your father." Andrew smoothed Edmond's brown hair back into order—he was well on the way to developing a cowlick to rival his father's—and gave him a nudge in the right direction before firmly blocking the door with his body. Edmond hesitated, eyeing the human with a more naked form of curiosity. But he knew to obey his alpha, so he scrubbed his tear-snotty nose and launched himself away.

The human cleared her throat. "I'm—I'm one of the servers. This guy said there was a mix-up and you don't need anyone?" She turned her body slightly to indicate Laurence, then back to

Andrew. "I mean, they didn't leave me a voicemail or anything, but I don't work as many events as everyone else, so I guess it's not that surprising. So it's a pretty exclusive event?"

Just the sort of questions they didn't need. Abruptly, Andrew wondered if she was getting hung up on the reason for her exclusion because she wanted something to make her hassle seem worth it. He couldn't offer her that, but perhaps he could soften the hassle itself. "Yeah, Laurence is right. We told them that when they arrived to drop off the food. I'm sorry it didn't make it to you." He got out his wallet and pulled out and offered a couple bills. "For lost tips."

The woman brightened. "Thanks, I appreciate it." With one more glance over his shoulder, she headed back to her car. On her way past Laurence, who was propping up the outside wall down from the door, she offered him a diffident smile of farewell in particular. He kept it from his face, but tentative hope suffused Laurence's posture, and he turned with her and trailed after with forced nonchalance.

"You do many weddings?" Laurence asked her as they fetched up at her car.

The human checked her phone, then shrugged and didn't use the excuse, orienting her body on him instead. "Nah, I just pick up hours when I'm not out in the field for my main job. I'm an archaeologist, actually."

Andrew leaned his shoulder against the doorjamb and considered calling Laurence back to face the serious discussion of his actions he clearly needed. But maybe being able to earn himself a little positive attention, even from something so beside the point as flirting with a human, would leave Laurence better able to hear what his alphas needed to tell him. Laurence wasn't a cruel man, but he couldn't allow the fact he was hurting to lead him into hurting others.

Darkness flickered at the corner of Andrew's vision, a trick of a blind spot or peripheral field somehow. "I see you've found an excellent excuse to put off figuring out what to say," Death said mockingly. "Punish him or counsel him, you know he'll not thank you for it." Andrew ignored the hallucination, which had tended to dog him in times of stress ever since it first turned up years ago while he was out of his mind from pain. With his worries about the Russians, he imagined seeing Death often now.

Laurence shoved his hands into his pockets. "That sounds cool." Silence stretched long enough for them both to look uncomfortable, until Laurence seemed to figure out he was supposed to continue. "I'm, uh, kind of between jobs at the moment myself."

The human dipped her head in apology. "No, sorry. I just couldn't believe you didn't make an Indiana Jones joke. Or ask if I'd ever been to Egypt." She laughed. "You kinda just won yourself major points with that, by the way."

"Oh. Uh, good." Laurence looked at his feet.

Andrew couldn't stand to watch this any longer, the awkwardness was too much. He mentally wished Laurence all the best and returned inside, pulling the door closed behind himself. He and Silver could speak to Laurence tomorrow.

Meanwhile, he'd better make sure no one was too upset by the temporary change in the Richmond sub-alphaship. Andrew scanned the crowd, picking out Susan and the guard he'd assigned to her vicinity, then settled his attention on possible brewing trouble of a different sort where the traditional and modern of the Roanoke sub-alphas had met in the persons of Billings and Sacramento. Billings was rangy and smug in his assumed expression of great wisdom, where Sacramento had the blond hair and sharp, thin angles of a model. Her expression banished any assumptions of air-headedness, however. Even with her new lover's calming influence, she often seemed ready to go on the attack at any moment when in public.

Billings said something Andrew didn't catch, leaning over Sacramento's ear. Some kind of insult disguised as patronizing advice, no doubt. Sacramento bristled visibly and Andrew swallowed a sigh. Sacramento hadn't been the first female alpha—that had been Portland—but Portland knew how to play the political game, and while Sacramento was great with her pack, she was damnably easy to antagonize by anyone of equal rank.

"Billings," he said, lengthening his last stride so he arrived before Sacramento could answer the insult.

Billings inclined his head. "Roanoke Dare. I was just asking Sacramento how things were going with that Russian hostage she's been guarding for you. What's the name, Tatiana?"

"You're asking the wrong person, then." As Billings well knew. Andrew matched Billings' insincere paternal smile with one of his own. "I don't believe Sacramento saw the Russian prisoner for…five weeks before the wedding?" He flicked a glance to Sacramento, who'd gotten her body language under control, if not her scent. Tatiana's influence was clearly working in some ways, at least.

"Six," Sacramento said, and smiled thinly. She didn't like that her lover had to live up with the Roanokes in Seattle, and he couldn't blame her, but after the initial protests she hadn't uttered a word of complaint. He and Silver trusted the truth of her defection, but few other Roanoke pack members had reason to, so it was better to keep her close and watch her carefully for everyone's peace of mind.

"Didn't I see her around here somewhere?" Billings glanced disingenuously first in the exact opposite direction from where Tatiana was standing over one of the tables of food, browsing with more concentration than necessary. "Seems an odd choice to allow her in while you tell all the rest of us to be on the lookout for Russians."

Sacramento must have transmitted some version of "help!" to her lover in her expression, because when Andrew next glanced at her face, it showed relief as her eyes tracked someone over.

"Because she would recognize most of her former pack's agents, because this keeps her under our control, because she'll be motivated to protect her lover..." Andrew lifted his brows at Billings. "Pick any one you like."

"The correct answer is 'all of the above,' by the way," Tatiana said as she arrived, and set her hands against Sacramento's waist from behind. Andrew was used to her accent by now, but seeing Billings' incredulous expression made a Bond girl joke bubble up all over again.

Tatiana was also blonde, but there the similarity between the two women ended. Tatiana looked deceptively round and soft for all the highly trained muscle underneath, and her Slavic cheekbones gave her face an elegant, Old World cast. Andrew introduced her, curious as to how Billings would react.

Billings gave her a dip of his head, expression somber and apparently respectful. "Delighted to meet you. Should I ever need to distance myself from...poor decisions, I'll know who to come to, to broker my deal."

Andrew was distracted from answering for a beat by the richness of Death's laughter by his feet. A single sentence, and

Billings had managed to imply that he disagreed with how the Roanokes were dealing with the Russians, that he'd break with them at the first opportunity, and that Tatiana was still a spy— all at once. And on top of that given himself the chance to claim that it was all just a test of Tatiana and he'd never betray his alphas.

"If they catch up with me, I'll make sure they know there's another betrayer they should take care of," Tatiana said, pleasant. "Loyalty is very important to them."

"Thank you." Andrew smiled at Tatiana and let that be his answer to Billings. The sub-alpha finally seemed to decide they were metaphorically hunting too far into human lands for his taste, and drifted toward the drinks with only a brusque farewell.

"I don't know how you guys come up with stuff like that. I'd have to spend all night before writing it out." Sacramento suppressed a growl to a mutter under her breath. "And then in the moment I'm just—ugh. Fuck me."

"Later," Tatiana said with sharp humor into the back of Sacramento's shoulder, then came around to stand beside her lover. "It's early training, in my case."

"Practice," Andrew said with a shrug. With a nod to the two women, he drifted onward himself, making sure to keep his steps casual enough that no one moved aside for him. He found no other knots around troublemakers for the moment, at least. As balance, he charted instead the points of family and true friends within the crowd, let it steady him against his worries.

Andrew's phone beeped, his warning that the actual vow ceremony was supposed to be happening right now, which really meant everyone would start getting into place now, and the ceremony would be happening in about a quarter hour. His job was to stay out of the way until space was cleared. And, he supposed, to trust the vigilance of those in his pack rather than wasting his own vigilance on monitoring theirs.

Boston ambled in the opposite direction from the movement of the crowd, fetching up at Andrew's side. Despite the weight of more than a century of years, his close-cropped hair was still black against the dark brown of his skin. He didn't need such external signs of age to lend him gravitas, however; that was all in his eyes. Which were smiling now, despite everything. Boston would be the one to "hear" their vows—normally a position filled by the alpha of one of the pair. He'd been Andrew's alpha once upon a time, when Andrew was a young man. An angry young man, and Boston had had no little hand in making sure he didn't let that warp him.

Andrew found he didn't know what to do with his hands, finally ending up with them shoved into the pockets of his slacks. Boston's lips twitched, and he set a hand on Andrew's back as they both watched the crowd sort itself out. "Nervous?"

Andrew grimaced. Healthily worried, perhaps. "I don't see any way the Russians could possibly get to Susan."

Boston broke into a full smile. "About getting married, boy."

Andrew considered elbowing him, but restrained himself. "I've done it once before, as you may recall." That had been when he left Boston's pack, traveled to Spain to be with Felicia's mother. Bittersweet, to think of that ceremony. It wasn't good to lock up all the good voices of memory, because of how she died, but that couldn't help but taint all that came before. That had been a very small affair, a mid-ranker and a mid-ranker, with only enough Were attending to form one layer of circle around them.

And this was the opposite, so large that layers lost meaning and what was left was a room full of people with a circular negative space, waiting for him and Silver to arrive. "I should have asked her sooner," he said without thinking, then followed the thought through to the end. He had few secrets from Boston. "So it didn't have to be political. Because it's not political. I can't…imagine what life would be like without her in it."

"I suspect she might forgive you." Boston exhaled on a laugh and lifted his hand to Andrew's shoulder, to squeeze reassuringly.

He certainly could make himself nervous, however, thinking too hard about it. Andrew countered quickly, to keep things on a teasing level. "You never know. I might wake up and discover this was all a dream. Or she might."

"If anyone was fated by the Lady to be together, it's the two of you." Boston propelled him firmly forward toward the aisle the crowd had opened to the empty circle waiting at the center of the room. "I think this is your cue, alpha."

A deep breath, and Andrew strode up his aisle as Silver stepped through hers.

3

In the circle of no shadows, the space of stars, and the press of
Were around her and her mate, Silver felt as near to the Lady's
touch as she had ever been since her wild self was murdered. In
the bright love of speaking the vows, she wished the Lady could
turn Her face upon them all. She would hear Silver's voice, even
with Silver cut off from Her, she had to believe it. But Death
was here, so solemn, and so she spoke to him as well as Dare
and that was all they needed, the two of them. That, and Death's
blessing as he bowed his head while everyone shouted joy in
human voices around them, as close to howling as could be
managed with safety.

Then some spell of breathlessness and heightened sensation was broken, and Silver clutched Dare's hands and did her
best to anchor herself to a world with its usual complement of
darkness clinging to the corners. Everyone fell upon the food
in earnest, nothing like the nibbling they'd been doing before.
It would have been traditional to hunt for their meal—as much

as tradition could be said to apply to something adapted from the humans so they could acknowledge Were mates—but there were so many here. Any pack with hunting grounds near to concentrations of humans had trouble enough as it was with overhunting. So everyone would eat in human, and would run in wolf later.

Tradition translated apparently also meant Silver and Dare must collect no food for themselves. With a little chivvying from John and others, Silver seated herself beside her mate to reign in state as tidbits were set before them. Dare managed perhaps three bites before restlessness drove him to his feet. "There's Susan, but do you see Laurence anywhere?"

"Not since you had to pull him outside," Silver murmured. Which Dare had not yet had time to fill her in on, come to think of it. "What happened?"

Dare allowed himself a rumble of a frustrated growl, then smoothed out his voice. "It looks like fear's making him hurt subordinates. I took the sub-alphaship away from him for now, so we can talk to him properly later. He must have taken Bryce's place guarding that door. He could have guarded it from the inside during the ceremony, though. I suppose he's sulking." He turned in the direction of the door in question, weight poised to stride off in search of Laurence.

Silver knew if she asked, Dare would sit back down, hold himself there. But she didn't see the need for it—they had returned to the part of alpha duties that meant projecting authority and whatever other necessary emotions, to be observed. She wanted time alone with him; time observed was not a loss. But she did lace her fingers with his and drag him down for a kiss before releasing him. "I'm not surprised he's trying to avoid us for the moment. And everyone else, for that matter. But do what you must, then come back and eat." She freed her hand to gesture a wide swath before herself. "I can't manage this all myself."

Dare pretended to turn away, then whirled back to capture her in a kiss of his own, a promise of chasing to come later in the night. They had only that touch, a relatively chaste pressure, and his hand on the side of her neck, heat of skin buffered by a few slippery locks of hair. But then again, she had every memory of their years together, the taste of him linking them into a chain of promise of far more intimate touch.

Dare rocked his weight back reluctantly. "You're right, of course. Instead, I should stop avoiding people myself, and speak to my mother." Over her shoulder, he nodded to someone, and when Silver turned to watch him go, he slipped over to his mother and pulled her aside for the private word he must have promised with the meeting of their gazes.

Watching them speak together, Silver was struck once more by how Dare's mother and his daughter, Felicia, had the same tame self body shape, height in their legs. Dare's mother looked to be asking him a series of worried questions, which he answered calmly. He seemed slightly exasperated, but not annoyed yet, so Silver judged there was no need for her to interfere.

She dropped a treat discreetly, near where Death lounged against her ankle, steady rise and fall of his flank shimmering the blackness of guard hairs. She didn't see him move, but the treat disappeared.

"The interrogation begins, I see." Dare's father stepped up beside her, looking the same direction. When she indicated the seat on her opposite side from the one Dare would eventually reclaim, Dare's father accepted immediately. He had the same dark hair as his son, but a squarer face. Of his two plates, one joined her accumulation, and he ate from the other without saying anything else. Silence stretched between them as she politely selected a nibble from what she'd just been given. Silver couldn't decide if the silence was comfortable or not. She always got along with Dare's parents when she met them, but Dare never seemed to particularly long for their presence, to make visits more than occasional.

"If it's your job to do the same to me, you need to work on your technique," Silver said, and Dare's father laughed. He pushed his plate away and actually turned to her.

"Everyone knows the Russians managed to poison the two of you a few months ago." He tipped his chin to his wife. "She's worried about lingering aftereffects. Me, I figure you both look fine, and if you're not saying otherwise, you're not going to admit to it because you get asked the question several more times. And no point me asking him anything in general."

"If the aftereffects are mental, how would anyone tell with you?" Death commented. Silver imagined kicking him. Given the dreams that the Russian wolfsbane had given her and Dare, mental, not physical, effects were the problem. But she felt stronger for having conquered that dream, and Dare seemed to feel the same.

"You and your son seem to be getting along well enough," Silver said. Inasmuch as she'd hardly seen them exchange more than two words so far. She kept her gaze on Dare and only gave her comment the slightest of a questioning lift. She was this man's alpha, but she wasn't asking as one.

Dare's father snorted. "Give it long enough. We'll start arguing. Cub always was opinionated."

His father certainly was, Silver suspected. Dare had a temper, which he kept under a control forged well with practice, but she'd never have called him opinionated. But if father and son had never learned to listen to each other, she had no doubt that by now one would never sway the other on anything.

"Well, Lady keep you." His plate now empty, Dare's father got up to leave. His nod of farewell was respectful, but unapologetic. They'd spoken, and in so doing, she supposed he'd offered an endorsement of her presence in his son's life as enthusiastic as he could personally manage. She acknowledged him with a nod of her own.

"Dare did not get his drive to be alpha from there, certainly," she mused to Death beneath her breath. He would always hear her, and she didn't wish to be obvious in speaking to what others could not see. Dare's parents were mid-rankers, solidly so, and happy in it. His father had opinions, yes, but no wish to lead with them. Not that rank necessarily passed within families, but a similarity of personality could, and rank held a great portion of personality.

Death snorted. "Neither did you."

The thought made her seek her father out, and she found him without trouble. In such a large group, Were still tended to knot by pack, or within distant families usually separated in different packs; he had neither, so he roamed here too. He did not seem troubled to do so, but Silver still beckoned him over.

He came with a grin, and even *more* food, sweets this time. He helped himself to Dare's abandoned seat, waited with exaggerated expectation until she picked up a new morsel and smeared all her fingertips. He beamed as she licked them, and the corners of her mouth.

"I'm sure I'll have to yield this place to your handsome husband soon enough, though." Teasing danced in his eyes as he drew out the word "handsome," and Silver punched him in the side. A laugh bubbled up, like when she'd been small and he'd swooped her up just when she'd sneaked up on her brother and planned to jump out at him. Laughing memories weren't enough, but neither were they nothing. He loved her. She remembered that.

"Have enough to eat yourself? It wouldn't feel right to share any of this, but you could wait until I get up and dive on the carcass." Silver swept her good arm over the food once more, but she saw her father was looking at her bad one instead. Or more properly, looking while trying not to be caught looking. Seated, keeping it in her dress pocket set her elbow to an awkward angle, so she'd placed it across her lap.

She hesitated for a breath. Did she want to show him? She supposed she might as well get it out of the way. "How much do you know about what happened to me, then? When my brother died. You knew the right name."

She closed her good hand around her bad wrist, and lifted it to set it on the palm her father held out. She twitched her fingers. Enough strength to keep something like her necklace chain from falling, but no more.

"You two are the Roanokes. There's a lot of gossip about you." Her father pressed his other hand down on top of hers, then turned it over to show the inside of her arm. Silver knew what he was looking for. Going that far made her grit her teeth a little, but she pushed up her sleeve to show where the snakes created by the liquid silver had reached upward from her elbow, yearning for her heart. Dare had slit them open, let the poison drain out, and now only the scars of their shed skins remained.

"Isn't there anything you can do to help it heal?" Her father traced a scar with his fingertip.

Silver flexed her working shoulder muscles to pull her hand

out of his grip. She didn't have any leverage, but he let it go immediately anyway. "No, I enjoy having it be this way," she snapped.

"There is something you can do. You know that." Death slipped beneath her dangling hand. She imagined his fur must have tickled her fingertips, but such light sensation was below the threshold of what her bad hand could manage.

"The Russians…" Silver pressed her lips together. Her father had no particular need to know any of this, but perhaps she had a need to tell someone. Everyone else who knew had discovered it along with her, and had never needed to be told. "The Russians cut out silver scars, and the body heals unblemished. But I do not heal properly. I *see* differently. That is not something that can be cut out. Perhaps it would not even work on my arm. It is too great a risk for an unknown benefit. Do not imagine that I have not considered it." She didn't realize that she'd used her alpha tone on the last until her father dropped his head and his wild self tucked its tail.

Silver sighed, tucked her bad hand away, and put her good on top of her father's when he lifted his head again. "If you are so desperate for painful details, speak to my mate. I don't want to go over them again."

"Of course." Her father held still beneath her touch for a beat, then pulled his hand away and stood. "I think now it is perhaps time for the hunt, however."

Dare was striding for her with purpose, so Silver judged that her father was correct, and rose to meet her mate. The hunt would be the part of the wedding Dare would most enjoy if he allowed himself to, she judged, more than speaking vows in the sight of the gods in whom he did not believe. As for herself, she'd make it enjoyable by sheer force of will, even if being trapped on two legs made her slow and awkward in comparison to everyone's wild selves.

Dare smelled smug when she reached him, as if he'd remembered that he knew something she didn't. She shot him a glance, but he looked completely innocent as he laced his fingers with hers and called everyone to order, then tugged her outside. She checked Death next, but he whuffed dismissively at her, and trotted off. Something sweet, then, not trouble. Silver smiled, and lifted her face to the sunlight slanting down between the trees as they waited for everyone to take their places.

Guards first, in human, to watch the perimeter and make sure no humans happened on to them, as had been previously planned. Silver noted a few guards in wolf as well, likely added in case of Russian interference. It would have been easier to cover their home pack's hunting lands, owned by them in human terms, but they were too small for this many Were.

The remaining Were began to undress, laughter and chatter bright. Unhurried, they drifted into two groups, men on Dare's side, women on hers. In a wedding hunt, she and Dare would hunt each other, and everyone else would try to keep them apart. Until the guests finally took pity on the couple and released them to find a little privacy, firmly enforced until the next morning. Silver wanted to run already, thinking of it, and bounced on her toes instead. Dare grinned openly, dropped her hand, and retreated to a bit of a distance, though that didn't stop the smell of his desire from reaching her.

It was only as the groups grew more and more distinct that Silver noticed. The women weren't undressing, or shifting. More and more wolves surrounded Dare as he shrugged out of his clothes and switched to his wild self, standing tall and steely gray and beautiful. But the women around Silver stayed in human, even as they moved to ring her in, keep her from her mate. Silver frowned, composing her question, when Susan slipped in among the Were and strode to stand in front of Silver, grinning more than anyone.

"Why—?" Silver said, but she already knew, it was already bubbling up inside her into laughter with the rainbow edges the daylight stars had had.

"Well, we're the ones who are making sure you can't get to your husband, aren't we? Wouldn't be a fair contest if we weren't on two legs too." Susan embraced Silver, which of course was simply a ploy to give the men time to chivvy Dare away, into a run.

Silver released the rainbow-edged laughter and wiggled free to dodge through her pack members, after her mate.

4

Silver found a patch of sunlight and circled the guest house's table to sit in it and sip her drink as Dare banged around, organizing breakfast. It had been interesting to spend the night here—a home to their pack, and yet not. Frequently passed through, but rarely lived in. Scent traces were lighter, more polite, and the furnishings were cleaner, neater. But it didn't feel empty, either. They always seemed to have some visitor or other who needed the space.

She wished she could let this morning stretch long, delay the time when they would have to begin all over again. The Russian threat had not resolved itself, after all. Perhaps they were still gathering up the information about Susan they needed, or perhaps now, after her father's warning, they'd realized they'd have to wait some few days or weeks for the Roanoke pack to let down their guard. She hoped it was not the latter, as she didn't know how long they could keep up that guard in purely logistical terms. Susan and those who would do the guarding all had their own lives to be about.

Someone knocked and Tatiana entered cautiously from the direction of the path to the main den. Death skirted the spill of sunlight around Silver's feet and settled himself at ease well away. "And here she is to join the discussion," he said, amused. "Are you going to demand better intelligence from her? Or perhaps you'd prefer to take out your frustration on your father for his bad intelligence. He'd make a good target in general, abandoning you as he did."

Tatiana dipped her head respectfully, and Silver raised her eyebrows at her in a silent question. They did need her for this discussion eventually, but Silver would have expected her to snatch a last few moments this morning with her lover.

Tatiana must have guessed the direction of Silver's thoughts, because she smiled slightly. "Allison's asleep. I sneaked out." She strode closer, and then hesitated, which sat oddly in her muscles. Tatiana nearly always looked poised and ready to listen patiently. Her wild self, dark with white-tipped fur, went farther and had its shoulders hunched. "Before business, I just wondered, there's an Old Were prayer we say at home, for new mates…"

Silver held out her good hand to Tatiana, inviting her forward. "Of course." They'd had their disagreements about how to worship the Lady, but this sounded perfect. And it was clearly important in Tatiana's upbringing, if she offered it when the alphas might well be in no mood to take part in anything so linked to their current enemies.

Tatiana sat down facing Silver and took her hand. A lock or two of her fair hair escaped forward over her shoulder as she leaned over their hands. Dare's footsteps approached behind Silver, and the mouth-watering scent of meat just now ceasing to sizzle drifted with him. He offered her a strip, so Silver indicated to Tatiana with a jerk of her chin that she should take up Silver's bad hand instead. She hoped Dare, who didn't believe in the Lady, wasn't planning to object. "It's just a prayer, love."

Dare hmphed, smelling more resigned than annoyed. "Does it need both of us?" he asked Tatiana.

"That's how it's usually done, yes." Tatiana lifted Silver's bad hand gently, and squeezed back when Silver twitched her fingers in the hold. She eyed Dare, wary.

Dare licked some last grease off his fingers and offered a hand. He was polite enough to ask nothing about how long it would take, but Silver knew Tatiana was more than diplomatic enough to use the shortest version.

Tatiana's voice was low and musical, and her words hovered almost on the edge of familiarity—though not meaning—for Silver, as they always did when she spoke in Old Were. The Russians held it was the original Were language, and Silver had to admit that it did sound like children's rhymes her mother had taught her. Silver watched Death for his reaction to the prayer, but his ears were focused on some scrap of movement in the shadows, more interesting prey than pretty words for new mates.

Her father didn't knock when he entered. Silver could probably have heard him cross from the main den if she'd been paying attention, but the way Dare's and Tatiana's heads jerked up, it seemed they hadn't anticipated their next visitor either. He spoke a single word, of the same sound as the prayer, and Tatiana dropped their hands and snapped to her feet.

She demanded something interrogative of him in Old Were, but he shrugged his shoulders and opened his hands, as much at a loss as Silver and Dare. Death got to his feet and panted a silent laugh in appreciation, though.

"Anyone care to let the alphas in on this conversation?" Dare crossed his arms and stepped over to block Silver's father's path farther into the guest house.

"He called me an intruder," Tatiana said evenly, settling her weight back into something pointedly at ease. "Or that's what it sounded like he was trying to say."

Silver's father laughed. "Oh, is that what it means? I figured it for something along the lines of 'cat's bastard poking his muzzle where it doesn't belong.' Only more concise." When Dare's silence remained dubious, Silver's father continued. "I've done a fair amount of sailing in my time. Ended up at a Russian port once. Got called…'intruder' a good few times."

Silver almost recognized the meaning behind "sailing" and she gritted her teeth when the word dodged away from her at the last moment. Hearing it made her think of flying, but she *knew* that wasn't right. Lady damn it!

"Floating on the water." Death gave her a look of supreme disappointment. "You're falling behind."

She was, Silver realized, because Tatiana had started speaking while Silver was chasing after the meaning. "—years ago?"

Silver's father nodded. "Nine, yes. But I was following my own trail, doing a little drinking and resupplying. I didn't go anywhere near that guy, he hunted me down." Even without having heard all of it, Silver could guess at the gist of the exploit. Nipping at tails, running back out of range.

"Ha." Amusement slipped into a curve at the side of Tatiana's mouth. "You were *that* one."

"Suppose I was." Her father's good humor slid away. "But that means I know a little bit about Russian Were, so I'm wondering why the Roanokes' fabled hostage is chatting with them over breakfast, instead of locked up somewhere."

Rather than answer, Dare looked at her, and Silver wasted a moment in embarrassment. Reconnecting with her father at length seemed nice in abstract, until he started slamming his way into their delicate political maneuvers.

Tatiana slashed the air with her hand, anger leaking into her scent with the gesture. "My alpha broke the ties of loyalty between us before I ever did. Not that it's any concern of yours." She drew in a slow breath, smoothed a lock of hair back behind her ear, and the movement settled her body language back into confidence. "But perhaps you're trying to make up for missed opportunities to protect your daughter by manufacturing false threats now?" She smiled, sweet and probably calculated to goad. It matched the apparent sympathy of her tone.

"I made no claims I was sure about anything. I heard about a possible threat to their human; I told the Roanokes." Her father shrugged, though the smell of his thinning patience belied the nonchalance of the motion. "I judged they would rather me do that than wait for proof."

"Susan?" Tatiana's gaze flicked to them each in turn. "I just saw her making coffee at the main house. What's she got to do with it?"

And of course Tatiana was confused. Silver should have realized sooner. Tatiana was one of the guarded—though for slightly different reasons—not one of the guards. She wouldn't have been a recipient of any of Dare's direct orders as to Susan's protection, and the general gossip would have passed firmly around her. However much the alphas trusted their hostage, the rest of the pack trusted Tatiana as little as her father did. "Tell her what you told us," she prompted her father. She listened carefully as he did so, but if new details had shaken themselves free in his memory, they were buried in concepts she could not follow. In their division of labor by relative strengths, she judged that a job for Dare.

"Why are you all so worried?" Death sauntered among them, circling Tatiana's feet, then Silver's father's. "The human was not taken. The guards must have sent the Russians away, quaking with fear. The side of good has triumphed! Time to celebrate."

Even without his heavy irony, Silver would have wanted to kick him. Of course, with everyone watching, she couldn't respond to Death, but she imagined doing it. She was aware nothing in this world was that simple, that easy. Had the Russians used the Roanokes' concentrated attention in one direction to set things in motion in another direction entirely?

How could they possibly guess what direction that was, before the attack burst out to set its teeth in their throats?

Andrew noticed Silver's attention growing abstracted as Hugh wandered into the weeds of how he'd come to know the young Alaskans, and why that virtually guaranteed they'd tell him the truth. His job to herd him back, then. "I assume they didn't give you much of a description of this Russian man they talked to, but would they do it if you asked them now?" He tipped his head to Tatiana—she would be the one making use of such a description.

She nodded, body language loosening with a clear course of action in sight, but then her pocket buzzed. A quick glance at her phone stopped being quick when she stilled with such absoluteness that even Hugh cut off what he'd been about to say.

Another beat of buzzing from the vibrate function, then she silently placed it on the kitchen table. "It's not a number I know," she said, softly and rigidly controlled. "Alaska area code."

Andrew jerked his hand in permission for her to answer. Whether it was an Alaskan, or one of Tatiana's former pack who'd picked up a disposable phone once on the ground—and who else would have her number?—it strained credulity to think it was unrelated to their current problems.

A man spoke without waiting for a greeting from Tatiana. Andrew didn't understand a word, but he recognized the language as Old Were. Tatiana whitened, especially around her lips. When the man paused as if for an answer, she spoke in English. "Don't play silly games, Mikhail. You know English."

Silence stretched, and Tatiana finally gave in and provided what was apparently a translation. "Have you misplaced a human, Roanokes? That's careless of you."

Andrew clenched his hands. Tatiana had just seen Susan in the house. And he'd seen Susan himself at the close of the hunt last night. Between that time and this, there was no reason for her to have left the pack house—Lady, he doubted John had let her so much as out of his sight.

Tatiana pressed fingertips to her lips as she listened to the next flow of Old Were, expression going haggard right in front of them. She translated again. "That's the thing about humans. Easy to lose. Not like alphas. But a beta's wife, she's valuable nonetheless, yes? That's why we'd like to propose a little…extortion—"

Mikhail's laugh rolled out of the phone. "Trade, Tatiana. Trade. Good translator does not add opinions." Andrew could have sworn he heard Mikhail smile over the line. "I will meet you at your hunting lands at sunset, and we can discuss this in person." He ended the call.

Andrew slammed out of the back door. "Come," he snapped to Tatiana. He needed information, but he couldn't wait to check on Susan long enough to get it standing still. "Start talking. Is he likely here alone? Why call you?"

Tatiana jogged after him, self-control wrapped tight around herself and held with hands pointedly unclenched. "Most likely alone. One Tooth from the Lady's Jaw on the ground is most usual for missions in hostile territory, and Mikhail is more than skilled enough for it. And he called me to cast doubt on my loyalties. If you two lock me out—or lock me up—I can't feed you his pack's maneuvers, as it were."

Andrew jerked open the door to the main house. The noise brought John out from the kitchen, Susan padding after, tousle-haired and pajamaed. Silver's father shoved Tatiana aside to come up behind Andrew, and Silver followed a beat later. "No, no one's teleported away with me in the last five minutes either," Susan joked awkwardly, taking in them all staring at her. "What's happened now?"

Andrew growled. "If they don't have Susan, who do they have?"

5

Andrew wasn't sure what he expected to find, but he shifted anyway and ranged ahead of the others once they arrived at the hall to try to sift some order from the chaos of the scent trails left from the hunt. At first, he assumed the whiff of dry Were blood was from Bryce, but he hadn't bled on the ground, only on his shirt. And when Andrew rounded that side of the building, the scent resolved itself into a soaked-in puddle along the gravel drive, not beside the step up to the side door. Small stones with sticky brown residue didn't really stand out in a sea of gravel lying on damp brown dirt, but Andrew marked it out by scent. A puddle from the initial wound, then a trail that petered out within a few feet, undoubtedly when someone was put into a vehicle. And the area of initial blood flow was worryingly large. A Were could have survived that kind of wound, but probably wouldn't have remained conscious.

And which Were was currently absent, last seen in this location—with a human?

Andrew shifted back, cursing silently until he could do it out loud. "Has anyone seen Laurence since before the ceremony?" he asked as he pulled on his clothes and got out his phone, even though he already knew the answer. Laurence's phone rang, then went to voicemail, while Andrew collected negative answers from everyone, both verbal and frowns of confusion.

He shoved his phone back in his pocket and paced a few steps out of sheer frustration. All right. He'd been the last to see Laurence; he should stay and see what could be reasoned out from that information, with Silver's and the others' help, while someone else chased trails. He gestured the general sweep of the truncated trail for John. "See if I've missed anything?"

"Leaving aside why they would take Laurence—perhaps that was sheer opportunity—why would they say they have our human?" Silver joined Andrew, anchoring him with a touch on his arm as she watched John undress efficiently so he could shift.

"There was a human woman. She didn't get the message about servers not being needed. Laurence was hanging around, talking to her, smelling of chasing thoughts." Andrew grimaced. And he'd walked away and left them there. But how could he have known? "She was nothing at all like Susan, though." He nodded to the woman herself, currently stooping to fold her husband's discarded clothes a little more neatly. Andrew measured her height approximately on his own chest. "Much shorter. Black hair."

And then things aligned properly around one of Andrew's memories. Rather than relief, it only brought more anger. "But she picked Edmond up when he fell. If someone—like a Russian, say—had never met Susan, but knew about her Were son..." He could imagine it now: Laurence was fundamentally decent enough to protect a weaker human on general principles, and when he objected, the Russian must have taken him out and dragged him along to keep him quiet.

But how could the Russian possibly have gotten that close in the first place? Laurence also wasn't stupid, and upset and distracted by flirting or not, he'd never have ignored the scent of an approaching stranger. Coming up from downwind got one only so close, and it wasn't close enough to injure Laurence that severely.

Worst of all, however it had happened, was that Andrew hadn't even noticed Laurence was missing until the Russian had called. Hadn't even put it together until he smelled Laurence's blood on the ground. What kind of alpha failed to notice that? On top of not noticing the way Laurence's control over his pack was deteriorating before he went too far.

"But he was so awfully inconvenient, as I'm sure the Russian agrees," Death murmured, arriving through a gap in the tight-shut door to the hall. It was as if Death had created a shadow illusion of an opening and then actually stepped through. Though Andrew didn't know why he was noticing one optical illusion on top of another.

"This isn't the human's blood, is it?" Felicia leaned over the stained gravel. The heavy, black waves of her hair tumbled free around her face, and she sighed, straightened, and caught them back in a tail before starting again. Her expression of rather abstract concern shook Andrew's thoughts off their current trail, and perspective managed to shoulder its way in. Laurence wasn't dead; he'd heal, and it was in the Russians' best interests to keep things on that level as none of them wanted a pack war.

"Can you tell?" Andrew asked his daughter. If she couldn't, it was a skill she needed practice at, and she might as well get it now. The nonexistent trail wasn't getting any more nonexistent while they stood here, and the meeting with Mikhail wasn't until sunset. Maybe she'd notice something the rest of them hadn't, too. If they could reconstruct what happened precisely, that might give them some insight into the Russian's tactics.

Felicia indulged in a just-audible growl of annoyance, presumably at the teaching moment, but didn't otherwise object, which was a relatively recent step up in maturity. Lady, how was she almost twenty already? She bent all the way to the ground first, clearly trying to avoid fussing with her clothing, but eventually gave in and undressed and shifted. In wolf, she shook herself, sending up a shower of her black hairs, and nosed a few gravels over.

Tatiana had slipped a little way into the underbrush in John's wake to conduct a search of her own in human, though Andrew noticed she was careful to stay in sight as she did. She hurried back now. "Mikhail hasn't been anywhere around here. I'd stake my life on it."

John followed her back, shifted, then gave his report as he dressed. "She's right. No one I didn't recognize, other than the human. Most people weren't back here, other than those Alaskan cubs romping around."

"Yeah, they were hanging around—" Andrew cut off as the realization hit him with force of a body-slam right into his stomach. "They haven't met Susan. And if they were close enough to see when the human was talking to Edmond..." He traded a glance with Silver and saw the same thoughts there. Far from simply providing information to Mikhail, the Alaskans must have done his dirty work for him.

"They must have been overjoyed by the opportunity Laurence provided them," Silver murmured, voice low and tight. "No one questioned the smell of blood."

Andrew snorted. "I bet one would have punched the other and claimed roughhousing during an argument got out of hand, if they'd needed to. No one would have questioned that either." Having met the Alaskans, he certainly wouldn't have. In any case, managing scents that way was smart of them. Or smart of Mikhail in coaching them. Hugh might have a guess which of the two it was. Andrew shouldn't make assumptions based on the kind of Were who would think kidnapping a funny *prank*.

Or maybe Hugh had made a deeper, more wrong assumption long ago, in thinking that his drinking buddies wouldn't like to cause trouble and violence for its own sake.

Andrew pulled in a deep breath. Now they had a reasonable idea of what had happened, time to figure out the way forward. "We'll have to tell Mikhail they have someone of no value." He sought out Tatiana, holding herself back from the edge of the group, slightly white-lipped, and raised his brows at her. "The Russians don't strike me as the type to harm her or Laurence out of spite. More likely to cut their losses as quickly as possible." He paused, and Tatiana nodded a verification.

Andrew rolled his shoulders, and turned his attention to Silver. It sounded like a workable plan to him, but he needed to know what she thought. "They might try to strike again quickly once they know, but…" He shrugged. They'd be no worse off than before, and with at least one win to their account.

Silver was too distracted to reply at first. Her eyes tracked on nothing the way they did when she was listening to Death—or perhaps in this case she was seeking him out, for his opinion, because the thoughts visible in her expression were tangled.

"You realize this poor woman is going to have no idea what the fuck is going on. We'd have to make sure she didn't immediately run to the police once they let her go," Susan said, then bit her lip as the various Were possibilities for "make sure" probably spread out before her.

Silver made a canine gesture of shaking her head as she came back to herself. "Even if she doesn't run to tell other humans, the Russian can't let her go." She turned from Susan to take Andrew's hand, smelling of urgency. "She'll have seen Laurence heal." She gestured to the circle of soaked-in blood. "Could a human bleed this much and live?"

Andrew muttered a curse. He already suspected the answer, but he let Susan be the one to give it, authoritative. "Maybe. But a human who'd bled this much would have an ugly wound. She'll have to know something is wrong, even if they haven't done something like shift in front of her. They'd have no reason to be hiding, right?"

"They'd kill her and dump her the moment they know she holds more danger than value," Tatiana said, accent blurring sharp words. "You might get your Were back, or you might not, if he tries to interfere." She glanced behind her as if wishing there were a background to fade into, even as she spoke and brought herself to the forefront of their attention.

"We'll have to negotiate like she *is* Susan, then," Andrew said. He set a hand against Silver's back and felt her relax against it. She had to have known he'd agree, but Silver liked to have things out in the open and stated bluntly, so everyone could howl the same note. And this woman's situation wasn't so different than Susan's in the beginning, perhaps. Dragged into the world of Were through no fault of her own, she deserved to be shielded from its dangers until she could make her own choices about it. As the ones who'd done the dragging, the Were owed her that much.

Not to mention what Andrew still figured he owed Laurence.

Andrew turned to John, already flicking through the pack's fighters in his mind. Keeping everyone safe at the meeting but not pushing the Russian into violence against the hostages would be a delicate balance. Tatiana spoke before he could. "I should come along. I'll be able to spot his tricks."

"Something to discuss in private," Silver said, before Andrew could answer. He assumed that meant she thought the answer wasn't the automatic no he would have given. He was dubious, but all right. They could grant her a few minutes. She could definitely be an asset if she could keep her equilibrium around someone from her birth pack.

Silver put her hand on Tatiana's arm, pulling her down one of the gravel trails that led outward from the hall, then diverged onto one of bare earth probably illicitly beaten by hikers, not maintained by staff. Having achieved relative quiet with the shade of trees all around enveloping them, she let Tatiana go.

"Well," Andrew prompted, when the silence stretched more than a few beats. "Start convincing us."

Tatiana's lips thinned, then she leaned into a tree so she could trace the gnarls of bark with her fingertip. She tugged at one raised section with her fingernails, though it was too firmly attached to be peeled away. "I don't know what...*proof* of my use I could possibly offer, but I'm not going to run to him. If that's what you're worried about."

"No," Silver said. "But there's more danger than what comes from abstract loyalty for or against Roanoke, or Russia. Did you know this man well? Were you lovers?"

Andrew shot his wife—Lady, he really hadn't had time to

get used to that, applied to Silver, and it didn't look like he'd get the chance any time soon—shot Silver a sideways look. He hadn't expected that tack.

"Mikhail?" Tatiana managed to snap off a small piece of the bark. "I wouldn't call us lovers. We played chase. But I played chase with half the other Teeth in the Lady's Jaw." She flicked the bark into the undergrowth and turned her usual self-possession to stillness. "We don't generally have mates or children, and nights get cold."

"It's amazing how people who know our pasts can guide our steps simply by speaking of things we might like to avoid." Silver looked like she would have liked two hands, but she gestured her point with a hip, showing it deflecting the path her hand took without ever touching it. "I would not be surprised if he is *very* good at making you run in whatever direction he wants."

"So you're worried he'd taunt me and I'd be useless to you?" Tatiana's lips twisted, but she looked like she couldn't immediately deny the idea.

"Exactly." Andrew set a hand on her shoulder, then turned to go. There was no shame in it. It would be surprising if someone from her childhood couldn't get under her skin, at least a little, never mind someone who sounded like as much of an asshole as Mikhail had on the phone.

"Roanoke Dare, wait." Tatiana drew a breath, visibly choosing her words. "I can't promise none of his bites will connect, but I promise to be on my guard and not run where he herds." She slid fingers through her hair, then shook her head to settle the waves back into some kind of order. "But you said to convince you, and I have to more to offer than merely not being a liability. You have said you must negotiate, but I don't see you have anything to negotiate *with*. Whatever Russia wants, it will be something you do not wish to give.

"If, however, I was to appear to turn on you, to join Mikhail…"

Andrew had an impulse to plant his feet, though the shove off balance was mental, not physical. That was a hell of an offer. To play double-agent—or was it triple by now?—Tatiana would need a tremendous amount of emotional strength above and beyond what she'd already displayed in defecting. She might go in with the best of intentions, but what if she were seduced by the taste of home?

This wasn't so simple as being only about emotional strength, however. "So you join him. Would he tell you where the hostages are being kept, just like that?"

Tatiana smiled, small and sharp. She lifted a hand to rub fingertips between her shoulder blades as if soothing an itch. She'd worn the mark of the Russian Were spy organization there, until Andrew cut it out. He wondered if she was reminding them, or didn't realize she was touching the spot as her thoughts circled around home. "Perhaps, perhaps not. I won't play it too eager, or he'll get suspicious. But I won't be relying on him *telling* me anything either. I will watch to see where he goes, and if that doesn't work, I can certainly delay him, give you time for a search of your own."

When Tatiana first decided to stay, she'd told them she would not work against Roanoke, but neither would she work against her former pack. Andrew didn't know if this qualified, or if she'd merely be working against this particular asshole, but still. He wouldn't have hesitated, if it were a matter of Tatiana offering to protect Sacramento, but this was different. "Why dodge near the hunters for a human you've never met and a Were you hardly know?"

"Ah." The stalling syllable seemed to grow from surprise—pleasant surprise, perhaps. Maybe she'd been expecting a lengthy interrogation. Tatiana seemed uniquely unable to trust him and Silver to trust her. "Because if my former pack wins this battle and eventually the war, I will be in a very delicate position. And perhaps I can atone for another human woman I'd hardly met before I killed her." Tatiana shrugged. "I will take any oath on the Lady you wish that I will not betray you."

She knelt before Andrew could tell her it wasn't necessary, and murmured her promise with her thumb pressed to her forehead. Silver gestured for her to stand. "You'll go to him at the meeting, then?"

Tatiana shook her head. "Better if I don't tell you anything specific. You'll smell angrier if it's at least a little bit of a surprise."

Andrew allowed himself a bark of laughter. She was right about that. And he was truly grateful to her. Now they'd be going into the meeting with the Russian not quite so far behind.

Which was not the same as "ahead," of course.

6

They arrived at the hunting lands well before sunset, of course, for Dare and John to fuss and fuss over where their fighters should stand. Silver stood where they directed her and watched the sunset, as much as managed to shoulder through the dark boughs of surrounding trees. Death sat tall beside her and watched the east like the rise of darkness held as much colorful interest for him as the sunset did for her.

Tatiana waited in stillness as well, wild self hunkered down like one might wait out a blizzard when movement would only waste energy. She kept well away from Silver, probably correctly predicting what would make John and the fighters most twitchy. The distance was all to the good in any case, because she and Dare had reluctantly given their fighters no warning about what Tatiana was to do.

Dare settled next to Silver, fingertips brushing her back like he was considering an arm around her and then deciding on having both hands free in case of violence instead. The sunlight warmed in a brief burst straight into their eyes as if in one last frustrated farewell for the night. "Death must be overjoyed at all the excitement," he murmured, low.

"He likes it better than he would a honeymoon," Silver said on a breath of humor, and tipped her head from the light to the path leading up to their position. Night tucked in around them.

When the Russian kidnapper arrived, stopping some distance short to walk up to them slowly, he moved like someone dangerous. A snake that strikes too fast for one to escape the fangs. Silver judged that he *wanted* them to take that impression—the period between learning such skill and learning that you didn't always want it to be visible was short indeed. His hair was darker than Tatiana's, brown tinged with a golden shade that evoked her pure gold. They also shared a high, elegant line to cheekbones and features that was sharply attractive even in masculine form. His wild self was undistinguished gray, but very lean, built for speed.

"You have something of ours," Dare said, leaving her for a single step forward toward their approaching opponent. Silver let her head drop, watching the kidnapper tightly from an upward angle. She and Dare hadn't planned this specifically, but they both knew the steps to this particular dance. Let her go underestimated while Dare growled and snarled as their opponent would expect.

"I will return them, for right deal." The man's rhythm of movement might have been perfect, but his rhythm of speaking was not. His accent was not terrible, but he hesitated in places, wrong-footed. He smiled, so suddenly it reminded Silver of the snake strike she'd been thinking of earlier: a pure attack. "I am Mikhail. You are Roanokes, I guess." He looked at Dare briefly, and Silver much longer, stillness settling over him.

"You are too notorious to stand in the shadows with me," Death murmured to her. He stood tall and regal at her side, ruff bristling up from the power in his shoulders. Silver had expected him to circle the newcomer, nip at his wild self, not ally himself so obviously with her. It made her think again, think of what Tatiana had said the Russians thought of her. The Lady, born again. Or a Were posturing as such. The sheer blasphemy of it gave her a shivery feeling, but Silver pulled at the tie holding her hair back and shook it free anyway. With the pure white shimmering in the weaker light put out by stars and humans, the Lady not yet risen, the kidnapper's eyes widened, just a little, in reaction. Her blow had connected.

Mikhail bowed, extravagantly, to Silver, though he flicked his gaze to Tatiana. He asked her a mocking question in their shared language. Tatiana translated rather than answering. "Why did you not tell us the rumors were true?"

"The rumors that—" Silver tried to say it, to dismiss it, to laugh it away, but the words twisted her voice too tight to escape.

Mikhail held a hand to her like a man wishing for warmth, though the Lady gave no warmth in any case. "The Lady—" This time, his words in another language came with a growl of frustration, and he clearly intended Tatiana's translation. "You bear the Lady's touch, Silver." He knelt—*knelt*—and bowed his head. "When this matter is sorted out, come back with me. Shed your light on those of us in the homeland. You would be treated with nothing but—"

Tatiana's translation stuttered out, and she and Mikhail exchanged contemptuous phrases, rapid-fire. "Respect," Tatiana finally finished for him, teeth gritted.

Silver knew she should take the respect the man was showing her now and use it, use it against him, but she couldn't.
Even had she not been barred from the Lady, had she not ached
for Her touch every full and every other moment between, she
would have hesitated. The Lady was not a convenient mask
for Her children to don when it suited them. She was so much
greater than that, and Silver would not sully Her with the act.
She bit the inside of her cheek, and let Dare answer in her stead.

"That's *Roanoke Silver*, Russian. Why in the Lady's name
would she ever agree to go along with her enemies just because
they flattered her?" Dare snapped, crossing his arms. Mikhail
stood, and his earlier smooth danger returned to his posture.
More his natural state than worship, Silver guessed.

"Does not Lady always try to share Her light?" Mikhail
said for himself. His snake-strike smile returned. "Tatiana?"
He continued with her expressionless translation services. "To
business, then. I will return your human and your Were—I
heard he is a sub-alpha no longer, very sad for him—to his
hands." He gestured with a flourish to John. "When the two
of you have stepped down and returned all the packs to their
independent status without you. I will escort you to exile in a
place of your choosing, off this continent. No one need be hurt.
Is that not generous?"

And Silver and Dare stepping down *would* fracture the
packs. Silver wondered if Russia could possibly know how
completely. John, as their beta, would no doubt try to keep control, but he had not an alpha's personality, and while everyone
tolerated his human wife now, looking the other way as long
as she exercised power in someone else's name, for an alpha to
allow such a thing—

Dare said something in response to Mikhail, no doubt a flat denial, but Silver couldn't hear him, not when Death spoke over him. Death's borrowed voice held the frost of the void when he chose, and so he chose now. "All of this for a human you have never met and one of your most troublesome Were?"

Mikhail laughed and looked at Silver. She set her teeth and tried to read the content of Dare's words on someone's face. Clearly, she was meant to react now, but she couldn't because she was busy listening to one of the gods when she'd specifically decided she was not going to play that part. "I—" she tried.

But Death ran over her planned words, trampled them into the mud until she couldn't remember their shape. "And you are too cowardly to use your advantage. Tell him whatever he'll believe, promise him with false authority. If you break the promise later, it doesn't matter, does it?" He paced to stand before her. As a wolf, he should have had to tip his head up to her face, but instead he met her eyes straight on without seeming to change in size. Silver had to avoid that gaze, lest she trip and fall down and down into the void set within it.

"Death, *stop*." Silver held up a palm as if that could turn the power of that gaze aside, and everyone looked at her and she flushed. She hadn't been able to *think*, with Death's voice unending, and of course now he had her exactly where he wanted her, pulling the Russian's assumptions around her shoulders like a mantle.

She concentrated on an effort to see Dare's world, the others' world, but as always, such effort cast her farther into mists.

Death did not change, of course. Death was the same in any world, and no mist tendril would dare to caress the tip of a single shimmering black guard hair. People changed little as well, though now Silver felt she could see curtains of shadow in

Mikhail's fingers, slack against the ground for the moment, but ready to be tossed like a cloak to muffle and trip and smother his opponent when he wished. Dare held the Lady's light instead, low below the surface of his skin because Her favor made him uncomfortable. This way, he could pretend not to notice it. But the loyalty of a healthy pack could lend him no less brightness.

And Tatiana kept her light at her core so the shadows at her throat, around her voice, would not notice it. Whatever she spun into her voice, Silver could see the light she nurtured.

"You order Death?" Mikhail said, incredulous. His head dipped, as if he thought of bowing once more.

"Not with any particular success." Silver shook her head with more of a jerk than she'd intended. She would not watch Death. She would not let her eyes linger where Mikhail curled his fingers around his shadow cloak.

"You harmed our guard. How do we know that the—Susan is not hurt, or dead?" Dare rocked back a step to set a hand between Silver's shoulder blades, fingers spread to widen comfort as much as possible. He must have guessed at her mental state—that, or it was clear for everyone, including the kidnapper, to smell. Silver cursed silently, and Death laughed.

Mikhail held something out to Dare in his free hand. The guards neared as the two men closed enough for Dare to examine it, and then everyone stepped back again, like a slow, elegant dance. It had been something Silver could not understand properly, but Dare reluctantly made an affirmative noise.

"So you will not step down?" Mikhail turned to her next. His cloak of shadows and how he held it negligently over one shoulder seemed dashing now, almost flirtatious. Of course a man such as this would flirt with the Lady should he meet Her.

Of course. His tone carried perfectly even if his words needed translation. "Perhaps with time for consideration, you will see that the Roanoke pack is simply too large to survive in its current form, and accept the inevitable. Since exile is inevitable, why not come, with your Lady's light, and extend your grace to those who are presently confined in discomfort in Russia?"

"Or with time to consider, you will find a justification for your own cowardice." Death settled in lower, watching. Silver clenched her teeth. It wasn't cowardice, so any reasoning would not be a justification.

In the Roanokes' place, Tatiana would not have trusted herself. But if they were not the kind to trust so completely, she might have found it easier to betray them. Or even to stand back, to not involve herself when the familiarity of seeing one she had trained with for half her life—even when he was so arrogantly self-assured, because Mikhail had always been that way—made her voice ache.

And yet. Lady-touched. Silver did not want anyone to say the term, anyone with eyes to see her face or nose to smell her scent could tell that, and perhaps she would have preferred no one even think it, but the longer Tatiana spent near her, the truer it seemed. Not reborn. Silver was as mortal as anyone. A great leader, but with weaknesses and blind spots several kilometers wide. But Tatiana saw Her touch in Silver's life, and sometimes wondered if it brushed her own.

To say the Lady *intended* her to help the North Americans, that was hubris. And yet.

"Did our alpha give you any orders in reference to me?" she asked, in English, and walked calmly across the space to Mikhail's side of their small standoff, many against one. Who could certainly account for the majority of those many if he so chose. She kept her hands low and loose, letting the breeze draw tendrils across her eyes and tug them away again without help from her, and let her voice hitch up on the last word. Just a hint of desperation. Not too eager, but longing for home, hoping for reassurance. Even knowing she'd go with him whatever he said, she did wonder in what way he'd try to excuse how their alpha had left her to die.

Mikhail's eyes flickered briefly to her, then settled back on Silver. In case she was a distraction, of course. "Tired of living among the heathens already?" he said in Old Were.

"Tatiana," Andrew snapped, rocking his weight forward, just as if he thought Tatiana were seriously considering changing sides. "You may recall Russia encouraged us to kill you," he growled.

A frown flickered across Mikhail's expression, and finally his attention bled away from Silver. "He means Father," Tatiana said, taking one more step forward. "Since there's no city to call the alpha after. Why, Mikhail? Why did he abandon me?"

"He did not." Mikhail's expression softened, very slightly, pained. "Never think that."

"What was I supposed to think?" Tatiana clenched her hands. She needed to be careful. She wanted that answer too much. Want an answer too much, and you couldn't judge the lie in what you received.

"He knew I would be here soon." Mikhail opened his hands to Tatiana. His voice held *concern*, Lady damn him. Was that acting, to draw her in? Mikhail played parts, the same as any of their alpha's Teeth did, but rarely more than one layer deep. "I knew some woman could not keep you here, even if they said there was one."

"I am a tooth in Her jaw," Tatiana murmured first in Old Were, then in translation for the others. Andrew had removed her brand, the one marking her as a Tooth, at her request. If that reminder didn't reassure him she was still on his side, nothing would. "I didn't know how much I would miss home—" She strode abruptly out of the Roanokes' reach, into Mikhail's.

"You cat," Dare snarled.

Mikhail laughed and took the final step to meet her. "You should have grabbed Silver when you were close, to drag one with us to exile immediately," he said in English. Tatiana reached for him, then pulled her hands back. If her longing for a reunion had been genuine, she still would have known this was not the time for it.

Silver muttered something, drawing everyone's attention back. She pressed her hand briefly to her face, slashed it down. "Death!"

It was not that Silver spoke to Death that frustrated Tatiana; it was that she tried to hide it until the failure to do so was all the more riveting. Any moment, the worship in Mikhail's face might turn to calculation. If he saw Silver's distraction as an opening, what should Tatiana do then? Stand back and let the North American guards—or Andrew himself—get hurt?

Sure enough, Mikhail stilled, but it was directly to Tatiana he spoke. "He told me to bring you home, but to expect no help from you. I did not truly believe it."

And where in the Lady's name had *that* come from? He'd believed her, she'd been sure of it, but she couldn't see any action she'd taken or neglected to take that could have changed his mind so quickly, so that left the no less ridiculous idea that he'd been playing with her the whole time, layers under layers. "Mikhail, what's wrong?" She switched to Old Were, to keep it private between them. "Yes, I went along with them to some degree when I thought I'd been abandoned, but I didn't give anything important—"

Mikhail made a derisive noise. "You watched me." He stabbed a finger at his own chest to match the violence of his words, in English so the others could understand. "*Me.* When she is crazy—" He swept an arm to Silver. "You watch me. Because she seems weak when I said to take her, and that *worries* you. Not makes you happy because it is advantage. I should have believed Father—"

"Father." Tatiana sneered the word and stepped over to place herself before Silver and Andrew. Her chances with Mikhail were well and truly dead, and into the void of disappointment with herself rushed a vibrating rage. She hadn't realized the breadth of what she'd pushed below the surface, but then she'd never had a chance to confront someone from home until now. "He may be our alpha, but he's not our blood. He's not your father, he's not my father. He is a tyrant who demands loyalty on the strength of a lie about being our family, and does not earn it in any other way."

Mikhail stared at Tatiana, lips slightly parted. On one with their kind of control, it spoke as loud as a jaw hanging open. "Tatiana…"

"His first plan could have killed me. And then his backup plan was to leave me to be killed by someone else. All because he fears an alpha with white hair." Tatiana lunged forward to spit the words in her former packmate's face.

Andrew and Silver both grabbed for her, Silver closer and connecting first. Silver could never had held her back, but even the movement from both of them snapped Tatiana out of it. She was panting with her rage, like a fool, and she couldn't afford that.

She'd wanted Mikhail to tell her their alpha wanted her to come home too, too much. But he'd sent a warning about her instead, because he knew how deeply he'd betrayed her.

"I can take you with me whether you like it or no, Tatiana." Mikhail reached to his sides where the sheaths had been hidden under his jacket, and drew out two curved blades. Rather than position them for use, he braced his hands up like an old-time boxer whose fists had grown a cutting edge. She wondered if the showboating was for her sake or the Roanokes'—she doubted they'd ever seen moon knives before, but even Teeth used them for only assassinations intended to serve some great, holy purpose. She certainly hadn't brought hers on her original mission.

Whose death had Father decided the Lady desired this time?

The fighters advanced and Mikhail sheathed the blades, threat made. If he'd intended to use them at this time, the first thing they would have noticed was the blood from two opposing cuts, moments before another two began to bleed. "Consider quickly, or you will not like next step." His bow to Silver was mocking this time.

When he turned back the way he'd come, the guards stepped forward as one. "Capturing me does not help you find your people. If you could take me. Or hold me. Then they might starve, I guess. Or you could try to follow, of course. Ask Tatiana how easy Teeth can lose any pursuers who try." Mikhail didn't even look at them. Dare held up one hand, and everyone held themselves in stillness until Mikhail had climbed into his vehicle and was gone.

Silence settled over them, sticky and uncomfortable. Silver still had hold of Tatiana's arm, and that suddenly made her feel like snarling. She deserved no protectiveness when she'd failed both sides and so, in the end, herself: she couldn't help find the North American captives, and she couldn't bring herself to go home either.

She shoved off Silver's touch. "So much for that idea. I'm sorry." At least that sounded mostly calm. "I didn't know he had come with moon knives."

"Moon knives?" Andrew visibly pushed frustration out of his expression and concentrated on the new information.

"Teeth only bring them on holy missions." Saying it out loud snapped her thoughts into a new alignment, though she didn't know if it was a more hopeful one or not. Mikhail must truly believe the rumors about the Lady reborn, whatever his orders from their alpha had been. Tatiana looked to Silver. "Which I suppose we could make this into. You could agree to go with him, at least until the captives are released."

Silver's lips thinned to whiteness. "I will not play that part."

Which she could say, if she wished. But from where Tatiana stood, given her own failure, it certainly looked like Silver might *have* to.

7

Andrew would have liked to curse at length and volume, but he chewed silently on the words instead as they drove home from the hunting lands. Any time it seemed they'd gotten ahead of the Russians, they arrived to find the Russians were instead three steps beyond that. Why couldn't Russia have sent a damn envoy to the wedding, so they could negotiate in good faith, instead of with teeth to the throats of hostages?

At the house, he started up the stairs for their bedroom, one of the few private places left now wedding guests had likely filled the guest house again, and were noticeably overflowing everywhere else. Rather than follow him, Silver picked her way through a veritable Hollywood epic battle of farm animals versus Hot Wheels set up on the hall's already much scratched wood floor. A couple older children were arguing flanking tactics while younger ones smashed opponents into each other.

Andrew backtracked to join her in the kitchen, clearing his path of a contingent of sheep with the side of a foot. She'd guessed what he was going to say, then. Fine. She needed to hear it anyway. Their options were too few and too poor to ignore any without consideration, at least. "You could act the part and tell him the Lady wants the hostages to go free. He seems like he might believe that."

"No." Silver yanked open a cupboard door, using it to hide her face from him as she rummaged among the cereal and other dry breakfast goods. "You don't understand what you're asking of me, Dare."

"I'm asking you to *think* for a minute. What other choices do we have? Tatiana's idea didn't work. Of course we'll search for the hostages—with everyone here for the wedding, we can cover a lot of area—but that will take time we probably don't have. What else can we do other than exploit this possible weakness of his? Unless you want to change your mind and decide the human isn't worth it." That would still leave Laurence, of course, so Andrew wouldn't be for it even if Silver suddenly spoke with a stranger's voice and claimed she was. "Mikhail showed me a picture of her with the newspaper headlines—a picture that was current, I mean." No way to explain to Silver more precisely than that. "He hadn't hurt her yet."

Silver slammed the cupboard door, end of a granola bar in her teeth. Andrew put out his hand automatically to open it for her, but she ripped at it with the wrapper still in her teeth and got the job done. "And that means it won't hurt her ever?"

Andrew pressed his lips together, suppressing his first, angrier response. "Of course not. If I don't understand your reluctance, explain it to me." He wanted to put an arm around Silver, but he stayed where he was and let her pace out her frustration. "Please, Silver. What's wrong with pretending for a little while?"

Silver took a deep breath and looked up, as if assembling her words like a pack for the hunt. "You don't understand because pretending has no *cost* for you. It's easy to pretend something that has no meaning. The Lady is real, Dare, and pretending to be Her would have a cost to *me*." She set the granola bar down on the nearest counter and thumped a fist against her core. "It's wrong, far more wrong than options and choices and our short-sighted mortal good intentions."

Andrew was trying to understand, he really was. Of course he knew Silver's faith was important to her, but then perhaps what he was missing was the wrongness of it all. "Why would the Lady care if you—?"

"Do not argue motives of gods you don't believe in!" Silver stepped up to him, balanced so she could rock out of the way if he tried to touch her. "It's not about Her, it's about me. If you were to—" She laughed suddenly. "Declare yourself Death incarnate, he would only laugh. But you could pretend to the Lady's words—though no one would believe you—and none would be any worse. I am not afraid of harming Her with pretense; I am afraid of harming *myself*. Why can't you see?"

Her voice wavered, and Andrew realized that this was one of the things he should stop trying to understand and just accept. Silver had said no to the plan, and that was enough. "We need to get everyone we can out searching, organized so we cover territory efficiently. It must be somewhere within a reasonable traveling distance of the hunting lands, if he was going there to feed them after speaking to us." When Silver relaxed her weight down, he pulled her into an embrace. His shirt tightened like her hand had clenched around a handful of fabric at the back.

"I thought I might invite my drinking buddies out this evening." Silver's father ambled into the kitchen, holding up his phone in illustration. "See what they might give in and brag about. Or even just where they're currently hanging out, in town."

Andrew had stiffened automatically at the interruption, as

ridiculous as that was when he and Silver had been having their discussion in a public area of the pack house, but he forced himself to relax again. "Do you really think they'd hang around near where they'd dropped off the hostages—unless Mikhail is still using them as guards." Hugh smiled as the connection must have sparked visibly in Andrew's expression. "That's a very good idea. He might not trust them enough, but then again, can he really risk leaving the hostages alone?"

Hugh tipped his head in acknowledgment, and he pulled his face into an expression of casual boredom as the phone rang on speakerphone, as if getting into character meant looking the part even when only his voice was transmitted. "Hey, Chuck. Feelin' thirsty tonight?"

A man laughed in response. Andrew didn't recognize the voice, but he wouldn't have expected to. His visit to Alaska had been years back, and he'd only heard the one of them say a sentence or so at the wedding. "Hey, Hugh. I thought you were bonding with your daughter or whatever. Tired of family togetherness already?"

Hugh gave Silver a twisted smile, and she reflected it back. Andrew tried to trace their resemblance further, as it was clearly the same smile, but he suspected her brother's masculine features had always shown their father's blood better than Silver's feminine ones did. "Everyone's got their tails in a twist about whatever prank that Russian of yours was planning. I got out of the way. Where do you want to meet?"

"Oh, sorry." Chuck made a reluctant noise. "We're back up in Anchorage, working on something. Probably couldn't meet you even if you came up."

Hugh met Andrew's eyes, and they were both so intent on the conversation that Andrew had to break the eye contact a bit abruptly before it got to the point of measuring dominance.

"Working on something? Come on, man. Don't act like you're fooling me. You helped that guy pull off his prank. I suppose you didn't tell me about it so you didn't have to split the profits? I'm hurt. You two owe me a night of drinking at the very least. Where are you staying?"

Chuck whined in discomfort. "Look. It is your daughter we're pranking, man. We didn't wanna make you feel weird. We're—"

"Come on, Chuck. No goofing off. We'll catch up with Hugh when we're done." The second man's voice approached the cell's mic from some distance and ended when he seemed to take the phone. "Gotta be serious about this job. Sorry, Hugh," he said. "No goofing off."

"Sure," Hugh said, and grimaced as he batted joking farewells back and forth. After hanging up, he gave Silver and Andrew a helpless shrug.

"Anchorage? They can't be involved any longer, then." Andrew suppressed a growl, mostly at himself for indulging in the hope that things could be that easy. "They must be lying. Or working on something unrelated."

Hugh scoffed. "Hardly. They're too transparent for the first and too lazy for the second. What about that Russian? Why can't the lie be whatever he said that makes you think the hostages aren't in Anchorage too? Why not put them somewhere well out of the way?"

"Because he'd have loved to crow about that," Silver said, but Andrew could see from her frown that she was still giving her father's suggestion deep consideration. "They're so far from here, you'll never find them, and so forth. Still. I know which side I'd suspect of lying myself." She gave a huff of a frustrated laugh. "As does Death." She transferred her gaze to Andrew.

"Surely we can spare one team to search there, while the rest spread out nearer to home?"

Andrew gave it consideration of his own, but quicker. "I don't think one team would make any difference down here, so we might as well." He pinched the bridge of his nose as he added another variable to those he was already balancing for the logistics of the search. "If they did take the hostages up to Alaska, they must have flown them in a private plane. Wouldn't have to be a big one, but they couldn't go commercial, and driving would have taken far too long. Laurence—" Laurence was the one with pilot friends, even if he'd let his license lapse, but of course Laurence wasn't available to them at the moment. "I suppose they could do human-style tracking from the airport or whatever private airfields are available up there."

"I'll get John. If you send him to lead the team, he can pick it himself so we don't have to worry about it." Silver jogged past her father into the house. For a moment, Andrew was rather surprised by her seizing the chance to make the assignment herself, but of course she wanted to pour effort into the search since she'd been the one to make the other possible plan unworkable. Fair enough.

"Thanks," Andrew told Hugh. Even if the lead didn't pan out, he appreciated Hugh's effort. Hugh seemed to take it as a dismissal, as he drifted out. Tidying instincts made Andrew pick up Silver's abandoned granola bar, and since the wrapper was already destroyed, he ate the bar rather than try to find a place to put it away. He should probably let the sub-alphas make their own organizational choices for the search parties as well. They needed to spread people as widely as was safe, and the sub-alphas would have a better read on which of their people should be placed in larger or smaller groups.

Death arrived from where the others had disappeared, striding into the kitchen as real as any of the pack members in wolf form, except for the way the floor seemed to shred away to mist and darkness where he stepped. "If she played the Lady, your part would be Death," he remarked.

"What, are you saying it would suit me?" Andrew snapped. He wondered if other people's imaginations manifested to mock them the way his did. "We're not playing any parts, Death or otherwise."

Death stopped at his feet and looked up. "Too short," he decided, and brushed past. When Andrew turned, he was gone, leaving only the smooth, varnished surface of the lower cupboard doors behind.

8

Later the next day, Silver took her lunch to eat outside, in their small patch of territory between the dens. Uncomfortably hot days would be coming soon enough, but now one could escape the discomfort of direct sunlight simply by walking into shade. She sat in the direct light and held on to the flushed feeling across her skin.

Perhaps she'd hoped unconsciously that it would keep Death at a little distance, but he lay down in the shade beneath her seat, and laughed that she couldn't keep an eye on him except by bending down or twisting around. She'd have liked to be able to brood in peace. She could not go out searching herself, of course, for reasons of safety, and Dare was similarly trapped with her because of the alphas' need to keep everyone organized from a central location. In theory, that should have left her space to be alone, but their visitors filtered back in between shifts for the wedding feasts, which she'd noticed had begun to cast a festival atmosphere over the whole endeavor. As if Mikhail were merely an opponent to be soundly beaten in some sort of game. She was avoiding a feast at the moment, not wanting to dampen the atmosphere that did no harm, in truth.

She could by no means share in it, however. No traces had been found, by John, who had left last night, or by those close to home. Frustration etched away the edges of Silver's every thought, as she had nothing to do but wait. If the hostages were killed, what response from Roanoke was even possible, short of war? Worse—if the hostages were found, what then? How could they get *ahead* of Russia?

But plan too far ahead and it ceased to be planning and became unproductive worry. She could do little herself at the moment, but having something done by a pack member, not the alphas, did not render it useless. With all of Roanoke searching, someone would catch a hint of a scent. Then they would deal with the problems of that day, on that day.

She had to believe that.

Footsteps approached, and didn't pass by as a pack member about their business would have when the alpha wore the kind of expression Silver imagined she did. She looked around and caught his scent at the same time she caught sight of her father. The skin around his blue eyes creased with concern. "May I join you?" he asked.

Silver gestured that he was welcome and looked down at her food on her lap. She should offer him some, but she had hardly any left. He waved away the idea before she could ask if she should get him more. He chose one of the outdoor seats and placed it so the sun would not be in his eyes, but struck up golden streaks in the brown of his hair as it angled across.

"How long are you going to stay? We deeply appreciate your help, but I know I haven't had much time to talk to you about anything else. With so much distraction at the moment..."

Even if Silver had had her undivided attention to give to her father, she didn't know what more she'd have said or done with him, so perhaps it was all for the best.

Her father exhaled on a laughing note. "Life is distracting." He avoided the first question, Silver noticed, but she didn't push him. Maybe he was waiting like her, staying until something felt…satisfied, about their relationship. Silver was starting to doubt that would ever happen, but she couldn't get herself to give up on the idea either.

Her father offered something across to her. "Do you know what that is?"

Silver frowned at the object. It was definitely slippery, of the wrong shape for her poisoned vision to identify. A depiction of two children smiled at her, the girl riding an adult's wolf form while the older boy clung to the adult's ruff. She started to touch his face, but some buried impulse told her that pictures took touches badly. "It's me and my brother." More deduction than recognition—what other children, one younger girl, one older boy, would her father show her?

Death roused himself and stood in the full light to examine the depiction himself. "You looked decidedly vacuous when young." He sauntered off to lounge in the shadow cast by the den nearby.

"And this?" Her father made some movement, and the picture changed, became a collection of angles and white against dark background. Against water, she picked out when she'd frowned long enough. The sea, perhaps. Gulls liked to travel the sea and screech at the waves as if their voices could stop the Lady's pull on the tide.

Her father made an encouraging noise, and Silver decided to try another deduction. "Is it where you go swimming?"

Her father stared. "Swimming?"

Silver pressed her lips together and kept careful hold of her temper. Just because her husband and home pack knew how to speak so she could understand didn't mean that others were confusing to be malicious. "You said before. Flying on the water."

"Sailing?" When she nodded, her father laughed warmly, but she could see his concern was only increasing. "Yes. This is a—" He tapped the picture and said a word Silver didn't know, and she shook her head.

He repeated himself again, and she shoved his hand with the object back to him. "If I could see your world simply by trying harder, don't you think I might have managed it in the *years* since I was poisoned? I appreciate that you want to help me, but the time to have done that was years ago. Even then, it wouldn't have worked, but at least then it wouldn't have been patronizing."

"Silver…" Her father fussed with the picture for a moment and finally put it away. "All right. I was just trying to help. Isn't that what parents are supposed to do?" he smiled weakly. "Make things worse by interfering in their adult children's lives?"

"Mm." Silver tried to settle herself into a more relaxed position in her seat, but it wasn't easy. "Meet any sea wolves?"

Her father huffed a laugh. "Yes, actually. Not like you mean, in the stories, swimming Were that never stop growing. But there are some true wolves that swim in the sea and eat roe. Off the coast of—" Another awkward pause, filled with things he seemed to finally realize he couldn't convey. "North of here."

Dare stepped outside at that moment, thank the Lady for the interruption, and Silver made herself not do anything so insulting to her father as to sit up straight and wave him over.

"Hugh." Dare nodded in bland greeting and settled himself sitting beside Silver, his silence pointed. It stretched until only someone asleep could have missed the fact that Dare was waiting for her father to remove himself so they could talk privately.

Her father declined, apparently. He leaned a little forward, hands clasped and wrists resting on his knees. "With no one finding anything around here, had you considered sending more up to join your beta's search?"

"We've got it under control." Dare purposely echoed her father's light tone. He remained comfortable enough in his seat, but his wild self stood, lip lifted slightly off its teeth.

"I have connections. I know Alaska himself. Maybe he could help, up there." Silver's father tilted his head a little as if avoiding direct light in his eyes, but it showed more of his neck, at least enough respect to keep the conversation going.

He was still trying to help, Silver realized. It made her want to put her face in her hand.

"If he did convince them to search at all, Alaska's people would only be itching to get back on four feet and running down their own prey again. My beta and his team will find the trail if there's one to find." Dare's voice twisted angrier than Silver had expected, and she reached out to touch his knee. She'd been plenty frustrated herself moments before, yes, but frustration was different than anger. Her father had good intentions.

Her father sat back, smelling of some surprise at the tone as well. "You never struck me as being too proud to accept help."

"You never struck me as anything, because I'd never met you before you showed up just when this batch of trouble started." Dare's wild self was snarling openly now, but Dare had gone a little calmer as he did when he recognized dealing with

some matter of pack business had involved him too emotionally. "With connections to everyone causing it. Been to Russia, a
friend of the Alaskans involved..."

"How dare you suggest I would work against my own
daughter." Her father surged to his feet.

Silver opened her lips, but her voice couldn't find any words
to shape itself to. Death stepped into her pause. "Aren't you going to defend your own father?" She shook her head: at him, at
the whole situation. She didn't know what to think. That was
the problem.

"You haven't exactly been around to build that relationship." Dare didn't get up. "If you'd been unconnected to all of
this, that would be one thing, but now the question has to be
asked."

"You've been talking to my nephew, I see." Silver's father
flexed his hands as if imagining smacking John.

"Why didn't you come, when my brother died, then?" Silver had at least the satisfaction of silence clearing away the ag-
gression of the others' words when she spoke. She swallowed.
This was hard, but necessary. The trail of their current snarling
led back to that, she judged.

Her father collapsed into his seat. His next words escaped
as a heavy sigh. "Puppy...I didn't come because I was sailing.
By the time I heard, it was too late, it would have been awkward
to show up then." His lips stretched up in something that was
too thin to be a smile. "Protective nephews would have asked
questions. So I put off visiting, and it only got more awkward,
of course. I should have come as soon as I heard, that would
have been understandable and not so awkward after all, but
now..." He shrugged. "From the rumors that trickled in, you'd
found a wonderful life for yourself."

Her father held up a hand when Dare would have broken in. "So hearing the Alaskans bragging about the money they'd make off the Russian was what knocked me out of my cowardice. You could say the trouble dragged me along with it. I am working against Russia, same as you." He pressed his thumb to his forehead.

Dare didn't answer, scent muddying, probably as he tried to decide whether to believe her father. Silver already knew she did. Because of the strong arms and deep voice that lurked in her memory. She didn't see how believing that would hurt anyone, whether it was true or not. If he was working with the Alaskans, what could he do that was worse than the Russian had already done? How could he get anything past them with Dare so on guard?

Her father stood, taking on more of his earlier casual confidence, his vulnerability disappearing like tears drying away so the salt-crust evidence was barely visible and you questioned if they'd ever been. "I'll let you get back to your planning."

"Wonderful even if I can't see what you show me?" Silver said it soft enough she wasn't sure if she meant him to hear it or not, but he did, of course.

He smiled just as softly and turned only partly to face her. "Wonderful even though you talk to Death. I mean, you found a mate who does too, so who am I to judge?"

Silver laughed. Of all the Were she'd ever met, Dare worked the hardest not to believe. "Dare doesn't—"

But Dare had frozen, and his wild self had tucked its tail between its legs. The stink of his panic—*panic?*—reached her a beat later.

"Dare? He must have misinterpreted…" Silver felt shaking start in her hand. She couldn't honestly tell if it was from upset or anger. At their core, both were so similar. This was all a mis-understanding. Her heart was pounding in reaction to a silly misunderstanding.

  Dare had to clear his throat to get words out. "I…was jumping at shadows. An optical illusion, that's all."

"An illusion of what?" Silver's father asked the question so blandly that Silver suddenly wondered if he'd made the remark on purpose, a lunge to flush suspected prey from the brushes. If nothing ran, you laughed it off. If something did…then your daughter knew what you thought it was only fair she know.

Because you were helping.

"Had you not been willfully blind, your father would not have had to force this knowledge upon you. Why are you angry? You suspected it all along." Death paced to stand equally between her and Dare. When the sunlight struck his coat, it disappeared, leaving twilight and confusion between them.

But Silver hadn't suspected it. She'd never suspected it, that her quirk that he respected, accepted with quiet forbearance when she knew he longed to lecture her about "optical illusions fed by otherwise inaccessible unconscious knowledge," was a quirk he should have *known* was not a quirk at all. That all his acceptance was utter hypocrisy.

She sought Dare's eyes, tried to find evidence there that he'd heard Death, that he was even now ignoring that lupine darkness between them. Death scoffed. "You truly think I am constrained to a single place and time, as a mortal is? What you see belongs to you alone. What he sees…" The guard hairs of Death's ruff rumpled in a shrug. "Or doesn't see, belongs to him alone. That is the way of belief."

Her shaking was definitely anger. Rage. "How could you let me think I was alone?" Silver needed to shout it in Dare's face, take her anger close enough that he could *feel* it, and Death moved aside to let her pass. "Standing on your hill of patronization, of *pity*, and looking down on me and murmuring comforting words and all the while you were the same. The same as me!"

Dare tried to catch her hands. "It's not like that, Silver. I never looked down on you."

He got her bad hand, she couldn't stop that, but she snatched her other away to smash into his chest, his shoulder, over and over. So *angry*. "But you see Death!" He hadn't admitted that in so many words yet, but she knew. She knew.

Dare caught her other wrist to stop her blows, but she wrenched it away and slapped him instead. The crack as his chin snapped to the side should have felt good, should have quieted some of the emotion spilling up and over and out of her, but it only fed it. Reason honed over the years, not instinct, made her stop, pull away. She dropped her hand, and she swallowed down the anger until it eased enough she could turn away from him.

"Silver, please. I'm sorry." He smelled sorry, his voice begged sincerely enough, but of course he was sorry. Sorry it had all come to light.

The same hard-won wisdom of years that had made her drop her hand whispered to her that she needed to leave. Leave and breathe and perhaps, when considered, Dare's actions would no longer seem the worst crime that could be committed, one mate to another. But now, now it was the worst and Silver kept walking away from him, kept going out past the den and among the humans' dens and paths.

She'd walk until she could think again.

Five years together and Andrew knew he had to let Silver go. Once he found someone to follow her discreetly, though. She shouldn't be out completely alone with Mikhail around. He hated to double up on someone's duties, on top of the search for Laurence and the human this morning, but there was nothing else for it. He jogged inside, and found Were scattered around, sleepy in the wake of the latest wedding feast. Pierce, his first choice for guarding Silver, was watching something on Sacramento's phone, which she was holding up for them in the corner of the living room.

Rather than noticeably break up the group, Andrew joined them, and looked at the phone without really seeing. He trusted Sacramento to keep her mouth shut. "Pierce, Silver wanted some time alone. I need you to follow her far enough back that she has some privacy."

"Certainly." Pierce dipped his head and rolled his shoulders back, taking his perfectly groomed appearance—or perfectly mussed, since he'd been off duty for the moment—and transforming it into the slick professionalism of a fighter. Andrew appreciated the fact that Pierce caught the nuances without Andrew having to explain them, and offered no comment.

Andrew scanned the room. Two people would be much better than one, but two was starting to trespass on Silver's illusion of being alone. Sacramento coughed apologetically. "There was actually something I wanted to talk to her about when the moment was right. I could go along to bring it up on the way back?"

Andrew allowed himself a sigh of relief and squeezed Sacramento's upper arm. More strength without more "guards." Perfect. "Please. I appreciate it."

Andrew pressed his lips together as they left. Knowing the others would be with Silver didn't make not following her himself any easier. But she'd be back in an hour, or two, and then they could talk.

Not that he knew if talking would help, this time, but at least it was better than screaming at each other. Lady, Silver was usually the calm one. She was good at it, he wasn't. He headed back out of the kitchen door to the backyard and rounded on Hugh even though he knew he shouldn't. "What in the Lady's kind light was that *for*? Are you happy now?"

"I didn't do anything." Hugh held up his hands, placating. "I didn't know that you had that kind of secret from your wife."

But he was damned smug that he'd successfully put Andrew in the wrong; Andrew could read that in his scent. If Andrew hadn't had secrets from his wife, the comment would have had no effect. Andrew was to blame, not Hugh. Damn his voice to the void.

And he *was* to blame. Guilt gained ground against the temper that flared automatically when he was shouted at. He'd hurt Silver and he didn't…didn't know how to put things back together again, make her stop hurting. He couldn't say he believed what they saw really was Death, because he knew his hallucinations were a manifestation of his unconscious as much as hers were.

But that didn't make them less…true. Andrew realized that was the word he wanted. The hallucinations weren't real, but that didn't make them untrue. More true, if you considered how they came from within, revealing the things you'd hidden from yourself. He'd been a coward to be afraid of what she'd think of him if he admitted what he saw, but he'd never thought less of her.

"A start." Death's voice came from behind him. Andrew whirled, completely on edge, but any hallucination wasn't visual this time. "I'd keep working on what you'll tell her, though, if I were you. Working hard." Again, Death's voice was behind him, heavy with sarcasm.

Andrew turned his movement toward Death into a snarling stride toward Hugh. How could he possibly have known, when could he have seen—? Then Andrew had it. After he'd pushed Silver on pretending to be the Lady in the kitchen. Hugh must not have left earshot as quickly as he'd appeared to. Damn his voice to the void. "And you had to do this now? When people are still in danger?"

"Is everything a political calculation with you?" Hugh dropped the "aw, shucks, what have I done?" look and straightened, expression hardening. Though he didn't outmass Andrew by much, his stance reminded Andrew that he must be in his seventies, with decades more of scrapping experience than Andrew, experience in human, probably in bars with his drinking buddies. Taking this physical would go badly, unless he turned it into a full challenge in wolf.

And a full challenge in his wolf would lead to much of Roanoke wondering why its alpha felt the need to challenge his mate's father while the mate herself was conspicuously absent.

And he'd just proved Hugh's point. "It has to be. I'm glad you, as a roamer, have the luxury not to take that into account—"

"I am taking into account my *daughter*—"

"What, like that will make up for lost time? I've been down that road with mine. Trust me, it's not so simple." Despite his best intentions, Andrew couldn't stop himself from getting right up into Hugh's face, vibrating with violence denied. "At least if you'd come to me first, I could have found some way… way to…"

Way to have not hurt Silver in the first place. Which didn't exist. Anger gave way to guilt again, within the whole tangled mess of it all. "Way to apologize." That used up the last clear words he had, anything else disintegrating into a jagged mess. He dropped his head and stepped back.

Silence for a few beats, then— "Perhaps I did go about this the wrong way." When Andrew looked up, Hugh was scrubbing a hand through his hair, head turned as if searching out an escape route. Which perhaps he was. Keep right on roaming until the heat had died down.

"Can you at least refrain from discussing this with anyone else?" Andrew caught Hugh's eyes, but Hugh looked away and conceded the measuring of dominance instantly. "Fear that their alphas are fighting among themselves while the Russians threaten us might hurt any number of people."

"I promise." Hugh pressed his thumb to his forehead, heavily formal now. "Andrew—"

"Don't." Andrew stepped past him to head for the main house. People would be expecting to be sent out searching again, for the afternoon. He needed to pull up his calm alpha's mask and go be very visible, while Silver wasn't.

9

Andrew was able to keep busy at first, coordinating the searchers leaving for the afternoon, but when they were gone, he had
little to distract him while he waited for Silver to cool down.
He pasted on a pleasant expression and took one of the house-
hold's tablets to the dining room table to look over the map in a
central location. Pins littered the local landscape on the shared
map, dropped by searchers on their phones when they finished
an area. Andrew laid the tablet flat and dragged the map around
in a futile search for obvious holes. At this stage in a search,
that wasn't really the point, of course—they wouldn't find the
original trail of hostages into their prison, not so late, but if they
had enough coverage, they could still hope to locate any new
scent of Mikhail the wind caught when he left his vehicle or a
building.

Portland, one of those still at the house for child care, nodded to him as she passed through, leaving him alone with no

one to impress with the calm alpha act, but nothing better to do either. The cat—either Silver's or Felicia's, each attributed responsibility to the other—wandered in next and leaped up to the tabletop, apparently attracted by a sixth sense of an activity it could disrupt. Morsel was a gray tabby, but of a cloudy, almost purple-tinged shade. She flopped long and used the corner of the tablet for a pillow. Her ruff fur obscured a whole neighborhood, but it wasn't like Andrew was really looking at the map anyway. He smoothed down a few stripes along her flank, though he really shouldn't encourage that kind of behavior. She purred smugly.

Tatiana drifted in next and looked a question at him. Andrew shook his head. No new developments when it came to the hostages.

Where *was* Silver? Pierce would have called if anything had happened to her, or if he'd lost her. Andrew checked his phone for any missed calls or texts. As if summoned by his thoughts, it rang, though that was less eerie considering how many times he'd checked it over the last few hours.

It was Felicia calling, not Pierce, so Andrew answered without particular panic. The young people had assembled themselves into a mini-pack that was probably doing more running around and roughhousing with each other than actually searching. He hadn't fought it, and had told them to range across the whole city rather than sticking to an assigned sector as the other teams were. "What's up, puppy?"

"Papa—" Beyond Felicia's strained tone, the diminutive set off alarms. Andrew shoved to his feet, the chair scraping across the already much-scratched wood floor. "You know Billings' son is searching with my group, right? He got a text from his father to come out to the hunting lands. But when we got there, we smelled blood and then we found Billings—" Her voice wavered.

Andrew strode to the opposite end of the room. Tatiana remained where she was, expression tightening. "Found him what?" Andrew focused on shaping each word with utter calm. Felicia was all right enough if she was making the call.

"Dead. Just…cut up." Felicia gulped. "I managed to shove everyone back down to the cars. We're there right now."

"Lady." Rather than think about it too hard, Andrew let his mind fall into the clarity of immediate action. "You did exactly right. Stay where you are, together. I'll be there as soon as I can."

"Mikhail's next move," Tatiana said as he ended the call and shoved his phone into his pocket. He didn't stop to answer, but she easily kept up with his strides toward the garage.

"Apparently." Andrew yanked open the door and fumbled his keys with a clatter onto the concrete when he tried to beep his car unlocked. "Cut him up."

"I know." Tatiana climbed into the passenger seat without further comment when he finally got the car open. It took Andrew until he was turning the key in the ignition to realize that she hadn't been reminding him she'd overheard the call, she'd been saying she'd already known how Mikhail would choose to kill.

"Cut up" was an understatement. Billings' tanned skin was crisscrossed with wound over wound over wound, except where they thinned out over his face, all the better to allow identification. Before this moment, Andrew would have sworn it was impossible, but now he found himself fully able to believe that a Were could die of blood loss. So many slashes. One must have hit an artery, eventually, but he couldn't pick out that one among the many.

Tatiana efficiently braided her hair back and snapped an elastic on the end of the tail. She crouched over Billings. Andrew didn't know she managed it. The scent of a dead body was one thing, but his every inhalation felt like it brought with it a fine mist of blood, for all that the underbrush Billings was lying on was nearly free of it. Such wounds should have coated every leaf—and must have, wherever he'd actually been killed, before being dumped here. Beyond the smell, the day was beautiful, late afternoon sunlight almost properly warm, and saturating all the colors around them.

And congealing the blood that remained on Billings' skin to greater rankness, as well. Andrew hardly wanted to talk, because that disturbed his careful pattern of breathing to handle the smell. He paced the outside of the clear space between great evergreen trunks, found a few diffuse traces of Mikhail—no shit—and Billings' bloody phone, placed neatly atop a raised knuckle of a root. As if there were any doubt who'd sent the text.

Tatiana took Billings' wrist with delicate fingertips and turned the hand over to expose the palm. It was relatively intact compared to the raw meat of the forearm that would have been held up defensively, except for a neat cut from thumb to pinkie, bisecting the main palm lines. "Signed his kill, of course. Cat's bastard."

"What?" Andrew gathered a deep breath and came to lean over the body too.

Tatiana angled the palm so he could see better. "See how it hasn't bled? This was done after death. A generation ago, there was some trouble with personal kills that were blamed on the Lady's Jaw. So we all started signing them so another Tooth could tell the difference. Of course, given that he's the only Tooth out here and North Americans don't know this style..." She snarled with disgust.

Andrew straightened and strode away again to try to find a little mental distance. He clenched his hand and leaned his forehead on it on the nearest tree. No, no, no, no! He needed to act, fast, but he needed Silver to talk to and he needed a pause to breathe clean air and he had neither.

Dammit.

He'd try talking it through, then. "I assume this was done with the knives we saw before?"

"Moon knives." Visible in his peripheral vision, Tatiana wiped her fingers the side of her thigh and stood. "Used for kills ordered by Father in his role as head of the priesthood. And for any ordered by the priestesses too, I suppose, though they don't generally meddle."

Andrew wondered if not for the existence of Silver making this a religious matter, if Billings' death would have been less cruel. But maybe if not for the existence of Silver, Russia would have stayed away, practicing his cruelty only on his own people. He shoved himself away from the tree to face Tatiana. "This is his next move, then. We won't go into exile, so he starts killing. Why not the hostages?"

Tatiana lowered a hand to indicate Billings. "To kill high-ranked instills more fear. Killing low-ranked instills more protectiveness and wish for revenge. I don't know for sure, but given that we learned our pack formations from the same alpha, as it were, that's how I'd read it."

Andrew looked at the sky. He wished he had a curse good enough for this. "And Roanoke Were, when fearful, put pressure on me and Silver to make it stop."

"Mm. And he will continue." Tatiana wiped her fingers on her thigh again, even though they'd looked perfectly clean the first time, a break in her casual manner.

"Until I stop *him*." Andrew turned for the cars, but Tatiana caught his arm.

"Not alone." The earlier crack gaped wide, and Andrew could see her own fear. "We're very, very good at this, Andrew. It's our whole purpose in life. Fight him alone, he wins."

Andrew clenched his teeth until his breaths made it back to even. She was speaking sense. Sense. He was listening. He was not giving in to the anger.

When Tatiana seemed to trust his calm, she spoke again. "It would probably be safest to pull everyone back to the pack house for now."

Andrew brushed off her touch to show how he didn't need it. "You're right, the hostages will have to wait. Billings shouldn't have been on his own in the first place, but I told the sub-alphas to divide their people as they thought best, so clearly he thought he could take Mikhail on alone." Would that his arrogance could have been disproved in another manner.

Andrew called Pierce as they jogged down the path to the cars. He kept the conversation short, conscious of everyone else he needed to get hold of, but Pierce assured him he'd ask Silver to head home immediately.

Tatiana took a couple longer steps to come even with him as he finished. "I assume you'll be staying here for the clean-up. May I...?" The pause sounded like one to catch her breath when hurrying, but she wasn't otherwise breathing hard. "May I go back to the house immediately? I know Allison's with Pierce, and will be heading back already, but I just want to meet her there..."

Andrew tossed her the keys. "Go. There's nothing for you to do here anyway." She sprinted ahead of him, pounding down to his car, and he fetched up in front of the half dozen young Were, Felicia at their head, instinctively leading and shielding both. Good for her. A young man with Billings' heavy shoulders on an otherwise long frame pushed forward. "It was that Russian, wasn't it? Just let me track him, and I'll—"

"Get killed the same way, if you're alone." Andrew definitely needed to keep control of this conversation right from the start. "But there is something you can do. I need you—" He nodded to the young man, but then focused on Felicia. "To help me with calling everyone else back to the pack house, all right? I've got to focus on the clean-up, so if you can make sure no one gets missed in passing the message, it would be a big help." Normally that would be John's job, but there was no need to bounce the message to Anchorage and back if Felicia could step up.

Wide-eyed nods collected, Andrew got out his own phone and took a few steps away as the group huddled together, divvying up the responsibility by who had whom in their address books already.

He had his own logistics to pin down, and quickly.

10

Silver finally acknowledged the Were following her on her way back to the pack house. She was still angry with Dare, but she did have to admit to herself that she knew him, and she knew that he wouldn't have kept that he saw Death a secret to hurt her. She checked Pierce's face first for any opinion on his alphas' fight, but he was as calm and professional as always.

"You can get back to what you were doing soon," Silver said, by way of a sideways apology without admitting that his alphas were in the wrong. He shrugged good naturedly, and shoved his hands in his pockets as he ambled. Sacramento, silent to this point, increased her speed to fall in beside Silver, rather than continuing to lurk with Pierce.

Silver drew herself out of her own thoughts enough to consider the other woman. She didn't have the manner of a guard, as Pierce did, so Silver assumed she wanted to talk about something. It brought another drop or two of calm to realize that Dare didn't think she needed so many guards. "Yes?" she asked, voice fairly even.

"Tatiana didn't sleep much last night. Came to bed pretty upset." Sacramento attempted an amble herself and failed miserably, unsure what to do with her hands. "Don't know if you can tell me much, but after too long, throwing a lot of completely directionless support at someone seems to do more harm than good. Lady knows *she* won't tell me what's bothering her. Obviously, it can't be fun having her former packmate here causing trouble, but I feel like there's more layers to it than that."

Silver supposed Sacramento deserved at least the basics. Her emotions protested her changing focus of attention, tightening up her voice as she tried to set her own problems aside, but thinking about dealing with someone else's did offer her perspective after a moment.

"Hush. We all know the world revolves around you." Death's barb had little sting, as it was chasing away the last of her selfishness, rather than puncturing it at full bloom.

Silver glanced back at Pierce. She trusted his discretion, but it never hurt to specify exactly when it needed to go into effect. He nodded, then looked at the ground with studied deafness. "He's certainly more than simply a former packmate. I'm not sure how to characterize him. Fellow warrior? Pack brother? Former lover? Last night at the negotiation, she pretended to rejoin him."

Sacramento blew out a large breath and pulled her hair back before remembering herself and releasing it again to fall around her face as Tatiana had convinced her to start wearing it. "I wondered if it was something to do with family." She bared her teeth, gaze distant. At what concept she was expressing her anger, Silver couldn't guess. "I suppose you two were worried she'd double-cross you."

Silver growled. "I would have thought you, of all the pack, could follow your alphas in trust when they choose to grant it. Her loyalty was not, and is not, in doubt."

Sacramento hunched her shoulders, scent turning apologetic. "Sorry. It's not that I—she doesn't trust you to trust her, if that makes any sense, and I guess I picked up on that. If you handed her perfect autonomy and her own alphaship, Tatiana would still be waiting for the hidden hunters to reveal themselves. Her upbringing's left her too twisty for her own good."

Which was as good a read on Tatiana as Silver had ever managed herself, so she smoothed the tension out of her shoulders and let any additional growls go. "Her former packmate didn't believe her, anyway."

"Oh." Sacramento fussed with her hair again and finally gave in and fastened it back.

Silver frowned, chasing the spike of relief she'd caught in Sacramento's scent. "Didn't you just finish saying how you don't doubt her?"

Sacramento freed her hands to gesture sharply with frustration. "I trust her not to betray us, certainly. But she might want to go home. Family is powerful. I don't know. She doesn't talk to me." Her voice took on notes of a wail, quickly suppressed.

"But you two—" Silver should have considered her words more carefully, but surprise caught her too. They'd been spending every spare moment together at the wedding. Had Mikhail come between them? But Sacramento's worry seemed of longer standing than that.

"Sure, she's happy to play chase." Sacramento smiled thinly. "Lots of chase. And talk about unimportant things. But nothing of any particular meaning. I can't get through to that part of her. She thinks her own thoughts deep and private." Sacramento gestured like flickers of thoughts behind her eyes.

"Go on, stun us with the wisdom of your advice," Death said, and danced out of the way moments before Sacramento kicked at the ground of their path. Because he knew Silver didn't have any, of course. She hardly knew what to say to her own mate at the moment.

"Maybe…seeing a packmate will help resolve some of her conflicted feelings about her former home?" Silver offered, at length. It was the best she had. She didn't need to say that it might take a very long time for Tatiana to learn to trust her lover, or that it might never happen at all. Sacramento knew that.

"Maybe." Sacramento hunched over again. "I just wish I could make her feel safe. I can offer her love, but I can't offer her the feeling of safety. She has to feel that herself."

Like love, Silver supposed, offered but not yet returned. "You're wise to recognize that's what she needs." She directed her steps closer so she could squeeze the back of Sacramento's neck.

Sacramento's upset eased so much at being called wise, Silver felt a twinge of guilt. It was true, though. Sacramento had thought things through.

An insistent noise startled them both, and Silver pulled back, but Sacramento ignored it, so Silver did the same. They ambled on in silence, but then another noise began and Pierce started speaking to someone at a distance.

"Fuck." Pierce caught up to them abruptly, herding without regard for rank. "That Russian killed someone." He increased his pace behind them, urging them to greater speed as well.

"Who was kind of garbled. One of the sub-alphas? Anyway, orders are clear: everyone back to the house, watch for threats."

Silver gritted her teeth. This was the Russians' next step, clearly. She glanced at Death, loping along with them now with such an easy grace he might have been strolling. "You'll know soon enough," he said, in his favorite voice, not in the voice of this new victim as Silver had hoped.

Silver smacked the side of Pierce's arm lightly to direct him to curve off into an overgrown patch of territory not currently claimed by humans. She knew the area around here better than even Pierce because of her wandering, and this was a substantial shortcut.

The three of them strung out to duck through a boundary of leaning wood, Silver settling between the other two from pure habit. No hint of scent, or scuffle of movement warned her until she whirled and blood spattered her like a slash itself as the heavy, wet droplets smacked into her skin. Pierce collapsed, flow from this throat turning from flood to trickle as the wound closed. Mikhail rid his knife of some coating of blood with an easy flick of a wrist.

If Pierce was healing, he was still alive. Silver collapsed after him to her knees, and when she set a shaking hand on his chest, it rose. Unconscious, too much blood gone, but not dead.

"Don't worry, he is too low rank for my purposes," Mikhail said, pleasantly. Silver looked up, belatedly considering that perhaps she should have run…but helping Pierce was more important, and she guessed that Mikhail would not harm one he'd called Lady-touched. Mikhail's shadows flowed from the core of his voice down his arms to his blades, where they smoothed the edges over as if whetting them, ready for another kill.

He held both knives loosely, blades oriented up over his knuckles, and smiled. "Now, her..." His next words Silver couldn't understand. Sacramento gasped and stumbled back a step to set her back against an unbroken section of the line of wood. Mikhail smiled wider. "It is you."

"What did he say?" Silver pushed to her feet and tried to get between Mikhail and Sacramento. He flicked a slash at the air in front of her, and she had to stay back.

"He said he's here for me..." Sacramento shook her head and glanced wildly around them before jerking off her shirt. No humans to see if she shifted.

Understanding aligned for Silver like a startled prey bolting from cover. "Tatiana has started teaching you? Puppy, that was a *test*. He wanted to find Tatiana's lover."

"Let's not go that far. Her current chase. Also sub-alpha, and I am hunting those. Very efficient. Two prey, one bite." He lashed out with one knife, and a red line traced across Sacramento's belly, once, twice as it healed up behind. She left off trying to shift and rushed him, but that only caught the next slashes across her collarbone and wrist. The second wound painted a layer of red all down her arm before it could heal.

Silver needed to keep him talking, she realized. Give Sacramento time to shift, or at least leave him distracted in the fight. "And the hostages? What have you done with them?" Lady grant they were not dead—though even if he said they were, he might well be lying. She could cling to that.

"Hostages are fine; their deaths would be irrelevant. You called all your high ranks together for wedding, hostages made you spread them out so I could pick them off. Very neat." In the briefest of pauses, Mikhail rocked his weight back so he could smirk at her. "I will continue to kill sub-alphas until you agree to my alpha's terms." Then he attacked Sacramento in a flurry, spreading that red layer all over her body, cheek and breast and hip. She could hardly do more than try to knock blows aside or take them on her arms rather than her face.

Silver rushed Mikhail too. With one arm, she couldn't take him down either, but if a few slashes went to her instead, maybe Sacramento would have time to shift. She could never win fighting as she was, Mikhail was too good with his weapons of choice.

Mikhail rolled his grip on one knife so the blade lay flat along his wrist. He punched Silver, up and under her chin, and she flew and the back of her head smashed into something hard and she could barely stand. When she'd blinked encroaching gray from her vision, he'd rolled the knife back and Sacramento was desperately smearing blood out of one eye from a cut along her forehead.

But in her other hand, she had a length of wood, and she caught the next slash on that. It was old, damp and rotted even without recent rain, but it took one cut meant for her, and another. Silver saw that Mikhail had to change his rhythm so his blades would not get stuck, but he adjusted as smoothly as if he'd practiced it before.

"Don't take her," Silver couldn't focus well enough to find Death among Mikhail's flashing shadows, but she knew he had to be there. "Please."

"That's not up to me," Mikhail said, and "That's not up to me," Death said, and Silver thought maybe her hearing was doubled like vision sometimes was when a blow had stunned you. But Death used a new voice he'd never used before, and

Silver knew it was Mikhail's other victim, if only she could recognize it.

"I have orders." Mikhail feinted to get Sacramento to raise her shield and he came down hard on her exposed arm, not to kiss with blood this time, but to sever muscle, destroy her grip.

A new female voice, shouting a challenge, and Tatiana thrust her way through tangled vegetation of former human order run wild. She berated Mikhail in their shared language, and he turned to her and laughed.

Sacramento seized her moment and smashed her length of wood across the back of his neck. It splintered, weakened by so many cuts. Mikhail rolled his shoulders and shook off the slivers like a wild self throwing off water.

And Tatiana brushed past him, a terribly miscalculated strike if that's what it was, but then she had one of his knives in her hand. She twisted back to face him and saluted him with the weapon. "If you're dancing today, you're dancing with me."

Mikhail stayed in their shared language this time, tone disdainful and slightly pleading in turns. Silver tuned him out and made her way along the line of wood to Sacramento, who was swaying. Silver couldn't tell if she was pale underneath the browning lines and smears of so much blood. Pure instinct had put Sacramento's hand over the worst gash on her arm, and Silver clamped hers on top. Experience with human bleeding of her own told her that you had to hold the wound closed, hold the blood in, if you could. She eased Sacramento down to sit before swaying became falling. Though the woman's eyes remained open, her gaze did not track on Silver or the fight.

Metal clashed on metal, and dance they did. Silver held on to Sacramento's blood and watched. It had a chill beauty, slash and block, lunge and retreat. Blood of his own kissed Mikhail's skin for the first time, caressing his jaw. He had no taunts now, just panting and clashing metal. Tatiana grunted when he marked her from heel of hand to elbow.

Neither of them seemed to know what to do with their free hands. Trained with two blades, Silver saw them think to block and catch themselves when they would have countered steel with skin. With the two so well matched in strengths and weaknesses, maybe Tatiana had a true chance, and Silver prayed silently that the Lady would favor her cause, not the cause of the killer, the kidnapper. Since it wasn't up to Death, he claimed.

When Tatiana scored the side of Mikhail's empty hand, he squeezed the blood into his fist and flicked the liquid at her eyes. Wincing to avoid it, she looked away too long and Mikhail swept her feet out from under her. "Fight dirtier, puppy," he said, and stepped firmly on her neck. She slashed once at this leg, then slumped, far sooner than Silver had expected. Too soon, too robbed of all her fight in the sprawl of unconsciousness.

He wouldn't kill her. Silver could see that from the way he stood. The two of them were as good as family. But she could also see what happened next, laid out as the simplest of trails before her. Once he was sure Tatiana was out, he'd finish Sacramento and sub-alpha after sub-alpha thereafter.

"It's up to you," Death said, an answer to a question she hadn't thought to frame, and should have, when he'd said it wasn't up to him. Yes. It was up to her.

Tatiana's hand with the knife had fallen limp beside her hip. Silver was careful to avoid it as she knelt beside Tatiana as she had Pierce. Mikhail's smugness was curling and darkening into worry now, like the edge of a burning page, leaving ash behind. Perhaps he thought Tatiana's lack of resistance a trick, but when he lifted his weight, then removed his foot entirely, and still she did not move, he dropped to a knee at her opposite side, ignoring Silver. He spoke her name, then a question in their language, and hovered a hand over her mouth to verify the warmth of her continued breath.

Silver drew the knife out of Tatiana's slack hand, settled it comfortably in her own grip, and stood. She would use this moment Tatiana had bought her. "I only need one. Seems like it was meant to be this way." She lifted the knife, angled it to catch her reflection and then to catch the sunlight. Not the Lady's light, but maybe she could draw it in and fill herself up and she'd wouldn't bleed inside to speak words she did not deserve.

She lifted the blade higher, closer to the sunlight and let him see her: white hair and a single moon knife and scent filled with protectiveness. To save her people, she would be the Lady reborn.

"Stop this." She imagined she was Death, speaking the words with a voice not her own, and Mikhail gaped at her. She cut the sunlight she'd gathered through the shadows in his voice, and he barely stumbled up and away from Tatiana in time. His blade came up, but he couldn't attack her, she saw in his whole body. A beat, and he lowered both hands, dropped the knife to bite into the grass beside his boot. "Lady," he whispered, eyes wide.

Silver swallowed against a dry mouth. "Yes," she lied.

So be it.

She drove him farther from the others on the ground, blade held before her. "Are the hostages alone, or are they guarded?" At his wide-eyed nod for the latter, she continued. "You will speak over the distance, say that the hostages are to be released. I will have no one held in my name! Tell your guards that I would speak to the hostages as proof of their freedom."

Mikhail hesitated. She could see the conflicting orders in the whole of his body, alpha against Lady. "What about exile after all? Will you go with him, perhaps?" Death said, placing himself beside her feet as a dark mirror to the position of Mikhail's wild self at his. "Then there is no conflict. But if you would enjoy it more, by all means, push until he breaks. Then you and he will both know which authority is more important to him."

And Mikhail knelt to her. He did not seem broken, but she wanted to scream at him all the same: no, no, no! When he spoke at a distance, she could not parse his words at first, but it seemed neither could the guard, for he had taken on a cadence of repetition when meaning seeped back in for her. "Yes, let them go! Tell them they must speak to their alpha."

"Roanoke?" said the voice Mikhail extended out for her. She recognized it as he who was missing, though his name was far beyond her at this moment. She didn't see that she rightly needed it, however.

"Are your guards truly gone?" Silver waited until his reply, cluttered with details she couldn't follow, coalesced into understanding on his part. All of the sub-alphas knew how to speak to her, more or less. Some remembered better than others.

"Roanoke Silver. It's just you there? Yes. The Alaskans are gone. We're free...wherever this is."

Wherever it was seemed quite likely to be far, as her father had suggested, given that the Alaskans were doing the guarding. "My cousin is looking for you. Now you are no longer hidden, he should be able to bring you home." Silver gave a short nod to Mikhail to show she was satisfied.

So they came to the real question.

Will you go with him? This source of coercion upon her and her mate was gone. She could order Mikhail to return to his home, and walk back to her own, to summon help to carry those who were injured here.

This source of coercion. Silver knew there would be others. The thought that had haunted her all along—perhaps even since they'd received word that there would be no envoy, that their attempt to talk was rejected—what would make Russia *stop?*

She and Andrew could not protect all their pack members, all the time. If she forced Mikhail home, Russia would send another, to begin again on the sub-alphas. One by one, they'd die. Or John would, or Felicia, if he wished other high-ranked targets who would shatter her and her mate's hold on power— no, shatter them both, full stop.

So to order Mikhail home, walk away herself, that was not a true choice, for it was one with consequences she utterly repudiated. What, then, were her choices?

"What could you accomplish if you did go?" Death said. He spoke but did not move, did not even *conceive* of movement with his body. Lest she read his opinion in some rock of balance forward or back, Silver supposed.

Russia, the alpha himself, he would not be ordered by a mortal playing at the Lady's words, Silver was sure of that. She could not walk into his presence and demand that he leave her pack alone because she asked so prettily.

But this one, he seemed ready to do many things only because she asked. What were a few questions, in that context? Silver stepped forward, beyond Death, to set her hand on Mikhail's bowed head. "Why does your alpha fear me so badly?"

"Roanoke pack is now large, and a threat—"

The answer came instantly, and Silver cut it off nearly as quickly. "You would have me think you actually believe that?

There is an ocean between us, and there always *has been* an ocean between us. Tatiana is conflicted to the very depths of her voice, about her alpha, but I do not think she believed that even when she first arrived with his words still directing her steps. She said he fears me, as the Lady reborn."

Mikhail was silent for a space, breaths measured. A muscle jumped in his jaw when he finally lifted his head. "Tatiana does not see Father's fears. None in the Lady's Jaw do. We all guess. But since she left, it has become more clear—there are not enough of us any longer. Middle ranks are restless, Father's betas cannot always hold order. It is not good to have some saying he has lost the Lady's favor, that another has it in the form of their alpha."

In his face, she could see it: conflicting orders resolved into something that was not precisely relief, but at least a rebalancing so his initial smoothness could return. "You could do *good*, if you come to Russia. Help reassure everyone, let them be happy again."

Happy. Such a word. Happy under a tyrant willing to kill one who'd dedicated her life to carrying out his orders, without a second thought. This, she could believe, of Russia. Turn restlessness inside against an enemy outside. Find the supposed Lady reborn and depose her, allow him to say she was not a sign of the Lady's favor after all. And across an ocean or not, a powerful pack would also be broken, as a pleasant side effect.

But where there was restlessness, under a tyrant, would there not be someone ready to depose him? Silver, borrowing the Lady's power for her words, could not tell an alpha to step down, no, but she certainly could tell all the middle ranks to support someone who would *force* him to.

So then that was the choice she had, to save lives: risk only her own, to travel across that ocean and seek to help depose

Russia instead. And pretend to be the Lady at all times, such a thought as made her voice contract in her chest with desperation, but that was a price she would pay, for her pack.

"I suppose it will be best if we leave now," Silver heard herself say. They felt like not her words even as they left her lips, dandelion fluff whipped away from her control. She had nothing with her for traveling, but how could she return to the pack house, smelling as she did, of blood, of their enemy? Even if Dare were not there, no one else would let her leave again either. They'd claim there was another way, if only she stayed to find it.

But there was no other way. So she must leave now, and keep close to Mikhail lest he think to circle back and finish Sacramento when Silver was gone.

Mikhail snapped to his feet at her words, collected his knife. She did not look at him, so *smug* in his expression, and she kept his second knife for her own, much good it would do her. But perhaps it would be a reminder of the Lady's presence he'd ascribed to her in his mind.

She leaned over Tatiana, found her senseless still, though her breaths came fast as if still fighting. That was a strangeness Silver had no time for, as long as Tatiana lived. Sacramento was similarly unchanged, seated against the support of wood without the ability to focus her attention. "Sacramento." There was another name, perhaps better to command her attention with, but her sub-alpha title brought her to look at Silver at least.

"This is important, puppy. I go by choice, because of the good I can accomplish. Dare must look to the pack, not to me. He must *stay*. Do you understand?" She could only hope he'd think along paths of reasoning similar to her own. If he followed her, with one sub-alpha dead and another seriously injured, the Roanoke pack would fracture as surely as Russia could ever have wished.

Sacramento repeated her message, more or less. Silver could find no more reason to delay. With Death beside her, she followed Mikhail, and did not allow herself to look back.

11

In the vision, Tatiana knelt on ash, among the black bones of the great trees that pressed in on all sides of the clearing fire had made. She knew it for a vision in her own bones, and none could say she did not know whereof she spoke; she'd had dozens since her life was nearly ended by an overdose of wolfsbane. Now, perhaps for the rest of her days, the echoes appeared, with nothing she could do to control them.

Though perhaps familiarity created a sort of control. Ash puffed up into dead snow that fouled her ability to scent but did not make her cough. The echoes were triggered by fear, most often, more than rage or other emotions strong enough to make one's voice forget its words. But she would not remember what had come immediately before this vision, so she did not try. These were the bounds of her world: within it, she would see what she would see.

The wind roused itself to a grand, white-speck-swirling effort, and uncovered what Tatiana had taken for a hollowed log before her, black turned to white in great, cracked squares like the ribs of the dead tree. But it was not a log now, if it had ever been; it was a body. A Tooth's kill, skin turned to red in long, slashed strips.

A woman.

White hair.

A touch, at the back of her neck, simultaneous with her realization. "Look what you did," Andrew said on a sob. He stood behind her, knee into her shoulder blade, and now his fingers clenched into her hair, wrenched her head to the side. He held a single moon knife against the pulse of the artery there. "Tatiana, how could you betray her so?"

It was a vision, it wasn't real, but her heart had stopped once in a vision. That had been real. It had taken human blows to that organ to start it once more. Tatiana did not remember her situation, but she knew those were not available to her in the waking world now. Despair clawed at her voice, opening rents that let the fear in to choke her. "I didn't!" she told him on a sob of her own. Silver. Not Silver, not killed like that.

"You let him! You might as well have killed her yourself!" Andrew's words tumbled over each other, so wild she could hardly understand them.

She knew this was a vision. A very few times, knowing that had been enough to show her the way out. If she could break free—but Andrew's grip on her head as she knelt was too firm to escape. So strange, to find that word in her mind: firm, as if it were a support, a reassurance of his protectiveness.

"I'm sorry," she said, and clamped an arm against the back of his knees, holding his legs against her body when she twisted violently, bending his knees and taking his balance with them. The blade kissed up a line of blood when he fell, but not to a fatal depth.

He lay where he fell, where she straightened to look down at him. He didn't fight. His face was such pure devastation, as if there were no more left to him than the burned wood around them. "We keep going," she said, and offered him a hand up. When he took it, she felt the cracks around the edges of the vision and delicately stepped through.

Grass. On her back, one hand flung wide. Scent of blood everywhere, drying tacky on her skin from healed cuts. Mikhail. Silver. Thoughts reassembled, Tatiana shoved herself up, panting. Lady's kind mercy, she hated the echo visions.

No, Silver wasn't dead. Or least, if she was, she wasn't here. Pierce lay where she remembered having seen him before she joined the fight with Mikhail. And Sacramento had collapsed up against the fence. Tatiana launched herself standing and into movement to her lover's side at the same time. Eyes open, tracking on her. Still alive, likely to stay that way since her wounds bled no longer. All right. Next problem. "Silver? Did Mikhail take her? How long was I out?"

Sacramento's eyes were glassy, and her skin was cold when Tatiana knelt and cupped her cheek on the side without a cut, thumb cradling her jaw. Shock. Not something werewolves generally managed to suffer from, but as a Tooth, she'd seen it before when blood loss came right to the edge. "It's her choice. I have to tell Dare—Roanoke Dare—to stay."

Silver's words, clear enough, even without her idiosyncratic way of naming her husband. Frustration flared up in Tatiana's chest for a moment. How could Silver possibly imagine any of them could manage to do *that*?

As least the frustration burned off some of the cobwebs left from the vision, and Tatiana lunged forward into the space of comparative clarity to set out logistics in her mind. If this vision had been as long as most of the other echoes had been, Mikhail would have had plenty of time to reach the airport by the time anyone from the pack house could arrive there. She should call Andrew out here alone, perhaps. Give him time to react as he would, before any of the pack would see.

From there—she supposed it would be in the Lady's hands.

When Andrew arrived at the pack house, he didn't even have time to check for Silver before his phone rang with a call from Sacramento. He hoped she and Tatiana hadn't just missed each other—he wasn't up to orchestrating any games of tag at the moment.

He waved the others he'd driven back with inside and shut the door from the garage into the house behind them, in case he needed the privacy. The automatic light blinked off, leaving him in cool darkness except for a blinding line underneath the garage door. It was almost calming.

"Roanoke Dare? Would you bring the car out here?" Tatiana was the one who spoke. Borrowed Sacramento's phone, obviously, but he was stressed enough it took a moment for him to put that together. She named an intersection in an older neighborhood about a twenty-minute walk away. Silver liked to wander in that direction, where developed land met undeveloped in places.

"Is Silver hurt?" Andrew's voice tightened. Mikhail could have gone straight from killing Billings—but Pierce was there to help, making any fight many against one. "Or Sacramento?" Was that why she wasn't calling herself?

"We're fine." Tatiana's voice was stretched thin, with what emotion he couldn't quite tell, though her accent was increasing. "I thought you'd wish to have the discussion of your next move where the pack cannot hear."

There wasn't much room for it, given the turmoil around Billings' murder, but a little relief seeped through Andrew anyway. Silver must be willing to talk to him again. Thank the Lady. He punched the garage door open once more, wincing as the expanding band of brightness reached eye level. "I'll be there in five minutes."

When he reached the intersection, he didn't see anyone standing on the sidewalk. He took a guess and turned onto the drive at the entrance to a large lot with a sign boasting of the townhomes to come. In the meantime, however, the gravel drive was hardly longer than a car-length, and scrubby trees and grass flourished all the way to the decaying fence belonging to the adjoining property.

Drying blood smacked him like a physical gust of wind when he opened the car door. Andrew closed his eyes against the image of Billings' body that flashed up, but that just made the image sharper.

Dammit. If Mikhail were there, he'd need to make sure the man didn't get into weapons range too quickly. He would have heard Andrew drive up, but Andrew followed the blood scent as slowly as he could, alert for someone sneaking in from downwind.

"It's all over, no need for that." Tatiana's voice lofted to meet him.

Andrew abandoned caution for urgency and crashed in through a low tangle of blackberries. "What happened?" he called back, though he couldn't see her yet. It came out pretty coherently, considering the chorus of *Silver? Silver? Silver?* at the back of his mind.

He shoved through a last screen of trees, snapping one trunk, displacing two others to whip their bad temper against his shoulders, and arrived at the edge of grass trampled into oblivion. Tatiana was helping Sacramento stand, both blood smeared but Sacramento markedly the worst of the two. Her shirt was off—had she been interrupted in the midst of shifting?—and some of the crisscrossing of cuts on her skin hadn't even healed, the worst on her arm gaping, but at least not currently bleeding. Pierce lay sprawled on the ground. He was sickly pale, but he was breathing, and when Andrew knelt beside him, his pulse sounded steady. Blood coated the front of his body below the neck, but no visible wound remained.

Andrew turned his head to the side, gagging against the smell in an effort to short-circuit the instincts that were screaming at him to chase, to bring down the dying prey that must be nearby. He didn't need violence right now. "What *happened?*" It became a snarl, despite his best efforts. Where was Silver?

"Mikhail bested me." Tatiana withdrew one hand and then the other from Sacramento, testing her stability, then moved to stand before Andrew, achingly formal.

Sacramento closed her eyes, seemed to ground herself, and spoke before Tatiana had a chance to continue. "Bested all of us. Silver—even you would have sworn she was the Lady reborn—she got him to release the hostages, call them for proof and everything. She told them John would pick them up. Then she went away with that Russian cat. She said it was her choice because of what she can accomplish there. She wants you to stay. Look to the pack."

"No." Andrew knew he should—should think, but he didn't need to think about that. He'd get her back. He couldn't find an exiting scent trail with this blood in the air, but if he walked the perimeter of the lot—dammit, Tatiana was in his way!

"They'll be at the airport already," she said, and again, when he tried to move around her. "You can't just leave the pack, anyway, alpha."

He snarled in her face. "And how *did* he best you, when you're so damn well trained? Next to Sacramento, you're hardly touched." He didn't honestly believe she'd betrayed them, but she'd still let Silver go, and now she wasn't letting him go, and if he hurt her enough, maybe she'd get. Out. Of. His. Way! She stared defiantly at him, just to the side of measuring dominance, and didn't move.

"Hey." Sacramento staggered into him, snapping his train of thought as he caught her, got her balanced again with a supporting hand at the small of her back. "It was one of her vision things, okay? You know, like she still gets when stressed after being poisoned by these very people."

"You never told us you still…" He didn't want the empathy, he wanted the clarity of his rage, but it seeped in anyway. The visions put you through hell, as he well knew, and she still had them? How often?

"It doesn't matter. I still bear responsibility." Tatiana tipped her chin slightly aside. She certainly anticipated a blow, but she wasn't flinching from it. Not like Laurence had.

Andrew whirled away from her, pressed fingertips to his

closed eyelids, trying to find the calm in the hurricane of rage meeting his own feeling of responsibility. He would never touch her. Never. Her or Laurence, whom he'd almost forgotten about in all of this, and he needed to think of him, and the whole pack.

Look to the pack, just as Silver would have said it. "We need to get all of you home. Once John gets back, then I can leave." He tried to laugh, ended up with something more like a choking cough. "I know where they're going, after all."

"Mm," Tatiana agreed. She kept her waiting stillness for a beat longer, then seemed to be convinced he wouldn't be giving in to the violence weaving into his every thought, making his muscles shake. She returned to Sacramento, leaving Pierce for Andrew to pick up.

At the car, when the others were loaded, Tatiana paused before getting in herself, formality back and clutched tightly around her like a blanket against cold that didn't exist in the mild, summer air. "They won't hurt her, Roanoke. Whatever my alpha believes about her being the Lady, whatever he might wish to do—the others would never let him."

She said it was her choice because of what she can accomplish there. What could she possibly accomplish among their enemies? But Andrew knew how Silver thought. She would be playing the Lady reborn against the alpha in person, to make him give up his vendetta against Roanoke, before anyone else was killed. So it clearly had been her choice—but it wasn't a choice Silver should have had to make. She shouldn't have had to do any of it. She'd said it would be more than she could take, to play the religious role for the Russians. And yet she was, because he'd told her it was necessary and then he'd driven her away, hadn't been there to help her protect their people. Once, twice over he'd hurt her, and he wanted to run to her, scream his apologies and offer himself in her place.

But he couldn't. And it was killing him. He could survive a few hours of this feeling, couldn't he? Just until John was back. Andrew slammed the car door far too hard as he climbed in.

12

A few hours became half a day, full flights from Anchorage pushing John's arrival until the next morning. Andrew didn't sleep, and didn't even try, spending the night pacing. Laurence was safe at least, they'd picked him up, but the human had gotten away. Andrew found he couldn't really care less about the human, as long as John arrived and could support Susan being in charge so Andrew could *go*.

Seeing Laurence climbing out of the pack's minivan where it had pulled up on the driveway of the main house brought Andrew back to a sense of his responsibilities once more, like coming up choking against a collar, chained to North America. The man smelled like he was in a bad state. Not injured, but worn gray like a white cotton shirt after decades of wear and washing. He was healed, but there were things that healing couldn't touch.

Looking at him, a memory hit Andrew like a punch to the stomach. The vision he'd had under the influence of wolfsbane had included versions of most of the people he knew, twisted into unhappier or at least far different forms by changed circumstances. He hadn't met Laurence in that vision, but he'd heard of him, abused too long by Rory until he fled to escape it. Hearing of it, he'd imagined a Laurence very much like this one.

Laurence stepped aside, letting out the rest of the team that had gone to Alaska, and waited, head hanging. Andrew embraced him. Laurence didn't wince, but he didn't respond either. "We took too long," Andrew murmured. Apologies didn't pass easily from alpha to pack member who'd been in disgrace before this all started, but Andrew did his best with his tone.

"Who did they want?" Laurence said colorlessly. "Your Russian hostage? I assume you gave her up and that's why we were freed."

"Tatiana?" Andrew stepped back but kept his hands on Laurence's upper arms. A laugh tried to form at the idea, but it hurt too much to voice. What a different situation that would have been. No easier, but Andrew selfishly wished it had been so. "No. They wanted us to abdicate and go into exile."

Laurence stiffened. "We tried to escape ourselves, Roanoke." Where he'd turned aside Andrew's touch and reassurance before, his tone begged desperately for it now. "The human was the one—she almost got us out, but they caught us…"

"Not your fault." Andrew transferred his hold to an arm across Laurence's back and nudged him toward the open garage door. Going in through the garage would get them to the kitchen with fewer gawkers. He hoped. "You need to eat."

"I've been eating," Laurence grumbled, and went passively where pushed.

"Eat more." Andrew maneuvered to keep his body between Laurence and the best sightlines down the hallway and from the dining room, but he smelled too many people lurking just out of sight to believe that he'd gotten away with it. Curiosity nearly always won out eventually in a pack house, and he was too tired to order people away.

When John joined them, Andrew left Laurence to deal with his own burritos when they came out of the microwave and drew his beta into the farthest corner. John scrubbed a hand through his hair, making it stand up even worse than before. He had dark shadows under his eyes, but ones easily attributable to long nights spent in the search. "Lady, it smells like panic in here."

"I'm planning to reassure everyone before I send them home and leave myself." Andrew drew in a deep breath to see if he was really reading the mood that differently than John, but the house smelled the same as it had since he'd pulled everyone back onto the property: too many Were pressed together and stressed because of it.

A baby's wail distracted Andrew and drew his attention to the doorway to the dining room where Portland was jostling Susan. Portland bounced Nicholas desperately, but Andrew could see he was drawing his mood from his mother. "I don't care if he's busy, I need to talk to Roanoke Dare!"

Her voice did hold panic, real panic, and Andrew stepped over to join the women. If Portland was worked up enough to try to push past his orders to Susan, who was essentially at beta status, he'd bet there were a lot of other sub-alphas listening carefully from around corners. Everyone smart knew that when a whole group had a problem, it was better to pick one person to bring it up.

"What's your plan?" Paradoxically, Portland's volume rose when she saw she had his attention, and she smoothed her son's hair over and over. "Billings is *dead* at the Russians' hands, and but for the grace of the Lady, Sacramento and Pierce would have been too, and Laurence looks like a two-week carcass, so he probably healed similar damage. It's all very well to pull us all together for safety, but what about tomorrow? What about next week? What are you going to do about the Russians, to keep us safe long term?" The longer she spoke, the more laying out the facts seemed to calm her and slot her back into her own sub-alpha role.

She lowered her voice, leaning in over her son, probably so those who deputized her couldn't hear this part. "And maybe since I'm the sub-alpha closest to Allison, I'm the only one to notice, but she and Pierce are definitely not saying something, and so I have to ask: *where is Silver?*"

They had a right to know, beyond the reassurances he'd been planning, he realized that now. All of them. Silver was his mate, but she was also their alpha. "Gather all the sub-alphas together," he directed John, though the words were also aimed sideways at Portland and all of her listeners. He doubted John would have to do anything.

Space was a problem, he realized a beat later. Keeping it to sub-alphas, letting them reflect the information outward would constrain things a little, but not enough. With time to plan, they'd have held something like this out at the hunting lands. He strode for the back door. The yard between the houses would at least give everyone elbow room.

A tide of Were flowed out behind him, staking out little patches on the gravel path or among the careful landscaping, ringed by high bushes on all sides for privacy. Nowhere was elevated, so Andrew chose his spot roughly in the center of the path's length. Portland had handed her son off to someone, and found a place next to Sacramento, who had healed up but was still markedly pale. John backstopped Andrew's shoulder, Susan set herself in the main house's back doorway as if daring anyone to contest her right to listen, and Felicia sneaked in from inside the guest house. He wondered idly if she'd started there or sprinted around the block, but he wasn't going to kick her out. She deserved to hear about his coming departure from him personally.

"You all know we have been under threat from the Russians for some months." Andrew shifted to catch gazes obliquely, without measuring dominance, but the sky was utterly cloudless today and the sun's angle prevented him from seeing one swath of his people without squinting. "That despite our best efforts, they captured Laurence and killed Billings. But Silver negotiated Laurence's release, and with strict assurances of safety, has gone to Russia to negotiate in person to make sure there are no more attacks. I will be following her on the next available flight—"

The rumble of shocked voices and gasps began competing with his words from the moment he said "gone to Russia," but by the end, he had to stop because he simply could not make himself heard over the babble of shouted questions.

Outside of the constrained space indoors, a breeze was beginning to clear away the dregs of old scents enough that Andrew could begin to read people's current emotions.

Panic was putting it mildly.

"What if that's what the Russians were waiting for? If they arrive when you're both gone and start picking us off one by one—"

"That's how you defend us? Both of you, just walk into their jaws—"

"And when they've assassinated you both—"

"Who's going to protect us?"

That last, Andrew swore he heard it in three different voices, overlapping too much to have taken up the cry as a purposeful echo. "What was that bullshit about leaving, again?" Death said. Andrew didn't allow himself to search out the shape of the wolf among the feet of all his pack members massed around him.

"What are you cowards whining about protection for? We need to go, *in force*, to save Roanoke Silver!" No weakness showed in Sacramento's voice as she pushed to the center, taking over some of Andrew's cleared space to shout at the others. For a breath, he was surprised it was her voicing the thought, but then he wasn't any longer. The Western packs, when individually autonomous, had skirmished a bit on their borders, but had mostly left each other alone. Before the first version of Roanoke, the Eastern packs had *fought*. The conservative voices who were usually the biggest pains in Andrew's tail were older, sometimes old enough to have been born into that period themselves.

One of that generation, Charleston, said it for them all: "No one wants pack war, Sacramento, least of all with the *Russians*. How easily did they kill one of our strongest already? Step back."

Andrew missed his cue to reply because the earlier words were still echoing in his mind. *Who's going to protect us?* He couldn't leave. Not yet. Not for days, until they'd given Billings' voice its color, and got everyone home and let them relax into the security built into their daily routines. Something in him couldn't—couldn't even breathe, couldn't keep on living and functioning even enough to call up anger to burn away some of the despair at even the thought of leaving Silver there alone among enemies.

"She told you to," Death said, emerging from among the shouting sub-alphas' feet, each moving out of his way as if clearing a respectful path without even realizing it. "You should listen to your wife more often. She's generally quite an intelligent person."

"Enough!" Andrew was alpha, had been alpha for several years, and his pack was going to *listen*. Hearing that in his voice, they did. Silence reigned but for the inescapable traffic noise surrounding a pack house even in the suburbs. "I see there is a need for one of your alphas to remain, at present." He wasn't sure if the formality helped or hindered the reassurance of his message, but he needed the rigid structure to find any words at all. "I will see to it that every one of you and your pack members are protected, my word on the Lady."

"How can you—?" Sacramento jerked toward him, movement arrested by Portland. The need to shake her off delayed Sacramento long enough for Felicia to eel up unexpectedly and speak into her ear.

"I get it, I do. Come to him with your idea when it's quiet later, though. That's what I do…" There was probably more, but Felicia tugged Sacramento out of range toward the guest house, and Andrew lost the thread. He made a mental note to follow up with Sacramento later, but he didn't have much faith the note wouldn't disappear two seconds from now like words written in sand as the tide came in.

For the moment, there was a funeral to schedule, guards to place visibly, any number of things to do that he could only hope would fill his mind up until Silver's situation at least didn't directly obstruct his breathing. And then in a few days, everyone would see how they could protect *each other*, with the betas right there to adapt the alpha's standing orders, and he'd be able to *go*.

A few days. Surely Silver would be safe for a few days. And he could keep from going mad for that long.

Hugh crawled out of the woodwork somewhere in the house when Andrew came back inside, hovering at the edge of his vision as he made the last arrangements, then followed him upstairs after he wound down. The older man fetched up on the threshold of Andrew and Silver's bedroom and waited for Andrew to acknowledge him.

Andrew considered shutting the door in his face—he would be within his rights, as the alphas' room was one of the few spaces they could be private amidst the pack. There was a reason Hugh wasn't actually coming inside. Standing in the open doorway was pushy enough.

Andrew flumped one corner of the rumpled bedcovers closer to being made and gave up. He didn't have anything to do up here, and being near Silver's scent was making his mood worse. He might as well see what Hugh wanted. "I don't owe you time or attention, wanderer," he said, looking up to watch Hugh's face in the reflection on the French doors to the balcony. His expression didn't change enough for the difference to be visible in the slightly blurry image.

"Perhaps not. What's next, Son-in-Law?" The disrespect in Hugh's tone made Andrew whirl to face him. "You just abandon my daughter there?"

Andrew crossed the room in two strides, stopping right in Hugh's face. "Soon, you cat's bastard. *Soon.* Just not yet. Weren't you listening at a window when I was explaining that outside? I'm sure everyone else was." He shouldn't even have answered, but anger had his voice in an irresistible grip.

"You're just giving them more time to hurt her." Hugh crossed his arms deliberately, though there was so little room between them that he almost bumped Andrew's chest.

With icy clarity, Andrew moved his weight sideways, turning Hugh's focus and Hugh's position as well. The moment he was lined up, he slammed his forearm against Hugh's throat, holding him against the door jamb. "They won't hurt her. They worship her. And as much as I hate it—and Death cast your voice to the void for doubting, because I *do* hate it—I am needed here, and Silver asked me to stay here—"

The need to make Hugh *hurt* for saying those things, to gasp and then weep with the pain of it, boiled up but not over. Too many years Andrew had known his temper not to know it now. He threw himself away from Hugh and turned his back and held absolutely still because he knew that was what he had to do. The effort wrung him trembling, worse than when he'd been listening incredulously to Hugh's words.

And Hugh did nothing. His scent remained tight, controlled. That shotgun hunter. He was calculating his slip-ups to some purpose again. To what purpose, though? "Do you *want* to be hurt?"

"I can take it." Hugh's voice moved like he had rocked a step forward, but he seemed to think better of the movement and settled back again. A pause, stretching, long, long. Andrew was perfectly prepared to wait Hugh out until he admitted what he was actually up to, and the older man finally sighed. "Thought it might get it out of your system, get you to articulate the reasons to stay out loud."

Andrew lifted a hand, fingers curling into claws with the effort of not turning around and slamming it into Hugh's interfering, patronizing face. "That's not how anger works, you dumb fuck." He could imagine Silver's interjection as clearly as if she'd been here, and he corrected himself as he would have done had she said it. "Fine, that's not how *my* anger works. Leave me to deal with it in my own way."

In the French doors, Hugh's reflection lifted its hands in surrender. Andrew searched the face for apology, even some conception of what he'd done wrong, but gave it up after a moment. Unlikely in the extreme. The best he could hope for was that Hugh would leave him alone.

Hugh didn't appear to be done yet, however. After a few beats of waiting for Andrew to turn back, he dropped his head. "I'm sure the Lady will guide my daughter, in Russia."

Andrew couldn't tell from his tone whether Hugh was really reassured by that himself, so he didn't object to the non-reassurance in his own case. The man could bend his voice to all the platitudes he wanted, and it wouldn't change anything. In the painful silence that followed, his anger drained away, leaving him numb beneath.

"Listen." Hugh dared a step into the room, set a hand on Andrew's shoulder from behind. "I have a hankering for some sailing again, sightseeing in Alaska and…around. Hopping along the coast. So if you, or Silver, or any North Americans should find themselves on a hostile shore without easy access to an airport…just give me a call."

If Andrew were honest with himself, it was a good offer—something they might never need, but would make all the difference if they did. A good intention. But then, all of Hugh's meddling had been from good intentions. It fell to Andrew to decide whether intentions mattered, to forgive or not.

Not forgiving her father wouldn't help Silver, though.

Andrew turned back, taking refuge in formality once more. He gave the barest inclination of his head, acknowledgment, nothing more. "Thank you."

Hugh kept his head down. "I could say I was amazed by how strong she's grown up, and say that she doesn't need any help over there, but you know the first part, and the second part—" He shrugged. "Don't really know if that's true."

A deep breath. "But I think the point here is that she didn't need *my* help. And I was a fool to assume she would, just because I'm her father. Or that you don't know perfectly well what you're doing, as an alpha of a continent. So I'm sorry."

A final nod. "Accepted." That was all Andrew had for the man, at the moment. Finally, Hugh ambled off for the stairs, leaving Andrew with Silver's scent and her absence.

13

The greatest part of the distance to Russia, Silver and Mikhail had to travel among humans. Those humans showed but little in the mists that were all she saw unless she grasped after the world of her mate, and Silver found comfort in that. She went were Mikhail directed—respectfully, always respectfully—and did not waste her voice or her attention on the humans packed around them. After a time, she was able to doze, and so not let the endless succession of seconds into minutes grow her worries beyond bearing. Mikhail, in contrast, seemed to walk a teeth-gritted edge of exasperation and anger until they arrived at a point from which they could travel just the two of them. He napped, before they set off from that point, having taken more than a day already in the traveling, but he seemed unable to properly sleep when his alpha was awaiting him. Speaking at a distance to warn that alpha of their coming had left him markedly off balance.

In the quiet between them in the last stage of their journey, with Mikhail focused on the manner of their traveling and their exact navigation, Silver tried to truly see this new place, or at least understand what aspects of it she might not be seeing. Strangely enough, it seemed to be suited to her sort of perception: where the green at home had a rain-washed gray as its foundation, all the summer colors here seemed based upon a blue so deep it crackled. The sky, the water beside the path when they came upon it, and then the forest of evergreens and rolling grass that had pulled the deep blue into itself and made of it such a green. At the same time, all the edges were sharper, forests had less underbrush, there were more spaces with a thinner covering of grass, and everywhere the hills broke up into rocks.

There were humans here, of course, to have made their endless paths and have left their buildings huddled into corners here and there, but they'd left little scent in the air, and grew fewer and fewer as they traveled. Silver drew in great breaths of air almost cold even in summer, and wondered if the world had perhaps been thus, when Death and the Lady walked among Her children still.

She thought to ask it of Death, stopped herself, then thought again. With the part she now played, could she not converse with Death whenever she liked? She had no wish to share even half of a private conversation with Mikhail, however. His alpha, even less so.

Death had been lounging beside her for the whole trip, head high, but now he focused the angle of his ears onto her. "We have almost arrived. Are you ready? This part you have chosen to play, it is certain to take more of you than you wish to give."

"I know," Silver said, and looked away at the trees blurring past. Let Mikhail make of those words what he would. Perhaps she had made a mistake, perhaps Russia would simply kill her, but all she could think of now was Dare. She buried her hand in Death's fur, to hold herself together. She hadn't thought of it in the moment, but what if he believed he'd driven her away? He'd hurt her, and she'd been so angry, but it had been the anger of wanting to shout at him until he *understood*, properly, what had caused the hurt, so he would never do such a thing again. It had been an anger of speaking together, then forgiving, not an anger of leaving. And now it was no anger at all, because she simply wished so fiercely to be back with him, or if she could not be back, at least to know that he was not killing himself with guilt.

Silver braced herself for Death's derision at the circling of her thoughts. He made no comment, however, and even set his muzzle on her thigh, unusual affection indeed. "We are here," Mikhail said, which was an end to all of it. Silver pushed her thoughts resolutely onto tyrant alphas and finding those who might wish to depose them.

When she climbed out and looked around, she found she once more could see more than she had expected. The pack— pack town, perhaps? Everywhere she found the scent of Were, not humans—the pack town was a loose collection of buildings with sides of weathered wood, at home among the trees. The cleared grass of room for tasks and cubs playing and gardens extended to a stream, yielding to forest not far beyond, though a wide path entered among those trees.

Look among the buildings and find the largest, and indeed, that was where Mikhail directed her. His wild self romped a few steps, tail whirling with the delight of being home, but quickly sobered again with a glance at Death. Death paced at Silver's side, not disappearing to explore as Silver had half expected him to do—but then again, he would be quite as familiar with this place as any other where he might need to take Were voices.

Inside the weathered wood of what could only be called a great hall, Silver found the gaps and vaguenesses she'd expected, aspects of the humans' modern world tucked away but present. She was more concerned that at the head of the room, beneath great rafters carved at the ends with wolf heads and along their lengths with the Lady's phases, stood nothing less than a throne. Wide windows along each side kept the room full of light, but the throne's dais and the rafters gathered shadows like cobwebs. Fortunately for her grip on diplomacy in the face of such teeth-bared hubris, the alpha was not presently seated in it. Instead, Mikhail led her beyond, to a suite of rooms accessed by a discreet door.

The alpha rose to meet them from one of two chairs around a small table covered with refreshments. He moved as gracefully as any Were as he marked a circle with a thumb on his forehead in greeting, but there were faint lines at his brow as if from a lifetime of frowns. His hair and close-cropped beard were fair, even lighter than Tatiana's, but viewed in movement, white strands shed the light differently only to smooth back into invisibility once more. In contrast, his wild self was grizzled, more white than gray, muzzle held low and each step taken with the pain of stiff joints. This was a Were with greater age than any she had yet met, Silver realized. An age that undoubtedly left him canny—if not precisely wise—instead of weak.

Silver relaxed her grip on the world of her mate even more, let the mists ghost up around them both that she might see her opponent as deeply as she could. She'd thought to find him filled entirely with shadows, as Mikhail had wielded, but she could find nothing in him at all. She flicked a glance to Mikhail, found his killer's shadows there still, roosting on his blades.

The alpha, she realized, had not a glow of the Lady's light, nor even a fleeting shadow of its absence. The mists did not bother to draw back from him, but neither did they stir with his movements as they did for everyone else. In his body, in his voice, he had only his mortality and utter, utter selfishness so deep as to have repudiated the Lady's light, leaving him with the nothing of the void.

Silver found that rather sad.

He did not fail to note her evaluation and turned it back on her, sardonic. She wondered what plans he might have planned, in the time since Mikhail had sent word of her coming. He could not ignore her, of course, but given how he'd turned Tatiana to first one purpose of his own and then another, Silver expected him to attempt the same with her. The question was, what purpose?

Silver pressed a thumb to her own forehead, marking a full circle there, as Russia had done. Tatiana had done something similar, half a circle, and Silver decided if this was something to do with rank, she wished to claim just as much as his.

"Silver!" He smiled, a dance of a laugh in his eyes allowing Silver to see where others might find him charming, or quite handsome.

"Roanoke," she corrected. Handsome was one thing, attractive was another. She in fact felt rather repelled, knowing the actions of the mind behind the smile. "My mate and I were deeply saddened you could not send your envoy to treat with us. I judged it time for a state visit to smooth matters between our two packs."

He held out both hands in greeting, and she allowed him one—which meant he simply picked up the other himself. She could have prevented it, but that was not yet the ground on which she wished to battle. "I am sorry for the circumstances that brought you here, Roanoke. They are certainly…inconvenient." He might have said "they," but Silver heard "you" layered atop. As no doubt she was meant to. "You do me much honor, coming here." She'd heard his voice once before, at a distance, but she was surprised anew by how little accent it carried.

"Have a care you remember that," Silver said. She did not glance down to reassure herself of Death, but she felt his weight against the side of her leg, a point of contact from which to draw strength.

"But the North Americans have used you very ill, leaving you so scarred when it is not necessary." Russia freed her good hand to gently brush up the sleeve of her bad arm, uncovering the white shed-snake-skin lines of where the silver poison had reached upward from her elbow toward her heart. He traced one, then angled her upper arm to better catch the light on it, concentration as deep as any healer's.

Silver clenched her teeth as she suffered his touch. She didn't know how to weigh diplomacy against submission in this place, where she was alone and did not yet know who might prove the allies against this man she'd come to find. But this man had laughter in his face still as he loped right up to the line—

And over it. "I've heard so much of your Lady-blessed grace, but nothing of your beauty," he said, and kissed the inside of her bad wrist.

Silver gave him no warning with a snarl or curse as she slid her free hand into her pocket and drew out the silver chain she always carried on her person. And thank the Lady she did, leaving as she had. She caught a length under and over her knuckles and as Russia straightened, she pressed it up to the underside of his chin. "Do you recall that it was during my *wedding* that you captured and murdered those under my protection?" That, she snarled.

Calmly, Russia let his skin burn, one breath, another, until the raw flesh odor of it made her want to gag. Only then did he step back. Her touched fingers to his wound, apparently judging it by the pain or small smudge of burst-blister blood he inspected on his skin, then said something in Old Were, ending on the lift of a question underscored by raised brows. Silver waited, chain and fist both held tight and ready, until her lack of answer in the face of his waiting turned painful.

"Oh! I am sorry. You don't understand me. How strange, the Lady reborn, and she cannot speak the language she taught her own children." Russia turned the full force of his patronization on Silver for a moment, then nodded to something behind her. Death's attention was steady on the alpha, so Silver risked a glance back to what he'd indicated: Mikhail's face, twisting into confusion.

How strange indeed.

Rather than push his advantage, having shoved her wrong-footed, Russia broke the moment instead. "Where is my daughter?" he demanded of Mikhail, striding past Silver to stand before the younger Were who abruptly straightened his stance, the better to bow more respectfully. "Did you think the alpha would serve as some sort of distraction, from your failure?"

"Tatiana?" Mikhail answered first in Old Were, but at a frown from his alpha, stumbled back into words Silver could understand. They had been a long time in traveling, with his lack of sleep, packed among the humans. And before that, he'd bled and healed, not insubstantially, in the fight with Tatiana. Silver suspected Russia had made similar calculations, and was using his conclusion as one more thing to turn to his advantage. "She…was against us. As you warned me, Father."

"So nice of you to only *almost* kill her, then." Silver tossed him to the hunters without regret, pacing to a better position in the room, setting her back against one wall to watch the two of them.

"I told you—" Russia spanned a hand across Mikhail's throat, dug his fingers in. "—to bring her back!" Mikhail, shocked, did nothing to resist him. With that grip, Russia lifted and threw. One grown man to another, there was not enough leverage to send Mikhail flying, but even the inch between his feet and the floor left him no way to avoid crashing into a chair and down until the back of his head smashed into the floor and left him stunned. "Not to hurt her in any manner!"

And not to bring an inconvenient enemy instead, Silver could also hear that buried in his voice quite well.

Mikhail's wild self licked at his face, whining, but Mikhail brushed it away without seeing it and staggered back to his feet. "I wonder how a pack could possibly be restless under an alpha such as this," Death murmured in the voice of a sub-alpha she could not quite put a name to. Silver didn't need the reminder: any sympathy for Mikhail was well tempered by the memory of his kill.

"Get out." Russia made a gesture as if to brush away an insect.

"No." Silver spoke without thinking, built up her justification on the fly behind the word. "I am without my own pack here. I should have…attendants, as befits my station. I will be the one to dismiss him, only when I wish." Station as an alpha, or as the Lady reborn? She hoped the ambiguity served her, as Russia certainly didn't believe she was the Lady. But beyond everything, she needed a witness, at least one, who did believe, with her at all times. She had no love for Mikhail, but he was presently all she had.

Russia gave a bark of a laugh, and turned away to his food. Silver was no longer invited to partake, apparently, if that had ever been his intention rather than using it as another subtle taunt. "Very well. Mikhail, take her to where she'll be staying."

On the tramp across grassy spaces and linking dirt paths outside, not a single Were was in evidence, save by scent. The eeriness set her teeth on edge—an alpha might suggest or even order such a thing of his pack, but where were the children peeking out of windows, the adults crossing her path on important business that couldn't wait?

She began to worry someone might have been turned out of their home for her, but when they arrived at the small cabin embedded among the others, it smelled like a place used for guests. Many different traces of people, all ephemeral under a dusty stillness to the air that persisted even after a thorough cleaning.

Mikhail threw open the door extravagantly, then collapsed to a seat in the common area. Silver explored to the extent of opening all the doors, finding bedrooms and bathrooms only, radiating from the central space. A good design, for Were. She supposed the nearby buildings were likely quite similar, with a larger common room to allow more bedrooms.

Mikhail rolled up one pant leg to check his calf, presumably for remaining bruises. "You really want trained Tooth to fetch for you?" he asked, tone dipping close to petulance near the middle. Some part of his alpha's jab about her lack of divinity must have connected.

Silver chose a seat of her own. As accommodations in the midst of one's enemies went, these were comfortable enough, though she would never grow used to the carvings of the Lady's phases tucked into every corner and beam. At least they had no depictions of the Lady or Death themselves. She knew from Tatiana the Russians didn't understand the blasphemy of such images. Now, Death diverged from her, to be about hunting of his own, which Silver hoped boded well of having some uneventful time to herself.

"Tatiana never said you were stupid," she said to Mikhail, and waited for him to bristle up as she'd intended. "It is inconvenient that I am here, as he said. But I could still be useful to him, he thinks. If I truly hold some of the Lady's light, he cannot in good conscience turn me to his purposes over my objections. If I am truly mortal, nothing more than an accident of injury, I have no strength in serving those purposes. To use me, he needs *doubt.*"

Something softened in Mikhail's face. He set a hand upon hers, reverence fully returned. "Father only tries to protect us."

Death nipped at the flank of Mikhail's wild self as he passed on his way to stand before the front door, expectant. "If you knew the number of voices I have that said such words just before I took them…"

As if summoned by Death, or at very least expected, a knock sounded on the door. Silver remained seated, as befit an alpha. Mikhail raised himself with a groan to open it on a woman, older than him and deeply confident, and another man much of his age. Much of his dangerousness as well, Silver judged as they both entered. He was a big man, square of jaw and shoulders, but he moved with lightness, alert to everything around him. His wild self also bulked far larger in the shoulders than any true wolf ever would.

"Do you have permission to be here, Irina?" Mikhail sneered at the woman. She had hair of the same golden shade of everyone Silver had yet met from this pack, but braided tightly up into a band across the top of her head. Her wild self looked practically diminutive beside the new man's, but was by no means delicate. Its fur tended dark, but nowhere near Death's black.

And she had Tatiana's bones. Leaner, certainly, and perhaps a little longer through her whole face, but the resemblance was unmistakable. Silver spoke the name without intending to. Irina looked to her with such desperate concern coming into her scent, Silver made the decision to trust her in that moment. Tatiana had proved her trustworthiness through visions, pain, and blood, and this woman clearly not only loved her but must have made Tatiana who she was. And Tatiana had never named her sources, but she'd been getting information about what was going on in Russia from somewhere.

"My daughter, yes." Irina shook herself, turned back to Mikhail. "Of course I have permission. I'm surprised *you* have it. I hear you failed to bring our alpha something he demanded." Her accent was stronger than her daughter's, requiring Silver to listen for several beats before she found of rhythm of it, but after that, each word was correctly chosen.

"I requested his presence." Silver rose, caught Irina's gaze to see if the older woman could read the words behind the ones she'd actually spoken, about the need for such a presence. Whatever Irina read, the connection slipped away from them both into a measuring of dominance. It grounded Silver, in a way, for she knew, unshakably, she was an alpha. Touched by the Lady—who could say? Alpha, she was the one saying it, and had proved it over and over.

And Irina was no middle-ranker herself. She yielded first, respectful, but Silver had seen the strength below, as yet not put to public use. "Mikhail has need of rest. Would Alexei suit your purposes as well, Roanoke?" She gestured to the man she'd brought with her. "He is also a Tooth. I'm afraid he speaks little English, but he understands it as well as any here."

Mikhail stalked up to Alexei, revealing the bigger man had an advantage, albeit a slighter one, in height as well as size. Mikhail stood a little too rigidly, just a whiff of posturing. Alexei changed his stance not at all, even as the two men exchanged a few rapid-fire verbal barbs Silver couldn't understand.

Trust Irina, trust the one she'd vouched for—more than that, likely selected and brought along for just such a purpose. Having suspected that job would need to be filled. Silver nodded once, certain. Mikhail snorted and swept off, still limping a little from his earlier crashing fall.

Alexei closed the door without comment. Irina waited for Silver to choose a seat, then set herself on one nearly opposite, and directly so once she dragged it to her preferred angle. "Is my daughter all right? I don't care to get my information filtered through Konstantin. I haven't found the opportunity to call her unnoticed for quite some time."

Silver frowned. She didn't think that was a name she'd learned and forgotten. "Konstantin?"

Irina laughed, a little jagged around the edges. "Our alpha. Can't really call him Father, can I?" She waved a hand dismissing that and whatever had caused her dark humor. Silver certainly couldn't understand it. Because of her age, perhaps? But the alpha had seemed plenty older than Irina's apparent age, to Silver's eyes at least.

In waiting for Silver's answer to her original question, Irina leaned forward over her knees, concern back in spades. Even Alexei took a step closer to the conversation, apparently invested in what she had to say as well. Interesting.

Silver wished she had better news. "She was alive when I had to leave. But she'd come off much the worse in the fight with Mikhail..."

Alexei offered some comment in Old Were that Irina revealed with her answer, rather than directly translating. "Really? I'd have said evenly matched, but I'll admit, I haven't seen them spar against each other for many years. But I'd still have expected her to have left him with more unhealed cuts than that." Her attention sharpened on Silver. "Did she pass out unexpectedly, perhaps?"

"Not...unexpectedly. Too fast. Is it weakness? From the wolfsbane poisoning?" Silver caught a glance of things unsaid from Irina to Alexei.

Irina grimaced apologetically. "Could be. I'd need to ask her a few things to know for certain." She settled herself back with the air of someone corralling her worry into studied relaxation. "And her mate?"

"I'm surprised she told you about her," Silver said, carefully. She could hardly imagine that Tatiana would have, in the normal course of things, not when she confided so little in Sacramento herself. Irina's comment must be a snap of teeth in the dark, but if she knew her daughter sufficiently to come upon the truth, Silver didn't see her denial would serve any purpose.

And when Silver answered, it was Alexei, of the two of them, who reacted. Silver couldn't understand it, even when review of her words traced his surprise to the pronoun.

"Tatiana said not one word of her, and I heard her in every single one of the gaps between the words she did say." Irina cast a very pointed look at Alexei as well.

"Say lover, perhaps, instead of mate." Silver weighed a wish to offer all possible details to set maternal worry at ease, but left it to Tatiana in the end to reveal Sacramento's name or not. "She was also badly hurt because Mikhail guessed who she was, but she was also alive when I…left."

"Some alpha you sound, walking out with so many of your people bleeding out upon the ground." Death took a place between the wild selves of her two visitors, all arrayed like a little council of war.

Silver thought of ignoring him, but this part she was to play would be hard enough already. Why not make use of her weaknesses, turn them to strengths? She looked straight at Death, the silhouette of his ears held high where substance of the cabin met the nothingness of his lack of color. "And how many did I save from the same fate by doing so, Death?"

Irina and Alexei looked to where Death clearly was not, for them, then back to Silver with a sour tinge of discomfort to their scents. "Konstantin may not know what he's stumbled upon," Irina murmured, then blew out a breath, face turning resolved. "Come." She stood, held an arm to one of the bedrooms. "There is in fact a reason I gained the permission Mikhail was demanding of me. I will help you dress for dinner. I'm afraid he wants you to look exactly like an icon, but it seems you're ready for that."

"As much as I can be," Silver agreed, and rose to follow her. Alexei remained at the front door, deeply patient in guard duties were Mikhail had sulked.

Irina was an ally, Silver was as certain of that as she could be, but there was no telling ally to what degree. To offer kindness was one thing, to fight an alpha was orders of magnitude beyond that. But this dinner, though undoubtedly staged to some purpose of Russia's own, would also serve Silver's, introducing her to many Were.

From there, she hoped she could draw the rebellious ones she needed.

14

That evening, just over a day since Silver had left, Andrew walked in as much private space as the others could grant him, from the cars up into the hunting lands, where everyone was gathering to give Billings' voice its color. Smaller by far than the national park where they'd held the wedding, the hunting lands felt saturated with Were, as if someone on two feet or four crunched between every tall evergreen and over every downed log.

Andrew's head was full of his search for something to say at the ceremony—a voice was given color by personal, emotional anecdotes, but somehow Andrew didn't think "that time he insulted my mate" or "that time he agitated for independence at exactly the wrong moment" would fly. He glanced back down the path, away from the ceremony he dreaded, and wished he hadn't, because it duplicated the angle from which he'd looked at Mikhail in that spot, during the last sunset he'd seen from the hunting lands.

Footsteps approached from the side, Felicia angling in to join him. Andrew welcomed the distraction, though he wished he had more comfort to offer her. She smelled strained, and she'd fastened her dark hair back into a simple tail, something she usually did only when she planned immediate exertion. He drew her into a quick sideways hug with an arm over her shoulders. She pressed against him for a beat, then withdrew to an easier walking distance with her hand tucked into his elbow.

"Are you all right?" He hadn't talked to her properly since she'd seen Billings, he realized. There hadn't been time, but he should have *made* time.

"I'll be fine." Felicia slowed their shared pace, scuffing her toes through the dust and pine needles of the path, eyes on that instead of him. "You, though...you're scaring me."

The heavy light of the sun's last rays stabbed into their eyes through a break in the trees, disappeared as a new set of branches blocked the horizon, then stabbed again, leaving Andrew with an annoying pattern of afterimages. "And the others?" Much good he was doing, staying behind if his lack of emotional control was only putting his pack more on edge. He needed to do better.

Felicia made a frustrated noise. "This isn't a pack thing, Papa. It's a you thing. Everyone else is fine too. I think they see you being silently strong under the weight of the alpha's duties, not shut down and fucking scarily intense. Can't you talk to someone? Not to me, I know that's...weird. But to John or something. Isn't that something else betas are for?"

Talk to someone? Wouldn't that be nice. How could he possibly tell John he, Andrew, had been the one who drove Silver to it? The beta's job was to support, and listening was part of that, but what if what he heard changed his opinion of the one he was supporting?

But he couldn't let Felicia take on a burden she didn't deserve. "I'm worried about Silver, that's all." He pressed his hand down over hers, and then even given her slowed pace, they'd arrived at the gathering.

Time to send Billings' voice to the Lady properly. After that...something. Andrew was certain he could find some other duty to keep him going, anger and guilt locked down where they belonged.

As darkness deepened around the pack houses, Andrew didn't even try to sleep. Those who lived close enough had left after the funeral and most others were packing for an early start to the next morning. He almost felt as if he could breathe again, but he still didn't dare pace noticeably, much as he would have liked to.

He ended up in the garden between the houses. The temperature had eased down but still carried enough heat from the day to be comfortable without a jacket. No longer packed with sub-alphas, the garden presented as it was meant to, especially with the darkness softening the general trampling. Short solar lamps glowed along the gravel path they'd created between the two back doors when they bought the properties and knocked down the fence between.

The star-lined path drew him along without his intending it, and he let himself into the guest house, only to hear voices. No privacy here either. For lack of anything better to do, Andrew crossed through the kitchen and lingered just before the doorway to the living room to see who it was. Laurence was slumped on the couch in front of the TV, beer in hand, and a soccer game muted on the screen. Andrew couldn't see who was playing because Susan was in the way, glaring at Laurence. Rooms in the guest house were always a touch sterile, cleaner, with furniture that hadn't been roughhoused into submission, but all the recent guests had at least left the scents lived-in.

"I am stuffed," Laurence said, with edged humor, as Andrew settled with his shoulder against the wall just on the kitchen side of the doorway. Neither person seemed to have noticed him—not a surprise in Susan's case, but Laurence must really be committed to his brooding if he was ignoring the sounds around him to that degree. "I couldn't eat another bite."

"That's not why I'm here. You forgot the 'rest' part of the 'rest and food' werewolf panacea. Go to bed." Susan walked up to Laurence and made shooing motions, but he just stared at her. After a beat, he grimaced and knocked back a swig from his beer.

"Not really up to sleeping very well in an unfamiliar place at the moment. But I'll get out of the house and stop stepping on your tails soon enough." He slumped lower, and Susan's expression softened with greater sympathy. She took a sideways seat on the arm of the couch beside him and ruffled his hair. It came out awkwardly from someone not used to the Were context of the gesture, but Andrew hoped Laurence appreciated the spirit of it.

"Seems to me, you did the best anyone could expect in a really bad situation." Susan spoke to the silent shift of bright, flickering movement that was a commercial break on the TV. "You don't have to leave Seattle. I'm sure the Roano..." She stumbled painfully on what probably would have been a plural. "Dare would let you stay. There's plenty of room here." She gestured around to indicate the guest house.

Andrew couldn't agree more, and he was glad Susan had said it when he might have lost track of the need for it himself.

The grayness to the man hadn't lifted, and Andrew would be a poor alpha if he didn't offer support until it did.

"They'll want to get information about the human out of me." Laurence moved to hold his beer in front of his chest like a shield. "So they can track her down like some kind of security risk. Joke's on them, though. I don't even know her first name. We didn't have time for introductions, and then..." Laurence shrugged jerkily. "I sort of thought of her as 'the Susan that's not really Susan.'"

Susan exhaled in humor and shook her head. "That will never not feel weird." Then she smacked him lightly on the back of the head, blow gentle enough to be suitable for a cub. "But you really think I'd let any Were hurt her?"

"She won't tell anyone about us." Laurence picked up again too quickly, like he didn't believe Susan's reassurance, or didn't believe anyone would let her enforce it. "She's smart. Really smart. She was the one who came up with all the escape plans. She'd see how humans wouldn't be likely to believe her."

"I'm sure she was," Susan said, and petted Laurence's hair again.

"I couldn't protect her." Tears crowded into Laurence's voice, though he kept his head down so they couldn't be seen. "I *tried*. I was the physically stronger one, it was the Were that pulled her into that situation, it was only fair I protect her, but I couldn't..."

"Oh, Laurence, don't." Susan swallowed. Andrew could smell her distress from where he was standing, and he supposed it was from not having enough reassurances to give. Andrew couldn't think of any others. He wished Silver were here.

But she wasn't. So it was up to him. He pushed off the door frame and tapped a knuckle on it for Susan's benefit. Laurence flinched, then seemed to fold in on himself with the humilia-

tion of such a strong reaction when he should have heard Andrew back when he entered the house.

"Susan's right. Stay, if you can." Andrew found a seat to
avoid looming, settled himself to give Laurence time to pull
himself together. Susan nodded to him, and seemed about to
squeeze his shoulder in reassurance as well, then thought better
of it, and drifted out to give them privacy.

"What about the human?" Concern seemed to finally pull
Laurence up out of his huddle.

Andrew let silence fall again as he tried to decide how
much truth Laurence needed at this particular moment, rather
than later. "We can't just let her disappear," he said at length.
"We don't have to kill her, we don't have to interfere…but we
do need to keep an eye on her. What if Russia decided to track
her down? Mikhail has met her, hasn't he?"

Laurence sighed. "I know." He laced his fingers together,
between his knees. "I didn't really think of it at the time, but…I
know." He glanced at Dare, and a little life came back into his
expression. "I need to do what I can to support her choice to
walk away from us, not protect her by removing the ability to
choose from her. Like Silver, huh?"

Andrew froze. Until this moment, he hadn't thought of
things that way, but now they seemed transparently clear. Silver was incredibly intelligent, and she'd made the choice to go
to Russia, and she'd asked him to stay here and take care of
the pack. She'd made the decision to play Lady-touched, and
he couldn't protect her from that. "We'll watch, we'll wait. See
when we're needed."

Knowing the Russians, he still thought he would be. Sooner
or later. But he wouldn't follow her until she asked him to.

"Maybe I will stick around for a while. Get my head together a little." Laurence collected his beer and stood. He waited until he was almost out of the room to speak, so Andrew didn't spoil it by looking at him. He stared at the TV instead. "Not-Susan suggested I talk about my troubles as a sub-alpha to a human therapist. With substituted details." He didn't have to explain any further; Andrew knew exactly what he meant. All of them did it, with human authorities, or coworkers, or neighbors, translating over things that wouldn't make sense or would reveal secrets.

"Couldn't hurt," Andrew said lightly. Lady knew he didn't really know how to help Laurence with the fundamental problems he had with Were authority. "If you do, take note of what it's like. Then others can find out if it's useful for them, as well."

"Huh," Laurence said, like he hadn't thought of that before, and then disappeared into the house, probably up to the bedroom he was borrowing.

Andrew turned the TV's sound back on and tried to make himself care about who was winning. It had been Silver's choice to go to Russia, but if only it could have been without the weight of hurt caused by her own damn husband.

He wrenched off his ring and held it on his palm, thinking about throwing it at the wall or something equally juvenile and dramatic. It probably would make a hole in the drywall, though.

The back door opened and footsteps approached. Andrew assumed it was Susan, come back to check on them, and didn't move just yet. Maybe she'd go away if she saw Laurence had left.

"It will roll under something. And you'll spend the next hour throwing furniture around looking for it." Tatiana's accent brushed her words with gentle irony and it was Andrew's turn to start and almost drop his ring anyway.

"I'm surprised you're up with the ones pacing all night rather than sleeping," Andrew said. He tried to make it a joke, but it fell a little flat. Her lover was still here, and she could be in bed cuddling with Sacramento this minute if she wanted. It was hard not to let envy sour his words.

"Allison and I...had a discussion about how much of my emotions I keep from her. We're cooling down." Tatiana's lips thinned, but with a bit of irony that suggested she realized how constrained her body language was even now.

"And her wish to go charging into battle doesn't help, I suppose," Andrew offered. He should talk to her. Another responsibility to add to the stack of those he had let slip away from him.

Tatiana's expression lightened a little. "Oddly enough, that didn't come up. I think Felicia really got through to her." Her lips quirked up, irony becoming true amusement. "One hothead to another."

Andrew snorted, but couldn't avoid a little amusement himself. "You know where she inherited it from."

In the conversational lull, Tatiana delicately took the ring he was still holding and slipped it back onto his finger herself. "I wish I'd been able to go with Silver. They wouldn't have trusted me, but..."

Andrew rotated the ring automatically so the etched circle representing the Lady at full faced the palm, the traditional configuration for luck. Or the superstitious configuration. "So you still have wolfsbane visions."

Tatiana bristled, then sighed. "So you and Silver had a

fight." Andrew must have bristled in exactly the same way, because she laughed, as much self-directed as anything.

"I hurt her. And I wish I could apologize, I wish I could make things right with her, but I never got the chance before…" Andrew scrubbed the side of one knuckle over the corner of his eye to erase an errant tear. Tatiana's expression was still open, listening, so more poured out, though before she walked in, he'd never have predicted Tatiana would be the one it would pour out to. Felicia had been right. The pressure had been building for too long.

"Yes, I seem to see Death sometimes, but I didn't tell her because I don't know how to make her understand that I can see things and still know they're a function of a distressed mind. Dreams aren't real, they're just what our minds make up every night, so why couldn't they do the same thing in other situations?"

Tatiana took Laurence's former seat on the couch, her movement recalling Andrew to the present and making him trail off. It wasn't really her he'd been trying to convince with all that rambling, and she actually didn't seem all that unconvinced either, now he looked at her face. "In my former pack," she pronounced the words with great deliberation, as if reading off a formal speech written by someone who had no emotions about the matter, "wolfsbane visions are common. Albeit usually only coming when you've actually taken some."

She leaned her forearms on her thighs, looked at her palms, then turned her hands over to look at the other side. Her hair was French braided back tightly, so none escaped even with her head tipped down. "In the most simple terms, you are said to see what the Lady sends you. Those priestesses with a more nuanced view say that She helps you see what you need to see. But visions are not representations of the real world, past, present, or future. They're just..."

"Dreams." Andrew rotated his ring to invert his luck—though the etched new toward the palm wasn't really bad luck, just nothing in particular—and then returned it to its original position. "I started seeing Death long before I met you or drank that wolfsbane. It was when I came close to dying myself."

Tatiana shrugged. "There were priestesses before wolfsbane. Maybe there were visions, too. My echo visions come without it. I thought I might be dying myself, but they've leveled off. Only once in a while, when I'm most frightened, angry. That's what made me so useless in the fight."

Andrew touched her knee, impulse to comfort automatic. "Significantly less useless than not being there at all." He withdrew his hand, and they sat in silence for a while.

"I think—" Tatiana paused, as if waiting for permission. When Andrew at least didn't object, she continued. "That you two have managed for—what, five years?—now, to somehow completely understand how the other can believe, or not believe, while still continuing to not believe, or believe. Both of you. I think when you speak to Silver again, she might accept your apology."

"When," Andrew repeated. He'd decided to believe that. *When.*

15

The dress Irina helped Silver into was pretty enough, and better yet, as she discovered as she returned to the great hall, it allowed her reasonable freedom of movement. She expected something gauzy, easily picked up by the wind, in white as Death had been dressed in black when he appeared as a woman in Silver's wolfs-bane dream. Instead, the dress hugged her waist before opening to a long, full skirt, with panels of embroidery everywhere, white on white. She rather thought the design would have been even more attractive in bright colors.

The hall had filled since Silver had seen it last. This could not be the whole of the Russian pack—Tatiana had spoken of individual settlements run by trusted betas—but the numbers still filled the room to bursting. In their tame selves, people's hair was both golden, as she'd already seen, and a deep black often paired with quite fine strands. Among the wild selves, Silver found most often dustings of dark or light, as Tatiana had on the tips of her wild self's fur.

One table was set before the alpha's throne, another two perpendicular down the rest of the room's length. Everyone stood before their places, undoubtedly because the alpha yet stood as well. Silver would be at the head table with the alpha, of course; she didn't need Irina to direct her there. But before she arrived, her steps were arrested by the sight of an icon set in pride of place on a sideboard.

It was two panels of wood, hinged to each other, and what they depicted...Silver jerked her head aside, before she could fully take in the image of the Lady at the left. When the Lady had left her children, She'd taken the memory of Her face along with Her, so it might not cause them pain. To guess at it seemed the deepest of hubris to Silver.

On the right, at least the Lady was in wolf, shining white in every respect. Death knelt beside Her in human, another blasphemy. He was denied his human form as part of his pun- ishment, but he would mock Silver for worrying about such things as swirls of paint on wood. For all that, she noticed he had disappeared for the moment.

"Is she not the very image of Her?" The alpha's voice car- ried across the whole room, blowing all conversations flat like a gust over grain. They sprang back up again a moment later as stunted whispers.

Silver looked at the icon of the Lady. She could not help herself, she had to know if there was some truth to the alpha's posturing. Had he perhaps had this icon made from some pic- ture, precisely to compare well to her? But it was stained with the patina only time could give, and besides, all these Were must recognize it, know it intimately, or it would have no pow- er for this comparison.

The goddess pictured had white hair, yes, and a dress such as Silver's. At Her side, the great black wolf captured Death well enough, though being painted, it lacked the spark of irony in his eyes. The Lady's face...well, it was serene. Silver had never felt such serenity herself. These depictions, they weren't like people, she realized. As well to say the image of Death in human had her mate's face: there was not enough detail to be sure. Any viewer could find exactly the resemblance they wished.

She did not see the sense in attempting to refute the alpha at this juncture, however. She held her silence, and seated herself in the chair he indicated, at his side. A moment later, Death's weight settled itself onto her feet, as if he'd stretched himself out, long and comfortable. At the alpha's other side was Irina—the mate's place, Silver would have said, but that could not be the case here. Tatiana would not have neglected to mention such a thing.

The alpha leaned to speak into Irina's ear, apparent affection in the closeness, in the way his hand overlapped hers on the table. It was a gesture that felt oddly public, in a way Silver could not decode. Was he aiming to make Silver jealous? She thought she'd made her thoughts on that topic abundantly clear—she noticed, now she was seated close enough, that the mark of her chain under his chin had been cut away so the skin could heal clean.

But no, perhaps this was a strategy played out solely for Irina. She stiffened at his touch, making him smile very slightly and say something chiding. With weaponized dignity, she tipped her head in similarly public attention and offered him a few words in return. His point apparently made, he settled back, and Irina sipped her wine.

Everyone had a glass, up and down the table, apparently permissible to drink while they waited for something. Silver had a metal goblet instead, which she did not touch. When she and Dare had been poisoned by wolfsbane at this alpha's orders not so long ago, it had been in the wine. She would drink nothing that had been set out so specially for her here. Nothing, in fact, that the alpha didn't consume as well, as he'd been willing to sacrifice Tatiana to consuming the poison from the same source to reassure them it was safe.

Two women entered, marked apart by dresses much like Silver's but with embroidery in gold, and single, long braids. Tatiana had mentioned priestesses, on occasion, and Silver would guess these were two of them. The older of the women, with broad cheekbones, had a braid that reached nearly to the floor. She paused, looking from the icon to Silver, annoying but not surprising Silver, then moved on before Silver could read her reaction. She didn't know if dubiousness or belief would be more reassuring.

The two priestesses circled to step onto the dais from either side. The alpha pushed his chair back; Silver glanced quickly around, but no one else followed his example, so she remained seated as well. Each movement of both the alpha and the priestesses had a ritual quality, even though she could not understand the words they spoke as the alpha stepped behind his throne for a semblance of privacy for the moment when he switched tame for wild self.

As his tame self stood quietly by, a hand resting on the back of the throne, the wild jumped to the seat. The black-haired priestess set her hand upon his head, between the gray-aged-to-white ears pricked high. Her voice lifted, aimed to fill the whole room. All those present responded with a word in unison, making a rumble like thunder shivering Silver's chest.

The blessing over, the alpha returned to his clothes behind the throne. Was Silver of any mind to be impressed, she supposed she should be by the speed with which he shifted two times in close succession. The Lady would be full tomorrow—with no wild self, Silver tried to pretend she forgot the Lady's cycle, but that would have been a lie to herself—but if a dinner with the whole pack together such as this was commonplace, shifting so every time, even in the new, would be a feat of considerable strength.

When the alpha was seated once more, a few teens slipped in from what Silver assumed was the direction of the kitchen, carrying platters of food. The alpha received his portion first, then she and Irina did, two servers darting desperate glances at each other in their effort to coordinate so closely neither she nor Irina could be said to have been served first. Lady, but rigid hierarchy made everything so awkward. The priestesses collected pitchers to refill glasses in the same order.

The alpha cleared his throat as the process continued. "You will all have noticed our guest. I ask that you all speak in English tonight, the better to make her feel at home."

And by "ask," he meant "order." Silver didn't know if this was an extension of his mocking of her ignorance of Old Were earlier, but either way, she didn't wish everyone to struggle with unfamiliar words for her sake. "There's no need—"

But the alpha simply spoke over her. "I know I can trust all of you fulfill any wish she makes known, as if it was an order from myself."

I wish you to depose this cat's bastard, Silver thought, and then swallowed the words instead of the wine she wasn't drinking.

"I dare you to say that out loud and see what happens," Death put in, from beneath the table. Far from Silver's rising frustration, he sounded more and more amused as the alpha postured.

"Strong voice, strong words, strong actions!" the alpha declaimed, and then drank. Everyone else drank with him, and Silver saw no way around it now but to pretend. She raised her goblet to her lips, stopping just short of wetting them, then replaced it on the table.

Gasps rippled through the room and the alpha smirked. Perhaps if she knocked the wine into his lap, he might look discomfited even for a second. What now?

Metal. Hers was the only goblet, the only one of metal. Silver brought it back to her lips as if for a second sip and now she was looking for it, she could smell it plain. It was made of silver.

All right, then. Play the role. Goblet replaced, Silver lifted her hand slightly, turning palm to the room so they could all see her unburned skin. The whispers surged up, crested, then died back as she lowered her hand and turned to her food. At least that had come from a common source. She could eat without unreasonable risk.

"Are they not formidable?" the alpha remarked as they ate, conversational phrasing at full-room volume. "I am quite proud of my pack members."

"I'm sure you are," Silver said. She spoke down the table rather more at Irina than at him, because it helped a little, and she was rewarded with a spark of humor in the woman's eyes.

The alpha translated her words before switching back to English. "Do they not look ready to take down any prey, no matter how numerous or frightening?"

That was a much more dangerous thing to agree to, in the Lady's name. "I'm sure they're wise enough to choose their opponents carefully."

His translation went a bit long, this time. Silver tried to find a hint as to its fidelity to the original in Irina's face, but she was controlling herself better now.

While the alpha returned to his food, giving Silver the chance to get in a few bites, other conversations around the room staggered cautiously to their feet. After a few minutes, a young woman left her food to approach the high table along the aisle between the two low. She bowed before the dais, and the alpha gestured that she might approach.

Her steps brought her directly opposite Silver, where she struggled with words for a few moments. Finally they burst free, low for Silver and the alpha alone, perhaps all the more so for the fact that she needed to stand in full view of all to offer them. "You ask Lady if I blessed to…blessed with baby? Soon? I wish…much."

When Silver hesitated, groping for the right balance between reassurance and false certainty, the alpha stepped into the pause. "I'm sure the Lady knows your eagerness. It's not an honor everyone appreciates, yes?" His eyes were on the young woman, but Silver got the impression he was speaking to Irina instead.

Irina's composure cracked into rather poisonous humor. "But all of the pack's children are the alpha's children, are they not? You must be so proud of all of them."

Looking rather confused, the young woman bobbed her head and departed back to her seat. The dinner did not improve particularly from that point, but neither did it worsen. Mostly, it ground against Silver's nerves with so much she didn't understand, whether the words were spoken in her own language or not. The alpha carried some grudge against Irina, she was certain of it, yet he seated her so high in the hierarchy and smiled at her so often.

That was not entirely useful to her purpose here, but Silver didn't see anything that was. Beyond Irina, she simply was not close enough to anyone to sound them out or read their opin-

ions of their alpha in their scent or incompletely hidden ex-
pressions. Her earlier optimism seemed naive, given the public
nature of this meal.

And, if she were honest with herself, sleep while traveling
was not the same as sleep in a real bed. When the sweet arrived to finish the meal, Silver could have cried with the relief of it. Each individual cake was intricately iced on all sides,
white dots and flourishes on white, with a circle of half black
and half silver shine on the top. She almost hated to cut into it,
but eating kept her from having to speak for a little longer, so
she demolished every bite. She did not quite like the taste of the
dye that must have been used to achieve the icing's shimmer,
but the cake itself was delicate and delicious.

The lower-ranked pack members were gathering themselves and departing now; with her escape in sight, Silver relaxed a little, content to wait until the alpha stood. The black-
haired priestess approached from her other side, leaned in to
speak privately, setting a smaller glass of wine before Silver
as she did. It had a nicely rounded shape she felt vaguely she
should have recognized, with no stem. "I could see you wanted something without making a show of it." Her accent was as
strong as any here save the alpha or Tatiana's, but Silver had
somewhere in this meal found her feet in the flow of it, and
traveled smoothly from word to word.

It had been important Silver did not drink, but the priestess
was very kind. Besides, she could not presently remember her
reasons for abstaining so completely. Perhaps they had been
only foolish overanxiety. If so, why refuse this kind gift?

Silver sipped. That was better. Perhaps she should be careful, not to become tipsy, but she'd just eaten, and besides, fuzz-

ing out the world at the edges was almost necessary by now. Just as long as she didn't fall asleep at the table.

She could float for a space, until someone told her what to do next. And indeed, the black-haired priestess did. "You can come with me. I'll keep you safe."

Silver slipped out of the great hall, following the priestess's straight back and straight line of braid down her spine. When they reached a room that was smaller and more private, the priestess gave her back her own clothes, smelling of recent washing in unfamiliar soap. She changed and curled up in a comfortable seat, only to realize she'd forgotten her glass back at dinner. The priestess kindly gave her another.

"Have you forgotten me?" Death said. He seemed piqued, standing much larger than usual before her, the darkness of his flank fit to block out the whole room. "You know what happened last time you did that."

Silver did not know that, she realized. But she made him room to curl beside her as she thought about it. With a sigh, he settled to a size fit to tuck against her hip and watched the room's door with a tight gaze.

The alpha, when he entered, lacked his usual charm. The lines of his face settled quite easily into his frown. He demanded something of the priestess in Old Were.

"She is still awake because we knew some would have remained in her system from her previous dose, but not how much." The priestess refilled Silver's glass and approached. Death jumped down with a huff of annoyance, and she took his place beside Silver, but did not give her the wine just yet. "Puppy, we want you to know this is for your good, yes? And that it is being done safely."

The alpha growled something else, but the priestess carried serenely on in words Silver could understand. "And the dose in the icing needed to be quite small because of the taste in any case. Now we have done it safely and gradually, and this is the last glass. She does not need to sleep at all."

"Safe," Silver agreed. She did feel safe. She accepted the glass and tipped it back.

The priestess squeezed a hand on Silver's ankle where it was tucked up on the seat. "You will feel no pain at all." She rose, drew Silver up with her. "Alpha, you have no part in this." Her tone was as firm as the stone beneath the soil of the world, and he was thus dismissed. Silver wished she could borrow such a tone for her own use.

The priestess led Silver into another room, stopped before a table or a bed—which of the two, Silver wasn't sure, and she found the confusion did not bother her. It was high, but there was a pillow. The priestess assisted her to step up by a convenient chair and guided to lie on her back.

Silver's shirt had short sleeves, but the priestess turned up the fabric to bunch even higher around her shoulder, wiped her skin clean down to the cup of her elbow with gentle strokes of a cloth. Then she set Silver's arm long and flat, shed snake skins of her scars for all to see once more. "It is true you cannot move your hand, puppy, yes?"

"My fingers." Silver twitched them, on her bad hand, to the minor curl at the limit of her abilities, then relaxed again.

"Thank you," the priestess said warmly, and it made Silver so pleased she could help the woman that the feeling radiated through her chest so her voice felt nestled in a cocoon of blankets.

She watched the priestess as other footsteps came and went, someone handed the priestess a knife. Not a moon knife, a reassuringly small, straight one, though it caught the light as those curved blades had, and looked similarly sharp.

The priestess was right, Silver felt no pain at all as she pressed the knife into her skin, removed a thin strip, then another. The scars did not look like snake skins away from her body; they were far too red and wet. And Silver's side was feeling rather damp and uncomfortable as the blood lost its own heat and wicked away her own with it.

"We knew damage was deep, no need to worry," the priestess said. Her voice was rather strained, Silver thought. It was a little odd, because Silver wasn't worried over such a little discomfort as the blood puddling up and into her side was causing.

The priestess had handed away the knife, and now she clamped a cloth tight to Silver's arm. And then another. "My blood you have to hold in," Silver said, to reassure her that she was doing the right thing, but this time the priestess didn't thank her. She exchanged a flurry of words in Old Were with an assistant, and only then found a smile for Silver.

"You should sleep now, I think. Worth—risk." Her search for the right words rendered her rhythm uneven. She did not loose her hold on Silver's arm, but other hands helped Silver sit up a little, set a glass to her lips for her to drink. "Think of your happiest time for me, yes? You will have the very sweetest of dreams, and when you wake, things will be better."

16

By the time Tatiana went running with Andrew for the evening
of the full, only the Roanoke home pack—and Allison—remained in Seattle, and everyone fit into two vehicles on the way
out to the hunting lands. Andrew had been dubious about holding the regular run at first, but nobody else wanted to spend the
full without shifting. And no one had wanted to be around him
either, while he forced himself to stay in human so as to be able
answer his phone in six seconds instead of sixty after shifting
back.

Running flat out in wolf until he nearly collapsed seemed
to have ground a few more edges off what remained of his rather disquieting intensity after their talk the night before. He
hadn't even bothered to shift back, just waited for someone else
to open the SUV's back doors. Most everyone else took their
cue from him and extended the time they could spend in wolf
a little more. Tatiana had stretched out as much as she could

among the others on the carpet over all the folded-down seats, and Allison had warmed up enough to doze with her head on Tatiana's flank.

The low sun threw window-squares onto the opposite wall, curling to a new angle as they made a turn. A sensitive nose made any journey like this annoying, long term, but she could handle sharing an enclosed space with seven other Were for the space of the trip from hunting lands to pack house. As a space outside of the possibility of action, she found she rather wished it could stretch long. The pack house held only worries, and nothing to do about them.

A phone rang. Andrew's head jerked up, but it wasn't his ringtone. He flopped his nose to paws, apparently dismissing it with a growl of annoyance.

But Tatiana knew whose ringtone it was. It was hers, and two North Americans had that number, both of them currently within touching distance in wolf. It had to be someone from Russia, and they wouldn't be at the pack house for ten minutes or more yet.

Everyone else grumble-growled and tried lifting feet to find which article of clothing in the pile they'd sprawled on held the phone. Tatiana walked right on top of flanks and legs to get to the pile, earning a few negligently aimed nips as well as growls. Then she needed hands, but there was no privacy to shift in here.

She didn't see she had a choice, however. The ring finished one iteration, began another. No Were set their phone to go to voicemail too early, and the person on the other end would know to wait, but she didn't know the situation from which they were calling. What if a Tooth walked in on them? It couldn't be good news, Silver would have arrived a day ago, if not earlier. If her mother had planned to call about that, she would have already.

Tatiana tried to stay low to the carpet, and most people turned their heads, but she could feel their gaze on her skin as she shifted anyway. The embarrassment dripped through her chest, acidic. Russians weren't this crass, she just had no *choice*. At least the process was quick, in the full.

Andrew must have traced her conclusions about the call the moment he realized it was her phone she was going after, because he shifted perhaps two breaths later, as Tatiana was answering. Her mother's number.

She didn't bother with a greeting. "Is it bad news?" she asked in Old Were.

"It's not good. Is the other Roanoke within howling distance?" Her mother sounded very controlled, but that could cover many things. Tatiana didn't allow herself to imagine any of them.

"He's here," she said, in English. Someone punctuated the words with a yelp as Andrew put a knee wrong launching himself across the vehicle to hover over the phone as she put it to speaker and held it out.

"Silver?" he demanded.

"The alpha got the priestesses to cut the silver scars out of her arm, but she wouldn't stop bleeding. Now the wound's closed, but she looks very bad. Is this something you know about? What do you do about it?"

Tatiana closed her eyes. Now she knew the worst, she could imagine it very, very well. The Lady had two working arms; Silver's bad one must have been a false note that irritated the alpha.

"She heals like a human. So pressure. And stitches? I think."

Andrew's deeper growl rolled out over all of them, making the other Were flinch against the nearest walls. "Susan will know. Five minutes."

"I told you, we closed the wound. That's not the problem. Call me back," Tatiana's mother said, and ended the call.

John, who was driving, made it in four. Andrew used the time to pull on his clothes, no one yelping now even when he had to step on them. Tatiana worked a bit more carefully, waiting for her pants until they'd screeched into the garage and Andrew had slammed his way out of the SUV. As she'd expected, once he found Susan, he dragged her back, meeting Tatiana at a halfway point that balanced out to be in the hall just off the kitchen.

Tatiana thumbed the last digit to complete the call, then thrust the phone at Susan in turn. The human had changed out of the edged professionality of her work clothes, but her hair was still back in its tight twist at the nape of her neck. "Here's the human," she told her mother.

Susan bristled slightly at her phrasing and extracted her wrist from Andrew's grip, but her eyes widened as Tatiana's mother repeated the question. "You need a transfusion. Of the correct blood type. And none of you know yours, I suppose. Um. Fuck." She reached abortively for the phone, changed her mind, and pulled her own from her pocket. "Need a keyboard that's not in Cyrillic." She typed something, read rapidly. "There are supposed to be cards, that drugstores sell, for home blood-typing..."

"Any drugstore is too far at this moment," Tatiana's mother broke in.

"Andrew! You're making me slower." Susan, brave woman and true beta, shoved Andrew's chest with her free hand when he tried to read her screen over her shoulder. "I'm not finding a webpage describing how to do it, but as far as I know, historically they just put drops of the donor's and receiver's blood together to see if it reacts—like, clumps up. That's all the cards have, the antigens from each type."

"So we want a blood…"

"That *doesn't* react with Silver's."

Tatiana's mother switched to Old Were, calling directions about finding possible donors to someone else. Without a response in English, Susan looked worriedly to Tatiana's face instead. Tatiana grimaced as the call ended. In the stress of the moment, she lost her own English for a breath, before she fought her thoughts back into order. "She understood. And now she knows what to look up."

Silence ensnared the three of them, each staring at the others and thinking someone else would speak first, perhaps.

"I'm leaving for Russia on the next flight," Andrew said.

"I'm coming with you," Tatiana said.

"We probably shouldn't discuss this in the hall," Susan said, third beat of one-two-three that couldn't have been timed more precisely if they'd practiced it like a song.

Andrew jerked his head upstairs and led the way. John arrived to bring up the rear, getting details from his wife as they jogged up. As the last in, he closed the door to the alphas' bedroom. Andrew hardly waited for the click of the latch before he started giving orders: Susan would be in charge, with both John and Felicia to convey her decisions to the Were, and Boston on the ground to support them with the Eastern packs. Tatiana honestly expected John to erupt into anger, but he looked relieved, of all things.

The logistics for this side of the ocean left Tatiana at loose ends, fidgeting at being in the alphas' personal space. It was a tidy enough space, mostly huge bed and view through the French doors onto a deck, but every breath held their scent. She felt vaguely as if she should have been second-guessing her decision to go with him, but she found only unshakable certainty. Andrew needed someone who spoke the language, who knew Father's tricks.

Susan interrupted Andrew's directions with a frustrated gesture. "Yes, it's all very heroic, but what exactly are you going to accomplish over there, just the two of you? I've heard all about the dangers of pack war, but taking even a few other people..."

"A few other people aren't going to matter against a few dozen Teeth of the Lady's Jaw," Tatiana snapped. There were the misgivings she'd been expecting. What exactly *were* they going to accomplish? They could hardly sneak in to help Silver escape, either of them.

"I have no qualms about arming myself properly. I wouldn't want to bring a gun through customs, but I'm sure one could be arranged over there." Andrew crossed his arms, jaw set, though a muscle jumped in it, belying his apparent calm.

"That's..." Tatiana groped after the right words. She couldn't even blame the lack on the language barrier, it was the fault of unquestioned assumptions. That's uncivilized? Too human? Just not done? "Only practical, I suppose. But still. That's an advantage only when it's a surprise. What about all the rest of the Teeth that jump us when the surprise is gone?"

Andrew stalked a few paces to glower out of the glass to the deck. "So we're left with talking. Which worked so well for Silver, playing up being Lady-touched..." He whirled back. "What if I was to say I'm Death-touched? The 'Butcher of Barcelona' is still a story people kick around about me sometimes, isn't it? If you are so wrapped up in religious myths, why not present the one of Death returning for his Lady?"

Now Tatiana felt like Andrew had physically snatched all her words away from her, leaving her gasping with only the feeling that he was wrong, and she couldn't explain why. "Death-touched is…not a thing. If you're dead, you're dead."

"So no one can tell me I'm doing it wrong." Andrew smiled without warmth.

Susan stepped back to survey them both, then sighed. "Well, you've made an impression on her, anyway. Maybe this isn't completely—" She glanced at her husband, corner of her mouth tucking up in reluctant humor. "Prey-stupid."

"It's his choice to be as prey-stupid as he wants." John drew breath to say something else, then let it out in a frustrated huff. He pressed a thumb to his forehead. "Lady shine on your endeavors. We'll leave you to figure them out in more detail."

"You'll need to dye your hair," Tatiana said finally, when they were alone. She touched her temple, and Andrew smoothed the bands of white in the dark brown at his own. "That's what La-dy-touched usually means, not Silver's unique situation. Go all black. And cut out your scars." She prowled around him, lifted the hem of his shirt at the back. "Though you can't shift—your wolf form is entirely the wrong color—so it might be that no one sees your back. Better not to take that chance, however."

If they were going to do this, they needed to do it *properly*.

She returned to look at him straight on, mentally adding the dye, trying to imagine she was other than she was. How would she see him then? Father would never believe it, but the other pack members were their target. "Appearance isn't really the point, though. Can you act it? Like you really believe Death is real?"

Andrew lifted his chin. "Of course."

Too fast. She scrubbed her fingertips over her eyes. She was sure he'd approach the role head-on, like it was something that could be conquered by mere effort, but she'd been living with him as something near to her own alpha for several months, and he was *such* an atheist. "Convince me. Pretend I'm my alpha. Play it like you would to him."

She took a seat on the edge of the bed, thinking cat's bastard thoughts to get into her own part. Andrew looked away, drew breath to object a few times, but finally seemed to talk himself around to the spirit of the thing.

He stepped up to her, stood loose, ready for violence. "You will release my wife or I'll rip your voice out for Death myself." Tatiana could feel the pressure of his will behind it, like a storm on the edge of the horizon.

"That's just regular alpha." It took a lot of will of her own, but Tatiana yawned. Andrew surged forward, reaching for her, and Tatiana brought up one hand to beneath his chin, as if holding a moon knife. "And then all his Teeth jump you."

Andrew snarled at her and twisted away once more. "Of all the times I *want* to see Death…which is the sort of irony that would delight that particular subconscious hallucination."

"If you could choose to see him—" Tatiana cut herself off, but Andrew must have figured out from her intonation there had been more to that thought. She hadn't recognized it herself until it almost left her lips.

He was back in front of her instantly. "What?"

"In very small amounts, wolfsbane is used for what's called a wisdom ceremony, rather than a full vision ceremony, which is what you two inadvertently had. It frees your mind, lets the Lady speak to you, if that's how you conceptualize it. You're still conscious. Maybe—and it's a big maybe—that might help you. If I can get the dose right. You got such a large dose already, some of that will be lingering in your system." She dropped her head to frown as she started the calculations. "If I took the wine that's left over from what Father sent me with, to poison you, and burn off the alcohol…the concentrated wolfsbane would be easier to measure…"

She snapped her attention back up. There was no point going down that burrow if you didn't know what was at the end of it. "But it would be a great risk." Would she take such a risk herself, if it were Allison being hurt?

She didn't know.

Andrew did, however. He gestured aside her objections almost before she finished making them. "I'll pack while you make it." He didn't touch her, but she could feel his impulse to bodily drag her off the bed and throw her out of the room.

Tatiana went. A wisdom ceremony sounded awfully nice at the moment, though they had never particularly worked that way for her. She'd have liked to know if she was making the right decision, or only aiding someone she respected in self-destruction.

With their flight booked and suitcases waiting in the hall below, Andrew ushered Tatiana back to the bedroom. Night had fallen outside, and he didn't bother turning on the light, finding grounding in the muted tone to all the colors caused by using night vision. Tatiana was apparently quite resolved about controlling the wolfsbane dose, as she filled the little dropper in the cap of her bottle, eyed the level, and only then handed it over to him.

The bottle looked like one that had belonged to Susan, emptied out and repurposed. Something-something essential oil, purchased, he was reasonably sure, for some scent privacy, but that was between her and John. It certainly assaulted his nose, and left a strange, bitter aftertaste when he dropped the liquid on his tongue, though perhaps that was the wolfsbane.

Tatiana screwed the cap back on the bottle with more concentration than it deserved. "Do you want me to prime you with anything?"

Andrew shook his head. "What does that mean?" He couldn't honestly remember what the wolfsbane starting to work had been like last time. The glow before getting tipsy, maybe? He wasn't feeling any different.

"There's a period, when it first starts to work, when you're very suggestible." Tatiana tucked the bottle into her hip pocket, stepped up to him. He half expected her to angle his chin to check his eyes or something, but she was more respectful than that. Or more cautious, still feeling herself a not-quite-hostage to a foreign alpha, no matter how their goals had snapped into extremely close alignment over the past few days.

"I'm sure you'll see Death, and he'll tell you what you need to know." She said it with such intensity Andrew had to snort. If only stating things strongly enough made them true. He'd shout how he was going to rescue Silver from the rooftops.

While he waited, he stepped over to the dresser against the wall over by the entrance to the bathroom, to see if opening the various drawers would shake anything loose that he'd forgotten to pack. He reviewed the contents of his suitcase mentally and it was suddenly…oddly easy. One object linking to another, as easy as purring through a catalog with the side of your thumb.

They'd leave here, go to the airport—parking garage, sky-bridge, check-in desk, no checked luggage—like a movie montage, he could see each step. A feeling of confidence stole over him, pushing, shoving worries out of his muscles. If he could see three steps ahead, four, five, why was he worrying anyway?

He'd expected a lack of balance, a swooping feeling, but he'd never felt so grounded in his life. Grounded and ready to *run*.

"This is an excruciatingly bad idea," Death said. He strolled off the deck, through the closed door, as if having just now descended from the wash of real darkness fended off the skyline by the city's light pollution. "Not least because you'll be spending most of your time without a shred of judgment."

Andrew left the dresser to plant himself before Death. Death was no larger than a real Were, but still he had no need to look up into Andrew's face. "Will it work?"

"It might. Of course, any foolish thing *might* work. Kneel." The command bypassed Andrew's conscious mind and brought him slamming to his knees, leg muscles answering to a new master. "You ask much of *me* in this scheme of yours, however. And, I notice, assume I will give it without even an attempt at persuasion."

"You were the one who put the idea in my head. If her part is the Lady, mine is Death." Of his own volition, Andrew went farther, set his hands on the carpet, bowed over them. He felt entirely outside himself in the moment: knowing Death was not real, knowing he was speaking to nothing at all, and yet doing it anyway.

"He was actually paying attention. How flattering." For all the shock of his command to kneel, Death seemed now to be almost pleased. He dropped his jaw in a canine smile. "That's not what I meant, however. It will be a considerable investment of time to stand by to feed you lines for however long this ill-conceived rescue takes. Are you under the impression I have nothing better to do?"

"Will you do it for Silver?" That was the best Andrew had. He knew he had no call upon Death himself.

"I cannot conceive of a way it could be boring, at least," Death mused. He shoved his muzzle against Andrew's chest, urging him to his feet with a sensation that was a lot like Andrew imagined being hit by a truck would feel, only compressed to such a density that it only vibrated your bones, didn't move you an inch.

"Follow my lead," Death said, and prowled around Tatiana. Who'd been watching this entire time, Andrew abruptly remembered. She looked a little wide eyed, a little white around the lips. Andrew circled her in Death's wake, and she turned to keep him in sight.

"How many Were have you killed?" Death said, conversationally, and Andrew did his best to match his tone when he asked it of Tatiana.

"What does that have to do with anything?" A frown came into her expression now. Aimed at him, not at Death. A strange feeling that was, collecting the consequences for words that weren't his.

"I could just ask Death, but this way, I get to see how many you'll admit to. How many you remember. Have you stopped counting? Should I ask Death for your total on your behalf?" With each sentence, the rhythm of it got easier, like anticipating the next verse after a chorus. Death led, Andrew followed, but perhaps not for much longer.

"This isn't about me, it's about my alpha. And I'm sure he's quite proud of every one of his kills. And he's probably ordered hundreds more." Tatiana drew back until she was against the closed door out of the room, trying to stare him down and not really succeeding.

"Ordered, and you carried out? Did that make it easier? You said you refused his orders finally, after a human. Was that one so different than killing a Were? Seems an odd place to stop, once you've started. And why waste the skills you'd build up? I'm sure you were *quite* skilled." Andrew didn't need to push into her personal space; he settled on the edge of it with Death standing by. Silent now.

The words came to Andrew anyway. "Nine is my total, if you were wondering. To make this fair. Doesn't seem like so many, does it? Eight and a half, perhaps. Silver helped with one. Seven made me a 'butcher.' Or perhaps that was tearing out their throats so Death couldn't find their voices. Not that it made any difference; the voice is not in *muscle*. But it's the symbol of it, you know."

"Andrew, please. Stop." Tatiana pressed her hands to her face, shaking becoming visible for just that brief moment, before she clamped down on it. "I mean. Roanoke. I think you've proved your point."

Confidence slipped away from him, leaving Andrew rather shaky himself. "I'm sorry. I went too far…"

"No, with Father, you'll need to go that far or farther. It's just what you need. Just please…don't use it on me, all right?" Tatiana lifted her chin high, a calm mask settling into place. Before she could entirely disappear behind it, he embraced her, whispered one more apology.

She clung back for a beat. He pulled away before she could grow stiff. "We have at least a little bit of time before we have to leave for the flight. Have you told Allison yet that you're going?"

Tatiana opened her lips, but words didn't come for a breath. "I...hadn't thought about that. She should hear it from me?" That least had clearly been intended to be a statement, but it trended upward at the end despite her best efforts.

Not that Andrew was a shining example of what to do, in a relationship. "I'd think so." He stepped back so they had room to open the door, then did it for her, and gestured her out, gallantly. She left slowly, conflicted emotions showing mostly in the slightly haphazard placement of her feet.

And Andrew, he was left alone with Death, who invited himself up onto the bed, sprawling across the whole comforter. He surveyed Andrew with something very near to a smirk. "The wolfsbane may have worn off, but don't look at me like you expect me to go anywhere, Dare."

17

Silver's grandchild squirmed in her arms, so she turned her upside down until she shrieked with laughter, then swooped her down to ride on Dare's back. The little girl gathered handfuls of his steely fur at his shoulders, making it stick up not unlike her straight-up puff of hair, black like Felicia's. "Woof!" she caroled. Dare refused to take off like a knight's mighty steed even when she kicked him in the ribs. Silver winced and gathered the girl back up again, holding her close where the child-scent of her filled each breath.

"Are you done yet?" Death asked, bringing his own shadows to the sun-soaked room that Silver hadn't realized until that moment had none of its own. But that was because it was a sweet dream.

Which she'd probably known all along, but acknowledging it now made the sun rather drain away. She set the girl down on her feet for Dare to usher off with a few guiding nudges with his muzzle, and turned up her hands. Over her bad one, she found she was wearing a long glove, crimson satin to above her elbow. Both hands worked, as they had in her last such dream, but at least she was otherwise herself in this one. "Is it important I go back immediately? Was there—?" She frowned. Had something important been happening?

"Wake up and see." With a flick of his tail, Death disappeared.

When she opened her eyes, her bad arm *hurt*. She tried to move it to a more comfortable position—and it did move. The pain flared up, settled back down when she stilled again, seeming more bearable, perhaps in comparison. She'd moved her arm with more than a flopping motion from her working shoulder muscles. This was...another dream?

She was lying on her back on the hard surface of a table, buffered only by a blanket beneath most of her body, though she did have a pillow. She wasn't wearing her shirt, but still had on her bra and other clothes. Footsteps intruded at an angle behind her head before she had time to chase and bring down the memory of how she'd arrived here hovering like a storm cloud at the edge of her mind.

"I'm so glad you're awake!" The Russian alpha, still effusive in his charm. He supported her in sitting up, but the aid seemed only a step in what he really wanted, which was to lift her bad arm by the wrist, examining it as he had when they first met.

The pain slashed over from her shoulder and down from her elbow and Silver had to breathe against it for a few moments before she yanked her hand away from him.

She could not see Death, but she could hear him growl. She couldn't remember when she had ever before heard such a sound from him. It was a vibration almost deeper than sound itself, fit to shake the foundations of the world.

Oblivious, the alpha laughed with pleasure, for all that she'd just defied him. "I knew it would work."

What would work? she almost asked, but she realized she knew the answer already. The memory arrived all at once, pieces linked haphazardly together, rather than in their proper marching order. The cake—worth the risk—a shining knife—how *dare* he, without her consent? This was beyond what she was prepared to stand, no matter the importance of the political goal. "You are going to send Me *home*, where they show better respect for Me," she told him with every ounce of imperiousness she could find. "You know nothing of how to worship the Lady."

That provoked the alpha into a laugh large enough he had to tip his head back to let the first bark free. "Oh, child." He tweaked the side of a thumb along her cheek. "You are no Lady reborn. The Lady has undoubtedly *touched* you, yes, but She never lets Her hand linger. You are left with a few tricks, which, while impressive and useful for swaying the gullible, do not mean you know anything of Her will."

He patted her bad hand where she'd tucked it along her belly. "And now you will be more useful, once you have recovered sufficiently. Irina!" He bellowed it, as if Were ears could not hear him perfectly well across even the length of a house, then returned to his former volume. "She will take good care of you."

And he strode out before Silver could find a reply.

Silver made it to her feet and achieved something of a balance fit for movement by throwing herself forward with all of her anger. "I will kill him! Kill him and have Death cast his voice to the void, to scream there unheard until the end of time."

Irina, entering, arrested her progress toward that goal with nothing more than an arm across her chest. "When you've rested."

Alexei followed her once more as well, a solid barrier across the doorway, but Silver was not yet ready to give up. "Do you doubt it? Death would do it, if I asked him." She searched for him, found him first by touch as he brushed against her hip, darkness to hold her up.

"If I made any such promise, it would be a remarkably easy one, because I know you never would." His voice had lost its world-shaking quality, for it was the one that belonged to the monster she and Dare had killed together, the Were who had poured silver into her veins. Another message, in parallel with that in his actual words.

"Wouldn't deny the Lady his voice," Silver muttered. "I'd still kill him."

Death laughed. "Exactly."

"Again, perhaps the killing can wait for another day." Irina eased her hold to one more supportive on Silver's other side, urged them both back into the room. Silver resisted, debating a greater effort until the woman's next, very quiet, words: "Your mate and my daughter will arrive soon."

Silver had told Dare to stay behind, but in truth, she couldn't deny that now the thought of his arrival was something to cling to while drowning. Thank the Lady. She sagged against Irina.

Irina accepted her weight easily. "You still see Death, then?"

And that was a question with heavy meaning, though Silver could not see why. "Of course...?" She dropped her bad hand to sink into the thick nap of Death's fur.

Her bad hand. She'd been so angry at the violation, she hadn't truly traced the consequences of it, good as well as the bad.

She brought her bad hand up, stepping delicately through the range of movement that brought the worst pain, and ending with her fingers curled, uncurled, clasped back tight this time.

When the pain was gone, she'd be able to *use* it. With hesitation, perhaps. She suspected it would be weaker, but even to be able to hold both of Dare's hands...

"They may have removed the scars on my muscles, but my wild self is still dead. My mind is as it always will be." Silver looked down at Death as she said it. And she would not change that, be other than herself, in her mind.

"So he was counting on, I suppose. If you are burned by the goblet at the next dinner, he will be decidedly petulant." Irina escorted Silver back to the table where she had awakened. Seen now, the blanket was rather creased and unevenly distributed, perhaps shoved under her from the side for greater comfort once the bloody work was done. The absence of her shirt was clearly explained by the need to clean up said blood.

Alexei spoke, and Irina provided his words: "May I?" Silver dropped her chin in assent, and he lifted her easily back to the table, to sit with her feet over the edge. Irina examined her bad arm with great gentleness, each step slow to give her time to pull away. Silver wanted to know more of its state herself, however, so she sat quietly, and frowned down when Irina had unwound the bandages.

Two thin red lines remained, remarkable only in were-wolf terms. They were considerably less than when Dare had first drained the worst of the silver from her veins by cutting shallowly. And the scars from that operation were gone, leaving only unblemished skin behind, something so strange as to seem almost an illusion of poor lighting or makeup.

"I think the clean werewolf blood has improved your healing. This is as different as night and day from even a few hours ago." Irina released a breath that shuddered a little on the way out in—relief? She turned away to gather a fresh bandage, but Silver frowned after her.

"Clean blood? What does that mean?" When Irina didn't answer, Silver drew her arm away from further ministrations.

After another beat of silence, Irina gave in. "Your mate will be telling you the story soon enough." She gestured, and Silver allowed her to bandage as she explained. "You bleed like a human—which you know, of course, but we did not—and you had almost no blood left before we realized. Your voice was nearly Death's."

Shocked, Silver looked to him. He sat tall, regarding her in turn with his eyes that held something of the void, but something also of the softer space in the night sky between stars. "When I take your voice, it will not be due to mortal *stupidity*. This I promise."

Silver bowed her head, acknowledging such a promise, and Irina continued. "I called my daughter and your human explained how humans lend blood to each other, and how to determine who has the matching type of it."

"I wouldn't say 'lending' is quite the word. They don't get to have it back." Death huffed his laugh, and broke the solemnity he'd used for the promise further by prowling off around the edges of a room as he liked to do in any new place.

Irina smoothed the bandage a last time then gestured, and Alexei retrieved a new shirt of approximately Silver's size, of rather plain cut and color. Irina assisted her in pulling it on. It hurt, but she could put both of her own wrists into the sleeves. She wondered how long it would be until that ceased to be one of the most amazing things she'd ever experienced. "Whose clean blood do I have, then?" Strange, to think of a piece of someone else being inside her, keeping her alive.

Irina stood back, indulged in a laugh hobbled by awkwardness. "I wish it could have been me. I didn't have the type, nor did Alexei. Konstantin didn't test himself. The first we found was—" Her lips twisted. "Mikhail." After the admission, she hurried onward, expecting Silver to grow angry again, presumably. "Konstantin ordered him into it, told the priestesses to take as much as you needed. That was a lot, so he needs considerable rest himself at the moment. He won't be bothering anyone for several days."

Silver scrubbed one palm against the other, for a few moments disliking the thought of his blood beneath her skin—but then she found the way to realign her thoughts. "He shed considerable blood from those in my pack. It's only fair he pay it back. And he hasn't even done that yet, since he took a life, and he still retains his." She laughed, liking that thought very much, and Irina relaxed.

Silver's laughter did not last long, however. It ran down, and so too did the strength anger had given her to push back the weakness brought on by having her blood changed out with another's. "It should not have been necessary. If I had been more careful—why not the cake, instead of the wine? And I, naive fool I am, ate it all. But if I was not so naive, I never would have come alone and expected to accomplish anything but my own ruin."

"No." Irina rocked a step forward, took Silver's hands. "He began this when he attacked you and your mate. What could you do, nothing? All of us who—" Her gaze slid sideways to Alexei, though Irina seemed reassured at whatever she found there. "Oppose Konstantin, we thought it would be pack war with Roanoke for certain, and it is only through the Lady's unearned grace and your native intelligence it is not yet. Until he suddenly moved against you, we saw him as *our* problem. Which is why he wanted a reason to turn his Teeth's attention outward, I suppose."

Silver clasped Irina's hands tightly in return. Both hands. So what she'd been looking for had been closer than she'd thought. "That is why I came. To lend my voice, with as much of the Lady's light as may inadvertently attach to it in others' minds, to such opposition." She realized her formality only belatedly when she caught a flicker of confusion on Alexei's face. "How can I help?"

Irina tipped her head, inviting Alexei closer to their conference, already low voiced but becoming even more so. "You already have. Konstantin plays games with implying you are the Lady reborn, but no one can deny you are Lady-touched." She freed a hand to brush a lock of Silver's white hair back behind her shoulder. "That *means* something to the priesthood. They promised you safety, and his orders almost had them kill you. Those who are true in their devotion to the Lady, rather than to Konstantin, are reeling. They will not follow his orders easily, if at all, if this comes to an outright conflict."

Irina's gaze drifted out of focus, tight on her internal thoughts. "His betas are all loyal, of course, because they were chosen to be, but they are at the other settlements, almost completely unsupported now he's pulled all the Teeth back here around himself. And he can't bring the betas here, because that'll leave no one out there following his orders. So the betas won't be much of a force."

"But Teeth are big problem," Alexei said on a rather sardonic note, accented but perfectly understandable.

"You said—" Silver had to trace her memories back, one step at a time. Many things Irina had said had been overshadowed by the thought of Dare arriving. "Tatiana is coming here too. She made her own decision, stepped away from her alpha, removed her Mark—could she convince others?

"Re—removed?" Alexei stuttered the word, and Silver thought at first he hadn't understood. Irina too, it seemed, for she offered a word in Old Were. He gestured the translation away, however, shock taking over his scent. "Her Mark?" He lifted a hand, tapped at the back of his own neck.

"Yes? The silver burn." She didn't think he was reacting to the inexactness of her phrasing, but she corrected it anyway. "Dare removed it at her request."

Irina's lips thinned with otherwise invisible upset of her own, but she placed a hand on Alexei's elbow. "We will speak with her, when she arrives. If Konstantin doesn't allow it, I will *make* him."

Silver flexed her fingers, feeling out the pain beneath the bandage, then forced herself to stop. That would not make it heal faster. "Perhaps I should be too weak, for further dinners, until that arrival." She looked around herself, suddenly feeling caged by the room and its table, though any whiff of blood had been sopped up and carried away on soaked cloths and her soiled shirt. But neither did she want to return to the bedroom he'd assigned her. "Is there somewhere I could go, that would be—" Safe?

Was there anywhere safe, short of returning to her home? And was even home safe, if nothing was done about the Russian alpha?

"If you agree, you can stay here with the priestesses." Irina nodded over her shoulder at the door she'd entered from. "The ceremonies are all outside, or in the hall, but this house is their living space. Even the alpha cannot enter without permission."

Silver gazed that direction as well, lip lifting in a silent snarl. "So he had it to be here when I woke." She touched delicate fingers to the bandage. "And they did this to me in the first place."

Irina reached to touch as well, did not complete the motion. "You didn't see Grace Zoya's face as you bled out under her hands." That was what had been worth the risk of sending her into wolfsbane dreams, Silver supposed, keeping the patient from worsening her own situation by absorbing others' fear.

Irina's tone held something of quivering panic of her own, remembered. She cleared it away as she cleared her throat. "They won't turn against him completely, not yet, but they will do everything to keep you safe. They won't fail a Lady-touched a second time. Not when you are so clearly doing the Lady's work."

Silver shook her head before she remembered she was supposed to agree to such foolish statements now. She was doing her best, but she didn't claim the Lady would agree. Alexei smoothed over any awkwardness by saying something in Old Were.

"Yes. Of course. Enough politicking, we should get you to a real bed." Irina led the way out. Rather than immediately follow, Alexei extended his arms to Silver, the gallant invitation clear. She took a beat to properly consider, then lowered her chin in a nod of assent. Alexei gathered her up, secure with his arms under her shoulder blades and knees.

They crossed into a central living space, not so different than the one in the cabin the alpha had first sent her to, though this one was perfectly round. Doors led off like rays, and seeing the pattern of the whole, Silver realized the room with the table had been subtly curved, though the sheer size of the building had disguised that fact.

"As well as something to eat," Irina said, selecting a closed door and opening it for them.

Just the thought of it seemed to hollow Silver out, leaving her shaky. Lucky she wasn't standing at the moment. "No!" she said, both to Irina and to her own stomach. She couldn't afford to eat anything in this place.

And framed in such a manner, it sounded absurd. How long would she be here? She couldn't avoid food—or drink—for days or more. But her hunger still growled and snapped and wrestled with her instinctive fear.

Irina stepped aside with the door to invite Alexei inside the small bedroom revealed beyond. She offered Silver a thin lifting of one side of her mouth by way of a smile. Her irony seemed directed outward, however, not at Silver. "I'll be your taster, don't worry." She pressed her thumb to her forehead in the formality of a deeper promise than that: safety, once more, in a different dimension.

Silver supposed she trusted Irina, mother of a not-quite-hostage, friend born of a common enemy, enough for that, especially given all the other ways in which she'd trusted her so far.

"Not that you have much choice," was Death's contribution, as Alexei lowered her gently to the bed. Silver also supposed he was right.

18

When they'd landed at the final airport, logistics kept Andrew going for perhaps half a day: a taxi to an empty pack house in town with a variety of vehicles stored for just this purpose. A collapse of a few hours, sleep clawing him and Tatiana both down after so long caged with the stink and stress of crowded humans. They set off the moment she judged herself safe to drive. The Russian pack's contact Tatiana dug up made purchasing the gun remarkably easy, but given Russia himself, on reflection Andrew found himself not actually surprised. They wouldn't normally need weapons, but he was certain crime connections made arranging their affairs to their taste, not the government's, much easier.

And now, more hours, albeit ones less constrained, with only one other Were in the vehicle and all the windows down to let the forest waft in. Well, one Were and Death, who had claimed the whole backseat, a looming presence taken to the edge of a threat because it was out of Andrew's direct vision. If Andrew did glance back, Death merely looked mockingly patient, as he had for the whole trip.

When worry about Silver began once more to get so sharp edged he couldn't breathe, Andrew pulled out the bottle of wolfsbane. He was supposed to be saving it, supposed to be stronger than this—or weaker, perhaps. The remembered fear and helplessness of the wolfsbane vision Russia had tricked him and Silver into, that was plenty strong, if he only surrendered to it and let that stay his hand.

But his worry was greater than that by far, and besides, it wasn't as if he were choosing another vision. He was choosing confidence, and equilibrium, both of which he sorely needed even now on the journey, before they arrived.

Andrew dropped another dose on his tongue.

He drew the handgun out of the case at his feet, checked it was unloaded, and then practiced ejecting the magazine and slamming it back in. If it came to this, shock at him using a gun wouldn't hold long enough for him to take much time reloading. And if Russia liked to hide behind his pack members as much as Andrew suspected he did, he'd definitely need to reload.

It had a certain rhythm, he found, as he did it over and over, smoothing the movements beyond the confident clarity the wolfsbane gave him into something almost instinctive.

Tatiana growled, but didn't loosen her focus on the road ahead of them. As if she'd actually forget the way home. "Stop!"

"Oh, sorry, is this annoying?" Andrew ejected the magazine a last time, left her hanging, waiting for the uncompleted slam.

Tatiana drew breath for a heated reply, let it trickle out instead. "Wolfsbane shouldn't be making you into such a fucking cat."

"Death's a fucking cat," Andrew said. "Probably because it's fun."

"Probably because most Were are too busy biting their own tails to listen to me otherwise," Death corrected.

Which was true enough. Andrew set the gun in his lap, and tapped a fingertip in the same rhythm on the car's windowsill. He wasn't looking at Tatiana, to see her worried look, but he found the warp of it in her scent anyway. "Can't you wait until we're almost there to be taking it? I told you'd I'd warn you when we were half an hour away. Why waste it now?"

"Why not?" Andrew took Death's point, however. Better to be a shit to a purpose. "But you're right, I should stop fidgeting. Let's talk instead. How did you leave things with Allison?"

This time, Tatiana's exhalation was less a calming breath and more a groan of pure frustration. "She was very...controlled. Which isn't like her. She claimed she understands why she couldn't come with us. I—I don't know. I couldn't tell if she was angry with me or not."

"She was hurt badly by your former packmate. That sometimes changes one's outlook," Death remarked, and Andrew relayed it. Better Tatiana was prodded by the real thing, not Andrew's pale facsimile of it. But then again, he was Death, and a fucking cat: "Introduce her to a really cute woman, then you'll know for sure."

Andrew had to laugh, and didn't repeat it, though Tatiana frowned at not sharing in the antecedent. "Let's not talk," she snapped.

"Fine by me." Andrew picked up the gun, seated the magazine, and waited for her wince in anticipation of him picking up his rhythm again, before stowing the gun away.

"Are you planning to walk in with that damn thing your hands?"

"Mm. Good point. Pull over and I'll put it away." Andrew laughed when Tatiana moved them onto the shoulder before he finished speaking. It was a rural road, no one passing them anyway. He'd bet she breathed a sigh of relief the moment he'd shut his door, so the sound would be muffled.

After he rearranged his suitcase to put the gun's case at the center, another hour ticked over in silence. He could chart their distance from the settlement where the alpha lived by Tatiana's tension. Her back was too straight to touch the seat by the time the curve of the road brought them to the cluster of houses, trees held back to allow growth of the rolling grass surrounding them.

She pulled off at the end of a rough line of other vehicles on a swath of ground more dirt and gravel than grass, with a well-worn footpath into the center of all the cabins. Though some of the buildings probably deserved a grander name than that, as despite their rough wood siding, they sprawled up to multiple stories or over enough area to contain a whole Roanoke sub-pack.

Tatiana popped the trunk and left the keys in the ignition, then climbed out to lean on the car roof and open door to survey it all. After a final dose, Andrew left the car and pulled out his suitcase, then stopped to watch everyone accumulate. Or to watch the fighters accumulate, at least. Everyone young or with the look of noncombatants whisked very abruptly out of sight as his and Tatiana's scent diffused to the settlement.

"Happy to be home?" Andrew asked. They were already on display, so he left her suitcase for her to retrieve when normally he would have grabbed it at the same time as his own.

"Not particularly." Tatiana finally forced herself to shut the door, pull out her suitcase, and slam the trunk. A little too hard, but her expression was otherwise collected. She joined him, taking in the Were, in both wolf and human, collecting and drifting in their direction with a nonchalance that fooled neither side. "Lady above." She breathed the words under her breath. "Did Father—the alpha call in *every* Tooth in the Jaw?"

That was interesting indeed. "Would he have time to do it if he found out we were coming?"

"Someone would have met us at the airport, if that was true. I suppose he could have given the order when he found out Silver was coming—but why? He wouldn't think her a threat, especially not a physical one."

"Are we a physical threat, then?" Andrew grinned, showing his teeth to their greeting committee, and then started for them, striding in as if he had every right to walk right up to the alpha himself.

Tatiana jogged a few steps to come even with him, scent souring for a just a moment with real fear. "Don't taunt them, please. With everyone here, we'd be raw meat, bled out, before we could blink."

Andrew counted idly, stopped when he got up to twenty. Really, that was beyond overkill to ludicrous. "I'm sure they'd make your end quick," Death said, pacing along at Andrew's other side. "Not her, though. I rather suspect they're not best pleased with her at the moment."

Another excellent point. Andrew leaned his head into Tatiana's, to speak too low to carry. "If you want me to have coerced you into the change in allegiance, you'll want to drop back to walk at a lower-ranked distance behind me."

"Here, it would be in front," Tatiana said. Her chin came up, and she stayed even with him. At least he'd given her the choice, though he suspected she wouldn't like the consequences of it.

"Now you're getting the hang of it," Death replied to that thought. "No one wants to do anything for their own good. No one. Get used to it now."

They were about to crash into the first wave of the Teeth, so Andrew stopped abruptly, ready to catch the gaze of any who dared to meet his eyes and measure dominance with them. "Death has arrived to escort his Lady home, away from your pitiful semblance of hospitality. I advise you to get out of my way," he said, voice lofted high to reach half the settlement.

Without the wolfsbane's confidence, he might have run fingers through his hair, worrying the black dye might have taken unevenly in some spot he'd not yet noticed, or clasped a hand against his back, feeling the smoothness beneath fabric now the lumpy mass of scar tissue had been removed. But from his last examination in the mirror, he remembered in sharp detail the look of black hair lending his skin a sickly cast. He remembered the pain of the cuts as Tatiana excised the scars. He was ready.

The closest Teeth rocked their weight back, at least, in surprise at his words. Those in human were all dressed normally enough, casual jeans still fit for hard outdoor labor, but their jackets didn't fall flat to their sides, suggesting sheathed moon knives on a harness as Mikhail had worn.

"Father will want to see us," Tatiana said. Andrew started walking again, and the Teeth did give way, forming to an aisle directed at the two-story hall.

On his side, Teeth watched him, carefully, but maintained the distance they'd chosen. Those on Tatiana's leaned in. He couldn't understand the words they said, but he certainly understood their *meaning*, carried in tone and sneers and snarls right into her face. Traitor. Lapdog.

Tatiana ignored them with a face like stone, and then they were entering the hall. Andrew did not even attempt to suppress his bark of incredulous laughter. The alpha was sitting on a Lady-damned *throne*. On a dais, like something out of the human middle ages with a provincial king who held court in his dining hall. The long tables, to be used for dinner, were even set away against the walls.

Here were the other observers, Were children and adults crowding around the edges of the room to watch the scene. No way to bring himself even with the alpha on his dais, so Andrew didn't try: he abandoned his luggage at the door and strode to the center of the room to position himself to play to the audience instead.

"Death has arrived to escort his Lady home, away from your pitiful semblance of hospitality!" Andrew reduced the range of his repeated words not at all for being inside. The alpha watched him with an opaque expression. Even without the white in his blond hair, he would have looked deeply old, though it took Andrew a moment to figure out why. The oldest Were he'd come to know well was Boston. Boston was a keen judge of character—to a frustrating degree, when you were trying to keep a few secrets of your own—and his whole manner proclaimed him as such. Russia, clearly older than Boston, perhaps even nearing two centuries, seemed as if he gazed out at the world that he *thought* he knew inside and out, but instead was an illusion built from assumptions that had worn out a century ago.

Russia had two Were with him on the dais. The first woman stood to his side with her hand resting on the back of the throne with forced casualness. A mate's place, which was odd, as Tatiana had said her alpha had no mate, and he would have guessed this woman had too much age and self-confidence to allow herself to be relegated to a mere chase of the moment. Whatever the meaning of her placement, she clearly liked it not at all; Andrew could read that in the tightness stretched across her knuckles.

Or perhaps it was particularly Russia's attention to the younger woman on his other side the older one disliked. That younger one, Russia was using to play a game of dominance by refusing to acknowledge Andrew's interruption of an unimportant conversation. The young woman, with one long, black braid down to her calves, was refilling his glass from the pitcher in her hands. Russia touched her wrist with a smile and said something into her, too low to catch even had it been in English. Andrew could guess well enough the content: *Isn't it adorable how impressive he thinks he is?* The young woman laughed, enjoying being drawn so intimately into the alpha's joke.

A deep breath, then Tatiana knelt at Andrew's feet and translated his words. He hadn't expected her to reverse her decision so quickly, but he was more than happy to back her in the role. He rested a hand on the back of her neck, a gesture outwardly controlling but comforting when built instead on trust. Or so he hoped.

That got a reaction, delightful in its unexpectedness. Russia sat forward, passing off his glass to the young woman and waving her away. The next moment he sat back again with forced casualness, lips thin. "You have my gratitude for bringing my daughter home to me," Russia rumbled. He spoke in English, very lightly accented, and Tatiana rendered his words in Old Were as well, tone mechanical.

"Home to you?" Andrew indulged in another bark of laughter. "Hardly. You told me I could do what I wanted with her, and so I have. She's *useful.* If you want to keep playing with your toys, you shouldn't toss them away so petulantly."

Russia's expression settled into its earlier opaqueness. "Useful? You've come to trade her for your wife, then." He made that a statement, not a question, already drawing breath for his counteroffer.

Andrew gave him no time to actually speak it. "My wife is not yours to trade. She is alpha of a pack of a strength to rival your own, not to mention that she is beloved of the Lady."

Russia settled into his feigned relaxation until it looked almost real. He clearly considered himself to be on firmer ground. "If she is so, she made her choice to be here, and has no need of your rescue."

Andrew gestured that aside with a flick of his hand. "And she has the right to reevaluate that choice after you almost killed her." He slowed to give those last three words their proper weight, listened carefully through the translation to be sure Tatiana did the same. "So am I here to enforce that right, as a partner, not a rescuer."

He could see Russia's next move would be to dispute that he had harmed Silver, and Andrew had no wish to battle on the field of how much danger she had or had not been in. Instead, he leaned into a jab. Sore spot, or well armored, he didn't care. It was the pack's reaction he was interested in. "Of course, you wouldn't understand the difference between partnership and rescue, never having managed to keep a mate of your own."

Russia held out his hand, and the woman beside the throne placed hers into it, face blank. "I recall I neglected to introduce you to Irina."

"Whatever corner you may have backed Irina into, a true mate doesn't spend her time contemplating the sound your neck would make when snapped." There had to be something

beneath that blankness, and Andrew judged it not a particularly risky guess to think it might be anger given Russia's behavior.
She narrowed her eyes at him, but he did not see disagreement
there. "It might help if you did not pursue casual chases in front
of her."

Russia stood. Smoothly, not an angry jerk, but it was telling, that he wanted that additional height over Andrew. "My
mate is irrelevant as, unlike you, I have no need for help in
holding my pack."

Andrew laughed. Such lazy snaps of the teeth were all that
were needed for this conversation. "Apparently you have need
of my wife's help. Otherwise, if you did not like the diplomatic negotiations she came here to carry out, why have you not
released her to return home? But then perhaps, like a mate,
you've never had the Lady's favor yourself, and thus do not understand that it cannot be *captured*, like a prisoner. Like Death's
favor cannot be *earned*, with sheer numbers of voices torn away
at your orders."

He looked then to Death, pointedly. He could not have said
Death looked approving, precisely, because he had the manner
of someone anticipating the stumble and humiliation of both
sides with equally wicked delight. But he panted in a canine
grin, and even lowered himself to playing along. "He thinks
the voices of his enemies—numerous as they are—will hide the
waver in his own. But age will only increase that waver, and he
will be mine, 'ere long."

Andrew lifted his gaze back to Russia. "He tells me he has a
message for you." He repeated the words, and jagged and sud-
den as a crack in a ceramic vessel heated too far, anger flashed
over Russia's face. "We will speak in private," he snapped, and
twisted his weight in one smooth motion into his first step toward a door set behind the dais.

Andrew lingered, soaking in the shocked silence. No murmurs yet, sadly, though a child or two whispered in what sounded like deep confusion at the very edges of the room. Tatiana pushed smoothly to her feet, and he allowed her to lead the way back.

The room they entered was clearly a more intimate space, but no demonstrating less posturing than the great hall had. Andrew would not have called it truly a living area, though it held chairs and small tables, angled around a fireplace. Russia was holding a low-voiced conversation in Old Were with two Were in human, discernable as Teeth by their stances even before he saw the blades at their sides.

"You should not be alone—he is alone—keep at least one—" Tatiana's translation was even more jumbled than the original conversation appeared to be, with three voices interrupting each other. At hearing the discussion shared with the opposition, Russia cut himself off and terminated the argument with a sharp gesture.

As they slunk out, the Teeth passed Irina coming in. Tatiana whined under her breath. Andrew reached to steady her elbow, walking the balance of control and support once more.

"Irina, this is no concern of yours," Russia said darkly.

"I wish to speak to my daughter, Konstantin." Irina kept her chin high, but came to a stop just inside the door, well outside of Russia's immediate reach. She didn't look at him, but Andrew still got the sense the name was a gift, and filed it away accordingly. He didn't need to be disrespectful just yet, but now he had the option.

Tatiana, after her first inadvertent noise, seemed to have shut down completely. Andrew hadn't expected her to indulge in tearful embraces given the current audience, but turning into a statue didn't seem particularly healthy. Russia had a table of nibbles set with a chair a comfortable distance from the currently unlit fire. Andrew abandoned Tatiana to flop into the chair and help himself. The little savory pastries were delicious, if a bit small. That just meant he had to eat more of them.

"I don't see my wife here," he prodded Russia. He didn't look properly annoyed yet, so Andrew picked up the pastry tray, shoved his chair back with a screech against the lovingly polished floorboards, and propped his feet on the table. He balanced the tray across his lap and kept eating.

Andrew got a muscle to tighten in Russia's jaw, but the alpha soon smoothed it out. "Did you truly expect me to just show you to her?"

"Eventually." Andrew smirked at him. "Meanwhile, it seems we are at an impasse." He could be patient, however.

Death was very patient.

Father—no, Tatiana supposed for lack of anything better, she might as well think of him in the North American style, as Russia—glowered at Andrew for a few beats, and then turned to her. His face softened into an expression he perhaps thought was conciliatory, and he held out both hands as he stepped over to her.

That snapped her muscles out of their frozen state, at least. "Don't *touch* me!" she snarled at him. "I was *listening* to the call where you told the Roanokes they might as well kill me. You *knew* I was listening. You don't get to do this 'oh, you've brought my daughter home' thing now."

"Tatiana—" Russia held out his hands for a beat more before he let them fall with a great show of reluctance. "I am so sorry. Had I known what I know now, I would never have countenanced such an action." He gave her mother a dirty look.

What would her mother possibly have been able to tell him—no. A connection tried to form in Tatiana's mind, and she refused to let it. "If you'd known what?"

Russia stared Tatiana's mother down until she finally sighed. "You're a coward, Konstantin."

"She won't believe me," he countered, then stepped back, pointedly looking from one to the other.

Her mother came a few steps toward her, but laced her fingers tightly together rather than reaching out. "He *is* your father, Tatiana. Biologically, not in the shared pack fiction sense."

Which Tatiana had been simultaneously suspecting and fighting to hold back the thought of for several seconds now. Not that the head start helped her significantly when it came to taking in the information when it was stated baldly. He— her mother—she'd never known who her biological father was, though as a child, she'd absorbed that it was some kind of secret. She'd thought perhaps he'd been a human. But her alpha— Father—

Andrew gave a slow clap, another, dropping his feet to rise and prowl over to them. "Oh, the poetic justice of that. You sent your own daughter to her death! You know, I begin to smell the resemblance now." He took Tatiana's shoulders, oriented her at the same angle as Father, though she was grateful he didn't drag her any closer to the man. "I'm not sure about the face, though. Give me a look of naked hubris, would you, Tatiana? Ah! There it is. I can see it now." He stepped back, hand to chin as if he were an art critic comparing forgeries.

Father ignored him utterly, crossed the distance to Tatiana, and embraced her.

She could only stand frozen once more. She wanted to—
to rip out his throat, she wanted to scream, or maybe she just
wanted to tear out of his grip and go scrub off her skin.

Merciful Lady, how could there possibly be anything of
him in her?

"I think you've overwhelmed her," Irina said. Tatiana didn't
know how her mother did it, but not a trace of irony could be
heard in her voice. "I can show them to their rooms, and they'll
be able to dress for dinner. I am certain Roanoke Dare is eager
to see his wife there."

Andrew polished off the last pastry set out for Father, and
gave that exaggerated consideration. "Barely acceptable. Tatiana, come." His grip on her elbow was as preemptory as before,
but she was even more grateful for the act now. She needed him
to hold her up, more or less.

"I look forward to it as well," Father said, and gestured permission for them all to leave.

Tatiana's mother led the way, not back into the hall or out
the back door, but upstairs. Tatiana had been to Father's rooms
a few times before, receiving missions as a Tooth, but never to
the second floor. She supposed she'd never thought about the
purpose of the rooms; his chases certainly didn't stay there. She
wondered if Andrew-as-Death was correct, and Grace Anna
was meant to be his next.

The stairs opened onto one main hallway, and the first
room Tatiana's mother opened and gestured into in invitation
was bland enough, a shared sleeping space with two beds, two
chairs, a small television, and a dresser and not much else. For
off-shift Teeth bodyguards, she supposed. He hadn't felt the
need for those before she'd left for North America.

Tatiana's mother closed the door with exaggerated care, but that only trapped them into the silence. She had too much to say to her mother, and so she couldn't find a way to say any of it. Andrew lasted perhaps five seconds of watching them watch each other before he growled exasperation and took a seat on one of the beds, no less proud in his posture than Father had been on his chair in the hall. "So, what, our luggage gets confiscated? You all have to smell us if we don't get clean clothes."

He was awfully cool given his weapon was tucked away in that luggage, but Tatiana supposed it was better to be, rather than making it seem like the loss of their possessions was important.

"Someone will bring it up," her mother said. She walked to the window, leaned one hip against the dresser below it, between drawer pulls.

Tatiana was almost certain she was the one who was supposed to start. Easier to talk about someone else, rather than the two of them, or Father. "What was that with Grace Anna for?"

Her mother snorted. "Konstantin is under the impression that by demanding I act as mate while he carries on chases publicly, he's punishing me. For hiding you." She nodded to Andrew, acknowledging how the truth paralleled his taunt. "The fact that she's a young priestess—as I once was—is also designed to hurt me."

And there it was, what Tatiana didn't want to talk about yet. All right. Try again. Something—neutral this time. She'd noticed her mother's braided coronet on the way up here. "Feeling regret for your days in the priesthood?" she asked, touching her own hair behind her ear. That wasn't very neutral after all, though. She'd always supposed her mother gave up the priest-hood when she got pregnant, but now it sounded like that had happened when she started playing chase with the alpha, in-stead.

And how long had that been for? For Were, children very rarely happened after just one chase.

Her mother touched the braid herself, shook her head. "Re-minding everyone of those days. Aligning myself visibly with the priesthood currently." She shrugged.

"That might have been English, but I'm still going to de-mand a translation," Andrew said.

Tatiana hadn't forgotten about him, precisely, but his voice still made her start. "Priestesses don't cut their hair, and wear it in a long braid." She traced the path down from the crown of her head.

Andrew tipped his chin to her. "I've seen you wear a French braid plenty."

"It's—" She'd come across the terms in her reading in En-glish somewhere, she'd swear she had. Probably in some trashy romance novel. "On the outside, not inside. Dutch! Dutch braid." Her mother's brows rose, and the whole situation and explanation abruptly seemed so absurd Tatiana gave a laugh that was more like a hiccup and turned into a cough when she stifled it.

A knock at the door gave her time to compose herself. She didn't feel secure enough to open it herself, and Andrew clearly wasn't going to, but her mother was already moving for it any-way. She was expecting someone, perhaps.

It was someone with the luggage, but that someone was Alexei. Her all-but-brother, the one who'd brought her into the Teeth when she was a gangly teenager, angry at her life, but unable to see how to change it.

Along with her mother, the one it had almost killed her to betray when she stayed with the Roanokes rather than trying to escape home.

"I'm sorry..." she said in Old Were, but further words stuck in her throat. Alexei looked the same as ever: strong, solid, grounded. She waited for any of the epithets the others had been throwing at her outside, but he only silently rolled the suitcases to the side, then shrugged off something that had been draped over his shoulder.

A moon knife harness. He extended it to her, and the moment she got her hand around one of the handles, she knew they were *her* moon knives. Even after all this time since she'd used them, the familiar balance still made them feel like an extension of her arm. She slashed the air and felt so near tears she hurriedly sheathed the blade and shrugged on the harness.

"Thought you'd feel better with those," her mother murmured.

Tatiana did, little as she wanted to admit that these trappings of the Tooth she no longer was settled her. But her skills were still her own, whatever she wanted to turn them to. "Thank you." In the small room, it was becoming more and more clear that despite her composure, her mother was very tightly wound, which also should not have helped and yet did. "How...?"

Not a very clear question, but her mother took her meaning anyway. "This story has been nearly forty years waiting to be told, I suppose. You'd think I'd be more ready. All right." She seated herself on the empty bed, spoke to the join between ceiling and wall directly opposite her.

"I was young; he was charming. I don't think I can explain it better than that, so I won't try. He had a game—has it even now, except he's shortened the interval, so more people have noticed it—where he'd focus entirely on one favorite and then when he was bored, he'd start putting her off. Breaking meetings with lame excuses, disappearing out of the settlement. He started that with me right about the time I figured out I was pregnant. He could have smelled it himself, if he'd been around and paying attention."

Her mother caught her lip between her teeth. "I remember some...instinct. I think it was the Lady, nudging me. I kept it to myself, and started watching, figured out who the new chase was. I went to Dominika—he'd told her he'd broken it off with me first, of course, she had no idea it was a lie—and befriended her."

Tatiana hadn't meant to interrupt, but Dominika was the name of her mother's oldest friend in Tatiana's childhood, and Alexei's mother. She stared hard at Alexei. "You're can't be—no. Of course not. You're too old." He was five or six years older than her, which would mean he'd been a child when his mother first got involved with the alpha.

Alexei grinned. His humor was very quiet, easy to miss in crowded situations, but she treasured those smiles in her memories. "I'm not, thank the Lady," he said in Old Were.

Tatiana's mother narrowed her eyes at him, but teasingly. "You're no help." Another breath, and she managed to step back into the flow of the story. "Dominika and I did everything we could to push up his timeline and then gave him a magnificent piece of theater, when he finally arranged it so I walked in on them together. Which is why he overlaps the favorites, of course. In hopes of fireworks, the bigger the better.

"And that gave me my excuse to storm off. Grace Zoya helped me find a place to stay, just a few priestesses in seclusion—you won't remember it, Tatiana. It was only until you were old enough I could lie about your birthday when I moved to one of the bigger settlements."

It was stupid, but that of all things was just *too much*. "My birthday?" Tatiana's voice squeaked at the end.

"Thirteenth of September, not of December, I'm afraid."

"Mother!" As soon as she heard it coming out of her own mouth, Tatiana mocked her own tone in her head—like she was fifteen again. Why couldn't she be an adult about this? But these were parts of herself, parts her mother had kept from her. "I can understand why you had to lie to everyone else, but why did you have to lie to me?" She found herself standing over her mother, who wouldn't look up at her now.

"Because I had to lie to everyone. *Everyone*, puppy. I had to, if he wasn't going to find out."

"Why wouldn't you want to know he's your father? I mean, he's such a winner, after all," Andrew said. At least this time, Tatiana saw Andrew's voice make her mother start as well.

After delivering the line, Andrew frowned, lifted fingertips to his temple as if fighting a tension headache. He dug the wolfsbane bottle out of his pocket and delivered a full stopper's worth onto his tongue.

"You just had some of that!" Tatiana had to admit to herself she welcomed the distraction, but that didn't make it less concerning. The idea had been for her to control his doses so he didn't get too much. He was no help to Silver if he fell to dreaming and never woke up.

She stepped over and tried to swipe the bottle out of his hand. He lifted it lazily out of the way. Rather than tussle for it, in front of her mother and Alexei, she tried to glower him down. "Give me that."

"Do you," Andrew speared her with a look from under lifted brows, "think it's an easy task, to sit here talking about some asshole's chases decades ago, when my wife is probably a few buildings away? When I could be cutting a path to her this minute?"

Tatiana twisted her fingers tightly together. "All the Teeth are down there, waiting for you to do just that. We have to talk our way through this, if we can. You can't just—"

Andrew snapped his fingers closed around the bottle, shoved it back into his pocket. "Exactly. So do you *really* want to take the one thing keeping me calm away?" When Tatiana backed up, he nodded once. "That's what I thought."

Whatever her mother and Alexei thought of the argument, they were keeping it off their faces. Had they smelled the wolfsbane in the bottle? She couldn't, but she'd been around Andrew so much, her nose had probably started filtering that scent out.

"Before you go committing my daughter to any fights…" Tatiana's mother stood, finally took Tatiana's hand, diffidence in her whole body. "I doubt you want to admit to it, but I can't let you put yourself in unnecessary danger. Do you still have visions without wolfsbane?"

"Yes," Tatiana snapped. If she didn't admit to it herself, she was sure Andrew-as-Death would be more than happy to provide her mother with the answer. "But unless you have a suggestion about something I can do about it…"

Tatiana's mother squeezed her hand, then released it and stepped back. "Of course, or I wouldn't have brought it up. Grace Zoya asked if she could observe one if at all possible. She has a few ideas for ways to at least decrease the frequency and strength."

Oh. Andrew answered before Tatiana could. "She'll do it." He transferred his gaze to her, silent question on his face: did he have to force her into it? She shook her head. To not have to worry about collapsing in a vision during a battle against the Teeth here would be—Lady's mercy.

"Can you trigger one?" Tatiana's mother asked.

Tatiana nodded slowly even as she thought quickly. "They come under stress, but I can try. If I could spar..." She glanced at Alexei. He touched the handle of one of his sheathed moon knives in assent.

"Good. Two doors down should have enough room. I'll get Grace Zoya." And Tatiana's mother let herself out.

"Well, I can't not come and spectate for this." Andrew pushed himself up off the bed.

Two doors down was some kind of common area, no more furnished than the bedroom, just a few couches. Tatiana had braced herself for awkwardness, but somehow none manifested. That was all down to Alexei—he was so even-keeled, she couldn't help but relax herself. She and Alexei moved the two couches that Andrew's ass wasn't currently holding down closer to the walls, then Alexei waited patiently while she limbered up, some stretching, some drawing of her blades to make sure the sheathes were hanging correctly.

When Tatiana's mother led her in, Grace Zoya looked exactly as timeless as Tatiana remembered her being for Tatiana's whole life. In the general mixture of the pack, her features were farther to the Asian side than many, and her long, black braid brushed her calves. She didn't bother speaking to any of them, simply nodded to Tatiana in greeting, then seated herself at the opposite end of the couch from Andrew. She was no doubt taking in every detail about him in peripheral vision and scent, while he evaluated her frankly, a mocking uptick to the side of his mouth.

Tatiana drew her blades, rolled them back against her wrists, and held up her arms, forearms straight up and down, side by side. Alexei echoed the salute, then rolled his blades down and waited for her to make the first move. As ever. She felt herself almost smile as she obliged.

She was rusty, no doubt of it, and Alexei rather overmatched her even at her best. He had reach, and could heal more of the small, kissing cuts they each accumulated as the flurry of slashes and parries settled into its rhythm. Pain, or wind of a missed blow, or the scrape of metal against metal, one of the three. Pain at shoulder, elbow, temple—that bled more than the others, Tatiana made sure to flick her head to make sure it didn't obscure her vision. Alexei wouldn't fight dirty, as Mikhail had, but even so, it was on her mind.

But the point wasn't the sparring, it was the vision, and if they simply wore themselves down with this kind of polite exercise, she'd get nowhere. Tatiana dropped her guard, and again, waiting for the deeper slash to her belly and then hip, but Alexei didn't take the openings.

She backed up, panting, and lowered both her hands. Her sense of the environment—or the possible threats in it, at least—got her oriented on Grace Zoya the next second, though she'd turned almost a quarter circle in the course of the fight. "I don't know this is going to work," she said in Old Were.

"Fight's not over until your opponent lowers his weapons too," Alexei rumbled and then she was hitting the floor because he'd swept her feet and her instincts got her hands more or less under her, ready to shove her way back to her feet but he had a heavy knee in her gut, and then one of his knives was at her throat. Both knives now, one on either side of her neck against the arteries, one movement in concert and she'd be totally gone.

She stilled, utterly, acknowledging his win, but he didn't let her up. It was perhaps only the space of a breath, but that moment stretched long and long, and she searched his eyes and began to fear. If he did think she'd betrayed the Lady's Jaw, betrayed *him*, one nick and he could tell her mother it was such a sad accident—hadn't she seen it herself, while they were sparring?—and she'd have what she deserved.

She couldn't see what he was thinking, but oh, she could guess. Why shouldn't he hate her for what she'd done? After all—

19

One of her father's endless dinners. One in a vision this time, Tatiana realized, but she couldn't quite put her finger on what was different about this one. Perhaps the mundanity was the point, night after night blending together so she couldn't see individual faces among the crowd, golden- and black-haired, at the lower tables.

"—and if you were to choose him as a mate, I would be very pleased," Father was saying, into her ear in her pride of place at his side. "He's one of my most loyal betas." She pushed around her food. This beta was a blending of all the dinners before as well, with not even a name. There were many "most loyal betas."

"And the last one? I chose him on your advice as well." Tatiana tried to find a face, but the vision kept it from her, only giving her the grinding feeling of *not enough*.

"You didn't like him enough, apparently, to play chase enough for a child. The Lady will not grant you one merely for *wishing* hard enough." Father sipped his wine, voice going dry with everything unsaid. *His* wishing, of course. Not Tatiana's.

Perhaps she did want a child. Not sufficiently for chasing only with *not enough* every night and forever, though.

This—agreement wasn't like her, however. Something in Tatiana was telling her that. Since this was only a vision, she pushed, to see what would happen. "I have my choice, Father. Alexei. He is the one I want." He understood her, at least. And wasn't his mother as powerful in the pack as any of these other betas?

Father's lip lifted in an uncharacteristic snarl. In this vision, she pushed, and he shoved right back, it appeared. "Only because he'll have his chases with men and leave you to yours. A *cub*, Tatiana. Is that too much to ask?" He was suddenly on his feet, yanking her chair out from under her, tangling his feet with hers so she was dumped to her ass rather than catching herself, and her reactions were so *slow*, she should be more practiced at movement than that, but she couldn't have said why.

"My Teeth will change your mind," her father said, and stepped back. By the time she was on her feet, they'd surrounded her, blades out, and she could only cover her face with her arms as the whirlwind descended to destroy her. Slashing lines of pain, thousands layered one over the other until she couldn't heal any more and the trickling, warm drip of blood smeared her whole body. She could only crouch to present a smaller target until finally the cuts ceased.

"More Roanoke's pet rabbit than lapdog," someone sneered. A cork popped, and oh, she knew what that would be, though why she should know the internal punishments of the Teeth, she wasn't sure. The stream the nearest Tooth poured from the bottle in her hands was no different than water if you couldn't smell it over all the blood, but then the vinegar cascaded onto her arms and back, and she *screamed* with it—

"I'm sorry." She sobbed it over and over, and Alexei was sitting on the floor and holding her and she didn't deserve any such thing from him, but she couldn't do anything except cling to him anyway. The cuts from the sparring were long healed, a little dried crust of blood flexing against her skin when she moved, that was all. "I betrayed all of you…"

"You did not," Alexei said into her hair. "*I'm* sorry. When I agreed to play my part to trigger the vision, I hadn't realized it would be so bad."

Grace Zoya knelt smoothly in Tatiana's range of vision, over Alexei's shoulder. Her braid made a neat curl on the floor beside her foot. "Puppy, may I ask you a few questions? Then I will leave you to letting the vision fade away."

Tatiana nodded with a jerk, freed a hand to scrub away the worst of her tears. By the Lady, she would make this have been worth it. "How long was the vision you had when last you took wolfsbane?" Grace Zoya asked.

"I—" That did help. Analytical examination of memories, and calculation. "A few minutes? Not long. My heart stopped, and I came out of the vision when the human started it for me again."

Tatiana's mother made a small keening noise. It stopped abruptly, and Tatiana looked up to see her mother with her fist pressed against her mouth, holding it in. Hadn't she told—? No, she must have something like "nearly died," which was true but didn't sound quite the same.

"And how long was it until the next one, without wolfsbane? How long did that last?" Grace Zoya guided her gently through the timeline, waving it aside whenever Tatiana couldn't exactly remember. Laid out, they did not seem so many. Grace Zoya did not ask about the content, and Tatiana didn't tell her. That was where the pain of them lay.

"Thank you." Grace Zoya bowed her head to underscore the thanks, then rose smoothly to her feet. Leaving Tatiana to let the vision pass, as she'd promised, Tatiana finally realized. Never mind that, she wanted to hear if there was hope for her. Using Alexei as a brace, she made it to her own feet, but there she realized there was something much more important to do before interrogating the priestess.

Without words, she embraced her mother, who held her in return, so tight. "You made the right choice," Tatiana said. As the vision had shown her. Tatiana couldn't bring herself to describe just why she was so certain that it had been the right choice to hide her from her father now, but her mother seemed to understand. "I'm sorry that you've been left worrying about me, dealing with the fallout of what I've done—"

"Which was a choice of mine, as well." Tatiana's mother didn't raise her voice, but she switched to English. "And don't you dare speak of betrayal again. You transferred your loyalty to someone who actually deserves it."

Andrew heard it, of course, as he was meant to, and spread his hands in an ironic little bow while still seated. Tatiana wished he wouldn't. It felt a little too close to Father's self-aggrandizement. "He's different when he's not high as a falcon," she murmured in Old Were for her mother only.

"So I presume. But you forget, I've met Roanoke Silver." Tatiana's mother eased back a step, cupping her hands to the sides of Tatiana's head. "You have become such an adult, I could not be more proud. I worried, when you wanted to be one of his Teeth, but it's clear enough now that Alexei was right, and I was wrong."

Tatiana heard a world of argument behind the words, which was another thing she'd never been aware of. When Alexei had suggested she start training, she'd taken the idea to her mother herself; her mother had frowned over it, and required of Tatiana a wait of a few weeks to make sure of her certainty, and then she'd granted permission. Relatively easy, from her perspective. Apparently it hadn't been.

"She was too restless not to be doing something. Skills are skills, now she can do what she really wants with them," Alexei said. Tatiana wasn't entirely sure she agreed—her death-grip on secrets, for one, that had been rather influenced by her time as a Tooth, and it hadn't served her well with Allison—but she couldn't imagine she would have been very healthy continuing along the aimless path she'd been on before joining the Jaw either.

With a shuddering breath, Tatiana leaned into her mother's arms again, holding the embrace in silence for several more breaths. When she pulled back, Grace Zoya was waiting patiently by. "Hit me," she invited, in English without realizing it.

Grace Zoya raised her brows at the idiom, though her lips did twitch in amusement when Tatiana provided her the paired literal translation in Old Were. "I'll begin with the caution: what I know of this, long term, is based on the experiences of priestesses who were much later in their lives. I do not think the visions without wolfsbane will ever leave you, I'm afraid. The threshold of emotion, to trigger one, you probably have a sense of that now. I don't know it will rise further, but given we had to trigger it rather artificially, that is not so bad."

Tatiana considered being annoyed, now she completed the connection with what Alexei had said before—play his part—but she was too wrung out to muster the emotion.

"If, however, you need to be sure you will not fall to vision at a key moment—there is something you can do. Balance the chances of a vision against the dangers of the suggestibility and decreased judgment, and take enough wolfsbane for a wisdom ceremony."

Andrew must have read something in Tatiana's reaction, because he pushed to his feet, though Grace Zoya's directions had been in Old Were. "Well?" he asked, and when she gave him the gist, he huffed another laugh. Of camaraderie, not mocking, this time. He tossed her the bottle, low and underhand. "Think we have enough, or should we beg for a refill?"

Grace Zoya plucked it away before Tatiana could reply. "Ah! I want to test that." Tatiana presumed she'd spotted the fact that Andrew was high fairly quickly. At least she hoped it was due to the priestess's specialized knowledge, not something anyone could figure out by smelling it on him.

Grace Zoya dropped a dot onto her skin before touching her tongue to that. "Not bad. You made it? From the wine?" At Tatiana's nod, she handed the bottle back. "You'd have made a good priestess. The bitter agent is a good idea, to discourage taking too much at once."

The bitter aftertaste from the essential oil stuck to the inside of the bottle had been entirely an accident, but Tatiana didn't bother disavowing it. Grace Zoya took her hands for a brief blessing, then showed herself out. Tatiana braced herself for further difficult conversation with her mother, but got only a quick embrace instead. "It's getting close to dinnertime, so I'll go help Roanoke Silver get ready," she said, and slipped out with Alexei following.

Andrew kicked back to lounge properly on the couch. "Remind me again why I'm waiting around for this dinner bullshit?"

Tatiana didn't feel any inclination to lounging herself, but the room didn't offer scope for much else. She shoved the wolfsbane in her pocket and gathered up, wiped clean, and sheathed her knives. "Because Silver will be there. And Fa—Russia as well, listening to every word you say to her, of course, but so too will the audience. Play to them, and maybe we'll make it out of here without violence."

"Mm." Having just made himself apparently comfortable, Andrew shoved to his feet. "I think I'm going to entertain myself in the meantime by attempting to stroll outside and seeing how many guards pop up and where. Want to come?"

Tatiana winced. "You're not going to fight them?"

"Harass." Andrew's grin widened at her deepening concern. "Only verbally. But very severely, I assure you. I won't even suggest you take any wolfsbane, so you know I'm not planning anything. Come on, listening to Death insult their intelligence, chasing skill, and honor will make you feel better."

Well. Maybe it might. And she didn't have anything better to do. "All right. Harassment." She freed her hair from its utilitarian tail and transferred it to a higher, messy bun instead. She had to fuss with her shirt as well to make the neckline fall as low as she wanted in the back. When she was finished, she saw Andrew's eyes widen with understanding, then crinkle around his smile of approval.

He came even with her and brushed a thumb along smooth skin. "There's a lot to work with there, if I have your permission to pull you deeper into the part you're playing."

Tatiana craned her neck to see his face. "I thought you already had it." Implicitly, at least. But perhaps he had the right of it. "Yes," she said. Explicit. It seemed she trusted him—even high—enough for that.

The stairs ran along a wall, with a view into a lesser-used sitting room and the back door beyond through the banister on the other side. Andrew took her elbow, grip overtight to direct her to the bannister side. The two Teeth below—Veronika in human, Sergei in wolf—had already looked up, probably at her and Andrew's footsteps in the hall, and rose now. They hadn't bothered with even the pretense of having other business that brought them to the alpha's house—Veronika had dragged a chair from a circle at the hearth and angled it to both observe the stairs and clutter the path to the back door, and Sergei had been sprawled over the rest of that path. Tatiana didn't know them very well, as when she'd left they'd been stationed at outlying settlements, but she thought they had at least some English. Not that they'd lower themselves to using it, she was sure.

"Oh, for the Lady's sake." Andrew lofted his voice down to them. "Why not go the whole way and start sharpening your knives meaningfully as you stare at me? I didn't know the Lady's Jaw needed to pull their intimidation techniques from the television school of meathead goons."

Tatiana translated, finding what little pleasure she could in her choice of which term most closely paralleled "goons," in the face of their hostile stares. Silently, the Teeth blocked their way, allowing not even enough space to step off the stairs at the bottom.

"No need to worry, I'm simply going for a walk." Andrew stopped half a dozen steps from the bottom, meaning the Teeth had to crane their necks up to him.

"No," Veronika said. "You are to stay upstairs."

Tatiana would have translated that too, but Andrew snorted. "I got the 'no' part myself. I'll have quite a store of Old Were obscenities and denials learned by the time this is over."

Veronika hooked a thumb into her moon knife harness on one side, unnecessarily, but Tatiana imagined it was intended to be readable to the uninitiated as the step before drawing the blade with her opposite hand. Her words, directed to Tatiana, were in a softer tone that didn't match the posturing, however. "If you leave his side, we will keep him from harming you."

Tatiana translated for Andrew again, and let that stand as her answer. Andrew laughed, and jerked her elbow to whirl her so her back was to her former packmates. The motion was so fast, so unexpected, she stumbled and had to catch herself with one foot on a lower step. "I'm sorry, were you deaf earlier, or simply stationed elsewhere without a single friend to report to you what I told your alpha? She is *mine*."

So this was where the permission came in. Tatiana hated the vulnerability of feeling their eyes on her back, but the satisfaction of hearing a gasp sustained her so she didn't wrench back before they'd had time to look their fill at her lack of Mark.

"Why?" Veronika said, low.

This time, Tatiana didn't translate, keeping the question and its answer in a space among the three Old Were speakers in the room, delineated by the shreds of their former comradeship, though she still faced the hallway above. "How is this different than how things were when Father sent me to North America? If I am to be used, I should choose the side whose purposes are served by my life, not my death." Which was a different lie in either case—now her father wanted her, and the Roanokes did not use their people. But neither of these things was she going to tell the Teeth, as much as she'd like to shake them by shattering the fiction that Father valued all his "children" equally.

Andrew guided her back around, changed his hold at her elbow to a parody of something gentlemanly, and patted her arm. "*I* don't break my toys." Neither Tooth was bristling yet, but Tatiana felt the anticipation in Andrew's stance. He was just getting started. "But seriously, is this what any of you trained for, standing around so you can loom for a little cheap intimidation?" Tatiana sank her attention into translating smoothly, waiting to judge reactions until Andrew had worked up to his full effect.

"This one is full of all sorts of interesting tricks. I think she'd be rather wasted on glowering." Andrew patted her arm a last time, then released her and went down one step, for more room to lounge after setting an elbow and hip against the wall. "You're trained to be *assassins*, are you not? But your alpha tells you to stand and glower, you stand and glower. Don't you feel the itch to be challenged to the edge of your abilities?" He smirked. "You don't have anything else, after all."

Veronika snorted, started to reply, but Andrew continued over top of her. "No, I've heard your voice enough already to know it will be a stunted, quiet thing I'll be taking to the Lady. What have you been using it for, besides saying 'yes, Alpha,' and 'no, Alpha'? You have no family in either direction, no acknowledged parents, no cubs, to live for or give life to. What aspects of living do you raise your voice to, besides killing?

"Tatiana tells me you try to fill time by playing chase amongst yourselves, of course. That means there will be cubs, if rarely." He tipped a hand to Veronika's abdomen. "What happens then? Do you leave the Jaw, settle down to domesticity among those you once policed and intimidated? Or is your baby *given away*, so you can continue in your usefulness?"

It was Sergei who reacted, in scent and in the baring of his teeth. Tatiana recognized his pain; her translation had been slow and uneven as she reeled from the same verbal blow. Sergei longed for a child, she suspected, and at Andrew's words had imagined having one, of his own, only to have it snatched away—

Her experience, on the other hand, was much less abstract: she'd asked to raise a Were child, after killing its human mother. Her last kill. Russia had refused, of course. Perhaps he'd been right, for the wrong reasons. Atonement was not a particularly good reason for motherhood.

She wondered if Andrew-as-Death had noticed she'd been caught in the crossfire of his taunting—or perhaps even intended it, to remind her of why she'd found a better place to invest her loyalty. But he had no way of knowing about the human woman's baby; she'd never mentioned that part.

She was sure, however, that having noted her reaction, he would be happy to claim such knowledge and intention after the fact.

"Our lives are the Lady's," Veronika sneered. "Our commitment to Her is absolute. Beyond family, beyond individual voices."

Andrew snapped his attention to the window opposite the foot of the stairs, as if hearing something outside. So convincing was he that he got an actual twitch out of both the Teeth, which made him laugh. The thin frown Veronika pasted over her simmering frustration enriched that laughter further. "Sorry, I thought I heard something. The Lady directing you to waste your lives shoring up a leader hollowed out by his own corruption, perhaps. But wait! Can it be, you have heard no such thing from Her, only took *his* word that's what She wants? You'd think if those were Her wishes, She might at least drop a word in the ears of her priestesses."

Veronika's sneer grew more pronounced. "We don't whine to the Lady each day for *proof* of Her will—" Footsteps coming up to the back door cut her off, and Mikhail's entrance distracted Tatiana before she could begin her translation.

He looked…"haggard" was the only possible word for it, when she shied away from "three-quarters dead." More than the pale, sallow tone to his skin, he moved with obvious hesitation, weakness even. What had happened to him since he'd brought Silver home?

He took in her and Andrew, and the way their path was currently blocked, and sighed. He swayed a little, standing still without the momentum of a destination, and Tatiana slipped by Sergei to steady him before she considered that the others might not let her by. But they did, and Mikhail only allowed her to take his weight for a breath before he pulled away, proud.

"I would speak to you, Tatiana," he said, oddly formal, then pulled her deeper into the sitting room, away from the others and also away from Andrew. The Teeth allowed that too, likely because it took her farther from the door. It was an insufficient distance to prevent them being overheard in normal circumstances, but Andrew started up again, perfectly happy to mock them even when they couldn't make any answer he could understand.

Mikhail drew her close, hands on both her elbows. She could feel in this touch he was too weak to hurt her at the moment, so she didn't pull away. When he swayed again, she took his arms instead. "Did Father do this to you?" He'd returned while the North American alphas still ruled, after all. That kind of failure was a lethal offense around here.

"No, I gave my blood to the Lady." For a breath, Mikhail looked as centered as she'd ever seen him, almost peaceful. Alexei was grounded; Mikhail was always on the move. That was how they were built, she would have said.

The blood Silver had needed. She must have needed a *lot*, to leave Mikhail so. The moment the thought formed, Tatiana knew she'd never tell Andrew that Mikhail had been the donor, to lead him to the same conclusion. "On Father's orders?" Two birds, one snap of the teeth. A failure punished and a current project sustained, at the same time.

And then Mikhail was in motion once more, metaphorically even if she still braced him as he stood. His expression tightened to a frown as he returned to what she guessed had brought him here. "The others are saying you were coerced. We both know that's not true. Give me a reason why I shouldn't tell them."

His voice was hard, but with a flicker of hope, Tatiana thought he might be speaking literally. All right. She'd try to convince him, try to make him understand. "Because you know the thousand ways, large and small, they'd punish a willful betrayer. I didn't—didn't realize how *angry* they'd all be. I know I'd never have time to try to explain that it was my loyalty to *Father* I broke, not my loyalty to anyone else here." Her voice was thinning out with the stress, and she dipped her head to make sure the change in tone didn't catch the others' attention. "They think those are one and the same, and they're *not*, Mikhail. At least set Father aside from the priesthood, from the Jaw, from the Lady, when you consider him, yes?"

Mikhail tipped his head away from her, but he didn't inter-rupt. Tatiana would take even that weak acceptance. "You—you wanted me to come home, didn't you? It wasn't simply Father's orders? What about now, knowing the choices I have made and won't change? I doubt the others would be sad to see me dead." More than the insults they'd snarled as she walked into the set-tlement, she'd smelled their emotions.

"Father wants you here," Mikhail said. "With his whole voice." It was not an answer, but Tatiana didn't renew her ques-tion. Perhaps she didn't want to know, and with Andrew-as-Death otherwise occupied, she had the luxury of deciding so.

She leaned her cheek against Mikhail's shoulder instead, drawing in a deep breath that hitched unexpectedly on the way in. Mikhail was most often a cat's bastard, like all the rest, but they'd shared so many years together, training, working, play-ing chase on occasion. She picked his pocket, in honor of the particular skill he'd taught her, and came up with what felt like a moon stone—not the human-named gem, but a small, smooth pebble, to roll between the fingers when thinking of the Lady.

She stepped back from him, brought it up between them. White, cloudy quartz, professionally smoothed far beyond what any stream might manage. "We all try to follow our own understanding of the Lady's wishes," she said.

She'd thought he might sneer at her, if he'd felt the lift, or snarl at her if his weakness had prevented him from doing so—she'd never have managed to get it at all if he'd been on his game—but instead he stared at the stone for a breath, another. Then he lifted it from her fingers, closed his hand around it, and left her, out the back door and away.

Tatiana returned to Andrew's side as silently. Maybe he'd understood. A little. She'd pretend he had.

20

When she heard the outer door of the priestesses' house open, Silver jerked to her feet and set her hand to the door of her little room. She shouldn't be in the common room, in case this was the alpha, but the moment Irina's scent reached her, she was out of her room in the next breath. "Is it not past time for dinner?" The priestesses had been pushing too much food on her for her to have noticed hunger—and she would have eaten enough food beforehand to not touch a morsel served under the alpha's auspices in any case—but the darkness outside was encroaching, even with summer's extended light.

Irina looked drawn, and when she turned from the few words she'd been exchanging with Grace Zoya, it seemed to be an effort for her to find English again. When she did, however, her words were as precise as ever. "Konstantin said you were too weak to attend in front of everyone. There was no way to contradict him. Even if we'd been alone, it would have cast doubt on our claim of weakness for you before. I'm sorry, I've been trapped at the meal this whole time. I only just got away. Grace Zoya told you—?"

"Yes. My mate and your daughter. Safe and sound, so far." And then she'd pretended insufficient knowledge of the language to catch the ensuing cascade of Silver's questions, only reiterated that they were to meet at dinner. And then the time for dinner had slipped away.

Irina could not claim such ignorance of the language, however. "How is he? Did he seem confident? Does he seem to have some kind of plan? If he did, do you think Russia noticed?"

"Let her sit," Grace Zoya said, with a hint of sternness. The common room had a great round table, large enough for perhaps a dozen priestesses at once. The three of them, in adjoining chairs, claimed only a wedge of it.

Irina made a wedge of her own on the tabletop, inscribed in negative space between the sides of her fingers and her spread thumbs. "He says he's Death-touched."

"He *what*?" Silver looked to Death, where he'd claimed a spot upon the hearth as if everything in the house had been built to honor him instead of the Lady. Why would he—when he could not even admit to *her* he saw Death—?

"It's a valid strategy." Death offered her nothing more than mild amusement for her to read in his eyes. "To meet Russia on the religious footing he himself forced."

"But Dare doesn't believe!" Silver grasped the man she knew and loved in one metaphorical hand and the idea of someone who would call himself Death-touched in the other. Try as she might, she could not force them anywhere near each other, never mind into occupying the same space.

Death laughed. "Poor man. You all but told him to play me! And now you object when he does?"

Had Silver really—she'd used it as a rhetorical illustration of her point, she remembered that now. But Dare would have known it was rhetorical as well. "But not believing is so...important to him." By the end, she realized her voice had gotten rather small. So important to him that of course he refused to admit to her he saw Death.

Death huffed an exasperated dismissal. "You're each as bad as the other. Why should one not overcome ridiculous mental blocks the same as the other, and for much the same reasons?"

And she was being deeply impolite, Silver realized, holding an extended conversation Grace Zoya and Irina could not participate in. She ducked her head in apology. "You spoke to him? Did he—have any message?" Or was that asking too much of Irina, ally as she was? Certainly, she was not a dedicated messenger, to spend all her time passing notes between them, across the settlement. But if Dare had happened to say something...

"He was around when I spoke to my daughter. You understand, at that time we all thought he'd be able to speak to you himself at dinner. After dinner, with Konstantin right there, he only had time to say that he left your cousin's wife in charge in truth, if not in name."

Susan, that meant. And better not to advertise the human had such power, even to Irina. And it was just the decision she would have helped him make, had she been there. John supported much better than he led. Silver's shoulders lowered as if someone had unwound one twist of tension from her back.

Somehow hearing, if not Dare's words, then very much his thought processes, brought it home to her that he was *here*. And she wasn't going to let him be kept from her for a second longer. "I'll go to him."

She rose, and gestured Death to her side, but Irina caught her wrist. "Not through the Teeth ringed around him. Please, Roanoke. Have patience."

"They are the *Lady's* Jaw, not the alpha's, are they not?" Silver knew she wasn't fooling either of the women in this room, but she drew herself up anyway, combed fingertips through her hair at her temples, emphasizing the color.

"Any displeasure from the Lady will most likely manifest at the end of their lives—that from their alpha will be immediate." Irina tugged at Silver, gentle but inexorable. "Weren't you saying to Death that your mate is attempting some political maneuver outside his usual comfort? If he's choosing that instead of a physical struggle, don't you want him to have the best chance of success in it?"

"I'm not going to wait forever," Silver growled, but she did sit.

"Now." Grace Zoya tapped the table in front of Irina. "Message is passed, your duty is done. A drink, perhaps?"

Some emotional structure collapsed in Irina's face, though she did not move, nor do anything so extreme as burst into tears. Her answer, though in Old Were, was undeniably affirmative.

Grace Zoya gathered a bottle and glasses, much as everyone had used at dinner. She didn't even wait for Silver's glance to turn suspicious. "Only wine."

When Irina received her glass, she tapped the stem with her opposite finger. "Ceremony glasses are rounded."

"And ceremony cakes?" Silver muttered, then immediately regretted it and was grateful when the women ignored her.

After filling all three glasses, Grace Zoya made a circle of her fingers over Irina's, fingertips to fingertips, thumb to thumb.

She spoke some blessing, some prayer, and as it continued, Silver let her vision slip more toward the realm not of her mate, the one of mist where Death walked. The Lady's light gathered into a semblance of Her round face in Grace Zoya's hands, and with each breath, Irina drew a little of it into herself. Its soothing effect was subtle, but clear.

Silver looked away, clenched her bad hand until the healing muscles wound up to screaming. It made it easier not to think about what she could never have.

But she'd taken it too far, the prayer had ended and tears were standing in her eyes. She saw exactly the moment when Grace Zoya smelled the salt. She braced herself for offense, but found only concern. "Why does the Lady's blessing make you sad?"

"With my wild self dead, I am barred from Her presence. You have some of the edge of her light, and it—hurts." More than that, she flinched now from the inevitable reassurances. The Lady loved her still! Silver had never doubted that, but should not that make separation from Her *harder*, not easier?

"I am sorry," Grace Zoya said solemnly. No more than that. Silver relaxed enough to sip her drink with the others. Or rather with Grace Zoya. Irina knocked hers back, then sank into herself once more, caught up in her own thoughts, or pain.

In time, when Grace Zoya gathered Irina to her shoulder, Silver rather thought she smelled salt as well. At length, Irina spoke as if the words were slipping free despite herself, just like the tears. "I only wanted that my daughter shouldn't hurt either. If I hadn't hidden her from her father, he would have been warping her all along. But if he'd known about her, he would never have sent her to die on that damn mission of his. If I hadn't told him, he'd have ordered her killed the moment she stepped back on his territory. But maybe he wouldn't have pushed the Roanokes so hard she had to come back."

Hidden her from her father—oh. *Oh*. Many things fell into alignment in Silver's mind all at once, an end to her confusion like she had been running to catch up with someone only to have them stop suddenly, so Silver slammed into them.

A hitched breath, and Irina's gaze grew more abstracted, going to the past. "She said she understands, but I'm not sure— she probably thinks I was like Grace Anna. Attracted to the power and the danger of it." She focused on Grace Zoya again. "She does know what game she's playing, doesn't she?"

Grace Zoya murmured an exasperated noise. "Grace Anna has been warned. If she wants to play dangerous games after that, so be it."

Irina relaxed fractionally. "So be it. It was different for me. While he has always been charming, in my day he was also kind. When you were the favorite, he *listened*, like you were the most important thing in the world. Or at least made it feel like he was listening. And he would fulfill the smallest request, as soon as you made it. That was what made the endgame so satisfying, I suppose. There was no pattern of neglect or dismissal, at least until he started to cancel meetings. That was a pattern, but all at the end. So it was so *bewildering*, when you found proof of the first lie, among his excuses." She ran down, attention gradually fading back to the here and now.

"I can give you privacy?" Silver would already have been leaving the table, but for the fact that Irina had spoken so she could understand.

Irina straightened, pressed at her upper lip, perhaps as a dam against further tears. "Your mate was...protective, of my daughter, that I could see. He played as if none of this was her choice, in public, and in private it was clear that was not so. If you two are to be her alphas, too far away for me to help her..." She accepted a refill of her glass from Grace Zoya, using the pause and mundane movements to pull herself together. "Please take care of her."

"Of course we will." Silver wasn't entirely certain if Tatiana would accept the ties to the Roanoke pack her mother perceived, but if Irina had the right of it, of course she and Dare would protect her as any other pack member. "But if you depose Russia, she could stay here, with you."

Irina jerked into a watery laugh. "Yes, we should speak about that instead, shouldn't we?"

"Perhaps we could—" For the subtleties, Grace Zoya leaned on Irina's knowledge, asking for and receiving a translation of a word or phrase without much disrupting the flow of her ideas. "Maneuver him into stepping down in favor of his new favorite daughter."

Irina jerked her head, emphatic in her disagreement. "He'd only control *through* her, and there she'd be, her life warped by him after all."

Silver watched the wine in her glass as she swirled it. This would take careful phrasing, with all of the stumbles of an unfamiliar language on the listeners' part, no less. "I don't think Tatiana is alpha material. That is not to say she is not high ranked, or cannot make the hard decisions necessary to lead. But she seems to feel the only one to be relied upon to take care of her, is herself. I don't think she can...offer her safety to others. For an alpha and their pack, it's an exchange of trust: you protect them, they protect you. If you can't offer that trust..." Silver shrugged. "But her mother knows her better than I."

Irina let her breath trickle out in what did not quite become a laugh. "I'm not sure I do. And you actually are an alpha on a similar scale. I trust your read." She straightened, looked to Grace Zoya. "What we truly need is for the priesthood to directly oppose him."

Grace Zoya's lips thinned. "That is not our job."

An old argument, well worn, Silver could tell that already. "Could you not reason with the Teeth, at least? You said they would not take their orders from the Lady, but what about appeals to their own decisions, their own choices? Russia does not particularly provide them with those, does he?"

Grace Zoya sank into thoughts that didn't show on her face, but Irina lit up almost immediately. "It worked for Alexei. That was mostly what I did, in speaking to him after Tatiana…had to stay with the Roanoke pack. The Teeth are trained to operate on their own, after all, when Konstantin isn't forcing them all into a small space to soothe his paranoia. They have to have minds of their own at least a little."

A few beats of silence more, then Grace Zoya tipped her chin down in agreement as well. "I will speak to the others about it, see if they agree." She rose, off about her own business in the house's common area and then into her own room.

So. That was a plan, but a slower one. Silver longed for more movement than that. "When will I see my mate, then?" she asked Irina.

"Dinner tomorrow is what Konstantin said." Irina's lip lifted toward a silent snarl, then she smoothed it back to at least neutrality. "It will undoubtedly be no more binding than his last promise."

"I will go early, then." Silver offered Irina a teeth-bared smile. "Escorted by the priestesses, of course, so that everyone sees me arrive."

This time, Irina did laugh properly. "Good." She pressed her thumb to her forehead, making a promise of the plan. "Let him try to wiggle out of that."

21

Andrew woke snarling, biting at whatever had wrapped him up in smothering layers. No matter how he writhed, he couldn't get free. He ripped at something with the full force of his jaws—

"Roanoke!" Tatiana's voice. "You shifted. In your sleep?"

It was a pillow he was biting, Andrew realized. His clothes he was tangled in. Rather than struggle free with four feet, he shifted back, the boost of the Lady being just off full making it the work of a few moments. "I was just dreaming." Or at least, he thought he had been. He'd only meant to nap lightly. He hadn't been able to sleep at all last night, cut off from Silver and surrounded by enemies on all sides. He'd paced the whole night. But today's enforced idleness had left him blurry, a state not helped by the wolfsbane, and a nap had seemed like a necessity.

After readjusting his clothes, he rubbed his opposite palm, trying to drive the remains of that blurriness away, and dived to the floor the moment his fingers found empty skin where his wedding ring should have been. The metal spat a point of light at him, where it had rolled under the bed. With that pulled on, he drew the wolfsbane out of his pocket and took his dose.

Tatiana stank of her usual mixture of disapproval and worry as she watched him drip the mixture onto his tongue. "You shouldn't be shifting in your sleep. It must be the wolfsbane starting to take hold."

She'd been using the time to create a crown of golden braids even more intricate than her mother's. Andrew rather liked the effect of it. He rose. "I told you, I was dreaming."

Tatiana's expression hardened. "When was the last time you shifted in your normal sleep? I certainly can't remember a time. But shifting in *wolfsbane* dreams, we know that happens." She didn't move out of his way, leaving them toe to toe.

He was taller, but Andrew didn't feel the need to loom over her to prove it. Death distracted him in any case, nosing into the bedding to tumble the poor, eviscerated pillow to the surface. "She's right, you know," he said. "It's not sustainable to keep taking it the way you are. You've been too damn much trouble for me to countenance you dying in your sleep."

Andrew knew it wasn't sustainable, of course. He'd known it for some time now. Mustn't admit that to Tatiana, however, lest she try to steal his supply from him. It was his risk to take, and she'd only whine about how he couldn't judge risks in his current state.

The wolfsbane was settling past his muscles into his bones by now, lending him not only confidence, but a certainty: they'd waited long enough, working with words.

Time for more than words.

"Hugh knows where to meet us?" Andrew sidestepped Tatiana and headed over to his suitcase, where he'd slung it on top of the dresser. After the excruciating evening spent alternately mouthing nothings and exchanging taunts at Konstantin's bait-and-switch dinner last night, he'd told Tatiana to contact Hugh with the nearest local port. They might not need the exit he'd offered, but then again they might.

"He does. What—?" Tatiana trailed behind him for a step, then rocked back when she saw he was taking out the gun case. "Roanoke—"

"No." Every particle of alpha authority Andrew harbored in his body and mind, he aimed squarely at Tatiana, and she fell instantly silent. "Strap on your pretty knives and take your own wolfsbane, or stand back and stay here, I don't care. I'm not going to give Russia a chance to cancel this dinner as well. We're going early."

He tossed the bottle at her face, knowing her instincts would force her to catch it. So it proved. She held it as if it would bite her as he drew out the gun, loaded it, and shoved extra magazines into his pockets. She swallowed, finally managed: "What does Death think of this idea?"

Andrew transferred the question with a silent lift of his brows. Death paced solemnly to stand beside the door, simultaneously too large for the room to contain and the size of a normal wolf, as if his blackness were in a very slow process of imploding. "You might kill yourself, or you might win the day. If you do nothing at all, it is certain neither of those things will happen."

"Sounds like approval to me." Andrew turned back and held the gun down and loose, ready, and waited for Tatiana's answer. A breath or two, he'd grant her that to conquer her hesitation.

She filled the dropper and closed her lips around it to draw the wolfsbane out. She closed her eyes, probably to let it settle into her bones too. "I never found answers, nor felt the Lady's

touch in wisdom ceremonies, particularly, but I find I can't object to feeling a little bit more powerful in our current situation."

She set the bottle aside on the corner of the dresser, then
started pulling on her harness, no jacket on top to disguise it.
Andrew didn't bother retrieving the wolfsbane—things would
be decided one way or the other by the time his current dose
ran out.

Two new Teeth were waiting for them at the bottom of the
stairs. As before one was in wolf, with a band of near black
along her back, and one in human, black haired as well. The latter was quick with his blades on spotting the gun, having them
up and ready by the time Andrew had come down a single step,
but that didn't help him.

Andrew shot for center of mass, rather than get fancy on
the downward angle with both human and wolf shapes to account for. One, two. The noise was nearly physical pain to Were
ears. Both Teeth reeled back, but Andrew waited to see them go
down, making sure they hadn't healed fast enough to come at
him as he approached.

The man in human collapsed first, less stable on two feet.
He clutched at his belly, blood making it as far as oozing between his fingers before the external wound closed over. But his
face was going deeply gray with suffering, and Andrew judged
he'd hit organs enough to create a delay sufficient for their purposes even if the bullet had already exited.

The woman in wolf more folded than collapsed, her bleeding hidden against the floor. Andrew stepped around them
both then, wasting no more time because others would be arriving to investigate the noise.

He slammed outside, to the fresh green smell of the surrounding hillsides and trees. No blood or gunpowder had

reached this far yet. "He said she was recovering with the priestesses. Where is that?" he asked of Tatiana. She'd pulled her blades, same as the Tooth bleeding inside now, and she pointed with a tip of one. A larger cabin, among smaller. Andrew strode for it.

Doors were opening in those smaller cabins now, faces peeking out at the noise. Most shut once more, smartly. Only one Were ran toward them, a priestess, in one of their white, embroidered dresses. Her braid barely reached her lower back. She came from the direction of the public door to the hall, calling out a question to Tatiana in Old Were.

"Wait." That for Andrew, then Tatiana snapped something back to the priestess. She pointed with her answer, and Andrew didn't wait for a translation. Back at the hall. Silver had been closer than he'd realized. Just the kind of irony Death most enjoyed.

He'd make this a hell of an entrance for a second time, then. Andrew ran for the hall's door, slammed it open with a kick so as not to lose any of his speed. The swell of voices held back by the wood ceased with a snap as those inside caught sight of him. Andrew took full advantage of it. "Civilians out!" Tatiana echoed him in Old Were, following as closely as if they'd rehearsed it.

Russia was back in his throne. Silver's chair, next to him, was merely a slightly ornate member of its species rather than a second throne. He didn't dare meet her eyes, or he'd lose track of all the intervening obstacles he had to clear to reach her. But she looked healthy, dressed in a different shirt than the one she'd left in, a soft cream color that only served to illustrate the pure whiteness of her hair, down loose over her shoulders.

The great tables were in people's hands this time, quickly dropped as noncombatants scuttled to the door behind the dais, hampering Teeth entering that way. A few braver souls skirted the edge of the room, and made it out the front door behind him. He made sure to give no indication he'd seen them, and the trickle in that direction soon became a flood.

"No," Russia said dismissively. "You do not get to choose where and when you come into my presence." A gesture, and all the Teeth in the room solidified around him, thirty or more, a handful in wolf but most in human. Ready for dinner, he supposed.

Having formed their tight arc, the Teeth then moved forward, aiming to sweep him and Tatiana before them and out the door, Andrew supposed.

More fool they.

He had an arc of his own, after all, three of them: himself, Tatiana, and Death, hulking pure night at his hip. "I do not have the voices of those on the stairs," Death said, in the voice of the first man Andrew had ever killed. "If that would change anything now."

That had been a different situation, sadly. Then, Andrew and Tatiana had been quickly gone, not within reach when healing was finished. He could not count on that here, if he did less than kill the Teeth before him. Still, a warning was called for.

Andrew lifted the gun, braced it stable, though he needed few niceties of aiming with as close as the Teeth were getting. "Death will have the voice of anyone who stands between me and Silver."

Russia laughed, and none of the Teeth even hesitated.

So be it.

Dare looked so very little like himself, Silver's next breath choked her on the way in. Black hair, set expression, weapon raised up. She couldn't see the truth of that weapon, but her instincts remembered its danger, though the Teeth did not seem to. Did they think he wouldn't use it? Her Dare wouldn't have, but she couldn't see him in this one's eyes.

A smash of noise hit them all, much worse than it had been a few minutes ago, when the anthill had been kicked, bringing all the Teeth into the hall in chaos. The scent of blood was a caress, not a smash, attenuated by the distance across the room on uncertain air currents. One Tooth fell and Death raised his head and howled in a new voice.

They'd kill Dare, her Dare still even if he was more like the icon of Death at the moment. Silver's knuckles went white around the stupid silver goblet Russia had pressed upon her when she arrived, posturing with her as proxy as ever.

And that was the solution she needed. Another smash, leaving Silver unnoticed as she flicked her goblet empty, spattering the boards at their feet. Transfer her grip to the rim, and swing at Russia's face. Not with the body, as wide of a patch of pain as that might be—Russia had proved he little regarded pain.

No, she swung with the base, curved edge cutting into the space between brow and cheekbone. Two arms' strength, she had available to put into the blow now. The base sank in, sank deeper than she'd imagined, with a *squish* and a scent not of blood but of something else wet and salty like solidified tears.

Russia made a keening noise, a scream that would not listen to his orders either and so oozed free. She shouldn't have found joy in the sound, but, oh, she did. It was too quiet for her purposes of distraction, however, among the crashing of Dare's weapon and the screams of those who died. The Teeth focused on Dare as Death howled again and again. At least they weren't getting any additional orders from their alpha.

Russia caught her bad wrist, yanked her closer by it, chair arm digging into her belly. In her hands, the goblet was arrested, under his control so she could not swing again. She bared her blunt teeth at him, did not struggle or pull from the hold. His eye was an ugly, weeping wound, not even beginning to heal, and she did not fear him. "Your bones can break, Lady-touched," he snarled. "Each and every one."

He tightened his hold until the bones in her wrist felt near to creaking like tree branches in the wind that would soon tear them free. Silver gasped and her good hand spasmed open, leaving her bad to fall to her side, carried by the weight of the goblet.

But that was not the end, this time. Not after what Russia had done. Her muscles moved to her call and before Russia could realize his mistake, Silver slammed the goblet's base into his other eye. A little off-center this time, with less power behind it, but how deep did she truly need to go? The eye still burst.

This time Russia screamed.

He did not release his grip, but it was the work of a moment for her to break it herself, pull back. The nearest Teeth turned to her and Russia now, but that only gave Dare better targets in their backs. He was so close, now.

Dare's exultant shout reached her in a space of comparative quiet while Russia panted harshly against the pain and perhaps the despair of his blindness as well. "Seventeen!" Silver thought perhaps Dare had shouted so before, mostly beyond the reach of her attention in the chaos of it all. She did not understand what he meant.

She didn't understand the names Russia called her either, but she didn't need to. He found his English again between Dare's "eighteen" and "nineteen." "Why would you do this to me, cat?"

"You wanted this fight," Silver said, acid in her words. It seemed none of them would be coming out of it whole.

Andrew was terrible at watching his back, so Tatiana did it for him.

She saw the first Tooth fall, the red hole in her head, and then she was facing the wrong direction, and didn't look back. From the assault on her ears, Tatiana gathered Andrew was shooting each Tooth who approached, and from the fact he was still standing, she suspected he was doing so accurately.

That, and she could hear him counting, starting at ten. She was honestly thankful she couldn't see who was falling, put names to deaths. After the initial shock, the Teeth weren't stupid, they shoved backward, trying to circle around. But there was no back enough to get out of the gun's range—though perhaps there was enough to get out of Andrew's killing aim, she wasn't sure, and clearly they had not thought of such—not without completely abandoning their protection of Father.

For those who successfully circled to his back, she caught their blows, either on her own blades, or on her own skin, to save Andrew's. She'd never fought under the influence of wolfsbane before, and it was amazing, granting her the clarity to sink into the sheer dance of it all, blow and counter. Andrew moved steadily forward and Tatiana did too, one backward step at a time to keep her back against his and protect him always. He must have changed magazines, for there was a pause, then one rattled to the floor to their side, no less a noise in the stunned quiet between shots.

Then she couldn't hear anything else again, between the shots and the screech of metal on metal, an auditory component to her dance. Block—block—block—purely defensive, that was what they needed. Andrew knew where he was going, what his goal was, and she'd get him there.

Then his back was gone from her press against it. Up, she realized a split second later. Stepping up onto the dais. She jumped up beside him, dared a quick look around now the Teeth had fallen back from her for at least the space of this breath. No more Teeth on the dais, only two crumpled forms that did not move. No more Teeth between them and Father.

Andrew closed the distance in two strides, rested the gun against Father's temple, where Father was pressed down over his knees, hands covering his eyes. Blood and fluid had seeped out between his fingers.

On feeling the gun, he seemed to find and grasp hold of all the strength of charm that had let him keep a pack for over a century. He straightened, steel snapping into his back. Andrew moved the gun with him, to keep its target unwaveringly the same. Father lowered his hands slowly, exposing the ruin of his eyes, as if admitting to his injury were another kind of strength. He tipped his head very slightly to Andrew, perhaps verifying with scent his conclusions as to identity. "You kill me, boy, and my Teeth will tear you to pieces."

Andrew didn't seem to hear him. "Want to be twenty? That's a nice round number. I think twenty is a good number."

"You can't kill me or you'll doom yourself!" Father shouted it, desperation creeping in. In the new, shivering quiet of stalemate, Tatiana opened her focus outward. Silver had risen to her feet and radiated such calm in the midst of them all. She must have been the one to blind Father, but clearly she needed no violence now to command respect. Tatiana's own knives and sleeves were less crimson than she'd expected, fabric gashed in a few places and stained with her own blood. The metal of her blades would undoubtedly tell the tale in scratches instead.

Her father was correct, she began to realize, more viscerally with each passing second as the scent of the effort of will needed for the remaining Teeth to keep themselves back seeped into the air. If Andrew killed him, he wouldn't walk away.

"I don't think he cares about that, at the moment. I don't think he *can*, anymore," she told Father. Not without a lengthy period of recovery from the wolfsbane poisoning his system, warping his decisions. "Yield to him. Tell him he can take his wife and return home safely."

"And then he comes for us, for our people, later," Andrew snapped. He was worse off than Tatiana had realized. And he was absolutely correct as well. "Perhaps it's worth the trade, my life for his."

Lady save them all, Tatiana couldn't see how Andrew could be convinced to make any other choice.

22

"If someone stops this, it will be you," Death told Silver. He used the voice of one of the fallen, the too-many fallen all down the center of the room to either side of the path Dare had walked to come to this moment, standing with the Russian alpha's life in his hands.

Silver didn't know if she would be successful, but the Lady and Death both as her witnesses, she'd try. That trade of lives was not worth it.

Soft words, she decided. To begin this. There had been too much noise, and too much shouting, and now the silence was too tight. "Love," she said, and stepped up to her husband. "Don't kill him, love."

Dare did not look at her, though he laughed. "Haven't you heard? I'm Death-touched. Perhaps that means this is what I'm meant to do."

She didn't touch him yet. Not with the weapon in his hands.

"But you don't believe. That means to be Death-touched or even Lady-touched is meaningless. Make your own choice."

"Perhaps I should believe," Dare said. His words were getting softer, which was good.

"You're delusional, if you think Death—" That was Russia, who didn't know when he should be quiet.

"Your kind of power doesn't *work* in this situation, Konstantin," Irina said. Silver had lost track of her when Dare entered, so she must have withdrawn to a safe distance from the weapon. One of the few intelligent enough to do so. Now, she'd drifted right to the edge of the circle fear of Dare's weapon at the alpha's temple held clear. "You won't stay his hand with it. Her kind of power is what we need. Stop interfering."

Silver let a beat of silence pass, to regather her voice's softness. These were private things, but there was no privacy to be had here, and she needed to say them anyway. "When I met you, you put nearly everything you had into not believing. When I fell in love with you, you still did. None of the best parts about you have anything to do with belief in the Lady."

"My lack of belief hurt you," Dare said. So quiet, she had to come right up to him to hear it. Natural, then, to touch his back, to settle her hip against his. Russia must by necessity hear their words as well, but he stayed silent this time.

"No, love. It wasn't that you didn't believe; it was that you didn't share it with me. I suppose you were afraid I wouldn't understand how you couldn't believe? Well, it made it seem like you wouldn't understand how I *could.*"

"No!" Dare turned, finally taking his eyes from Russia. "That's who you are." Silver prayed with every tone of her voice that Russia wouldn't try to jump him, blind or not. Any vio-

lence now, and Dare would use the weapon, without even looking. *Stay still,* she urged him silently. *Please, if you love the Lady,
stay still.*

To think, she was begging such an enemy as he to save himself.

"I know. So it's all right now, love. You don't have to be
Death-touched anymore," Silver said. She spread her fingers
wide, lifted her hand to his shoulder blade to extend her touch
as widely as possible.

"Something must be done about Russia. For the safety of
our pack." His muscles were loosening, but not the ones in his
arm.

So. That was the point upon which this moment would
turn, from bad to good. Or not. Silver lofted her voice once
more, the work of softness done. "The alpha is stepping down,
so he will be able to threaten our pack no more." But step down
in favor of whom? Even before Death's attention pointed that
way, Silver could think of only one possibility. But it would not
do to force someone into such a role, by announcing it first,
leaving them to refuse—or wish to, and feel unable—under the
weight of so many eyes, of so much judgment.

She found Irina, caught her gaze and held it, to dominance—and then dipped her eyes away, ceding. Irina's lips went
white with her understanding of Silver's meaning, and she
dropped her chin, assent. Silver wondered if perhaps the stress
tightening up around her eyes also was due to dubiousness that
Silver could justify it.

In that, she would take a page from Death's book—speak
as though any who doubted it were embarrassingly slow. "His
mate will take his place, as he has planned for some time now."
Silver lifted her free arm wide to indicate Irina. Providential

once more, that both of them worked now so she need not break the connection with Dare.

"I never—" Russia began, heated, because of course he couldn't stay silent.

"You wish to die?" Silver asked. She was beginning to wonder, truly. He had no answer for that.

"Mates come and go. Better to call them all chases and be done. Why is she different?" someone asked from the back. Their doubts given voice, the Teeth edged forward, not to the point of casting their alpha's life and good sense to the wind yet, but close.

"Because of their child, of course." Silver gestured Tatiana forward. "Does he have any others, in truth, not in name? Certainly I have not heard of them if so."

Tatiana moved with excruciating reluctance to the center of the dais, but once she found her angle, she used it to its fullest. She sat in Silver's abandoned chair, copying some small details of her father's posture, angle to his chin, the resemblance hitting Silver like a slap now even knowing what she already did.

Russia twitched, then twisted his head once more, awkward in his cobbling together of sound and scent to track their movements. He grabbed at Tatiana's arm, found his way to a grip on her wrist. "Tatiana—?" Silver could guess at his next words by their cadence: "Daughter, help me."

"No," she said. She did not pull out of his grip, perhaps to avoid a scuffle that would disturb Dare, but she chose Dare's language, not her father's. He whispered, urgent, and Tatiana's lips whitened in their press together. "Don't I want a father? I *desperately* wanted a father, as a child. But a good alpha would have been enough, instead." And she peeled his fingers off her wrist, slow and steady until she was truly free of him.

"I am sorry that it needed to be said in such a way, but Konstantin and I have been planning this together, and it must be said eventually." Irina strode to take control of the center of everyone's attention; Tatiana reached over and pushed Dare's hand with the weapon aside, confiscated it when it was lower to the ground; and Silver pulled him away, toward the door behind the dais. To think things could move so apparently smoothly now, after those moments of terror for his life.

"Do you know, when Konstantin was born, the *city* where the Roanoke pack is based did not even *exist*? The land was still in the hands of the tribes that came before." Irina had switched to Old Were, but Tatiana provided translation to them in a smooth undertone. She was getting practiced at it. Her hands were empty now, but Silver did not bother to see where she had discarded the weapon. Such a thing should not be used again.

Irina said something to Russia in a harsh whisper, and he remained in his former throne, collapsing in on himself. Tatiana's laugh at hearing it was no less harsh, and she did not provide a translation until they were on the other side of the door. "My mother told him he's blind now, and likely to stay that way from what she knows of silver wounds, but if he'd prefer she can always cut out his tongue as well."

The door behind them, only just shut, opened again on Grace Zoya, her normally measured steps falling into a haste that Silver could never have imagined the priestess managing. "When the power transfer has sunk in, they will want Roanoke Dare's life in any case, to balance those they lost," she said through Tatiana, wasting not even a fraction of a second on the unfamiliar language as she herded all of them before her with arms open wide. "You must go now."

Out the back door into fresh air, but Dare was dragging them all with his refusal to hurry. He yawned, leaned more on his arm across Silver's shoulders than she'd ever known him to allow himself to do, short of grave injury. "Don't think it could hurt to catch a nap before we have to travel."

Grace Zoya lengthened her stride to circle around and stand in front of him as Silver brought them both to a stop on the graveled path between the hall and whatever point would launch their escape. She spoke an order Tatiana, already far ahead, was slow to notice and translate. "Exhale."

Dare blinked at her, but complied at length. The curse Grace Zoya hissed on smelling his breath needed no translation. "Too much, too long. If you sleep now, it is the last thing you do," she said, choosing her own words in English. She hauled back and slapped him, force enough to knock him into Silver so she had to brace her feet.

He growled, almost sounding like himself for a moment, then the sleepy droop settled back into his eyes. Not like himself, not at all, and Silver was only just now realizing it, thinking back to the way that he hadn't said anything as they left the hall, no greeting for her, no opinions to add to their general plans. Barely aware of his surroundings.

"What do we do?" she asked Grace Zoya. Lady grant there was something they *could* do. She could already tell the efficacy of blows would wane quickly.

"Come." Grace Zoya led the way at a slightly diverging angle this time, across grass since they had not chosen this path from the start. She conferred with Tatiana, heads together, and Silver gritted her teeth and did not disrupt them to demand her translation in process instead of all at the end as they obviously intended. Dare was heavy and kept trying to stop walking and lean his weight completely onto her.

"A little help?" she tossed to Death, and he deigned to shoulder Dare's wild self along. Less supportive, and more body-checking it each time it tried to lie down, but Silver didn't object.

When they arrived at the priestesses' house, Grace Zoya left them, to gather supplies, presumably. Tatiana closed the door behind them. Any explanation was delayed, as Dare pulled away from Silver, seeing a chair, and Tatiana darted to interpose herself. "No, don't let him sit down. Even something like that could be the last straw, at this point. Grace Zoya says the adrenaline of facing down Russia was holding back the effects of the accumulated wolfsbane, but she doesn't see we can hope to match that with anything else. Silver—I was supposed to be watching his doses, but he wouldn't let me—I should have insisted—"

"Dare! Stop." Silver slammed her hip into Dare's when he leaned too much again. It didn't do much, but Tatiana taking an arm to draw him away and balance him between them helped. "I don't care how it happened right now. What did Grace Zoya say? What can we do?" She'd thought she'd saved him, and now it seemed his life was in danger once more—to fall asleep and never wake up, or to fall asleep and fall to the Teeth who would be coming for him, there wasn't any difference to it. Lady, she wanted to fall sobbing herself.

"We have to drain as much of his blood as we can, because that will take much of the wolfsbane with it. We have to hope it will be enough. Grace Zoya says there's no guarantees." Tatiana's face was bleak. Silver suspected Grace Zoya had said something not quite that, even less hopeful.

She twisted to see Dare's face. His eyes were open, even

tracking her for a second, but his chin kept drifting down, for him to jerk it back up. Permission from that quarter would not be forthcoming.

"Do it," Silver said. If he slipped away, let him slip while they fought for him, not while they watched helplessly. And clean blood had done her good, perhaps it would him as well.

Grace Zoya was there, with a great metal bowl, too ornately engraved to be sullied by such a purpose as this, and a knife. A juggling of weight between Tatiana and Silver, and Tatiana held the bowl braced against her hip while Grace Zoya drew one of Dare's arms toward herself. Silver almost had to close her eyes against the unbalancing feeling of an echo, but her scars were—had been—above her elbow and when Grace Zoya had cut Dare's sleeve away, she deeply slashed her line down the center of his forearm. It welled up and closed, welled up and closed, what felt like a thousand cuts needed to reach through werewolf healing, however deep Grace Zoya went.

And the blood gathered in the bowl, each new stream throwing up spattery drops from that below like something mundane and not the pulse of life, filled with what had also been killing Dare. It *stank* so, the whole room, stank of prey that was failing soon, and Silver refused to listen to her instincts on that head.

Grace Zoya judged the level in the bowl, lifted her knife after a last cut, then tossed it to a nearby table, to clatter itself out of their way. The red line grudgingly sealed itself, leaving only the drying drips of previous flow. Grace Zoya took the bowl from Tatiana and bore it away, but slower than Silver would have liked. "And now clean blood?"

"What—?" Tatiana was confused on her own account, so there was a delay long enough to drive Silver wild before she started conveying real information from Grace Zoya again, called out in Old Were over her shoulder. "A healthy werewolf can heal from as much as she took, that's why she was measuring."

"But clean blood wouldn't hurt—"

Grace Zoya returned without the bowl, hands still wet from washing. "You can't spare any. From who, then? There are only the two of us. If we are not the correct type…" She gestured that they should let Dare down. "Let him rest now. He will heal and wake up, or he won't. He is in the Lady's hands. When he wakes, have him shift to heal faster."

Silver was *not done* with this argument, but the door slammed open on them under a kick from a Tooth, and she and Tatiana lost hold of Dare in their surprise. Silver managed to keep enough of a grip on his arm to change his fall to a folding up, and she went with him, ending kneeling at his back where he'd curled onto his side. His breaths were slow and his eyes were closed, as if in sleep.

Irina shoved her way in after the first Tooth, but she couldn't hold back all who were behind her. The first man snarled at all of them, and lifted his blades. "Step away, I not hurt you also."

Silver bowed her body over Dare's, as if she could cover enough. As if the Teeth wouldn't cut her too. "Death, please protect him," she begged, because she didn't see she had anything else left to do. Even if she'd had his weapon still, she didn't know how to see it, never mind use it.

"This last crisis does not turn on my decision, nor yield to my influence." She couldn't see him, but Death said it in the voice she thought of as his own, no hint of meaning in his choice there either. Whose decision did it turn on? Silver's? The Tooth's? Or was it the Lady's influence he meant?

If there was nothing left, then she would beg for that, then. With every part of her voice. Though she was barred from the Lady's presence, she had to believe She would still hear her, if weakly, at a distance. She ignored the words swirling around her, most of them in the language she could not understand, and focused on the softest possible words, between her and the Lady.

"If you can hear me—please, help me save my mate. He killed only because he felt he had to. I know he doesn't—that he doesn't honor you, but he is a good man, and I will praise you twice as loudly in his stead, and—" Her words were all of them inadequate, but Silver kept grasping after them anyway, to pull her pure emotion into something focused. "He did this for me, and I couldn't bear it if he loses his life because of that—I would do anything for *him*, anything at all, only I cannot see what it might be, and if you could only show me…"

She was crying and hadn't realized it until it made her words thin out until they were barely gasps. With no audible voice left, she sent her prayer to the Lady with her mind.

better any of Our children who have killed live on to atone, rather than add yet another voice to those lost. as for belief, if a Were does evil in Our name, is it not evil? if a Were does good not in Our name because he does not believe, is it not good?

The voice was not a voice, not sound, it was pure light. Light that entered Silver with each breath and filled her so full of love some leaked free in each tear, refracting that light as it fell. After so much loneliness since her wild self died, Silver longed to the depths of her voice to turn, to truly see the Lady's face, but a touch on her shoulder settled her to absolute stillness. That touch that was pure light as well.

you are not barred from Us, Silver, it is only that without your wild self, to see Us would cause you pain. We wished not to cause you this pain, but in holding back from you, We have caused you pain of a different sort. it is the way of this world, as Death and I know intimately, but We are sorry for it

Silver shook her head, putting the answer in her throat, unvoiced, as it seemed she had forgotten how to speak. Never should the Lady apologize to her.

but you have shouldered a far greater burden than many Were are asked to bear, and have done it with love. if you will lend Us your throat for a few tones of Our voice, We would grant you what small gift We can

Silver closed her eyes and tipped her head back, opening herself to whatever the Lady might wish. She was a Were, one of the Lady's children, and the Lady need never ask. Two touches, as if graceful hands alighted on both of Silver's shoulders.

"*You will use your teeth to rip out no more voices in Our name this night!*" Even a few tones of the Lady's voice shook Silver down to her bones, as if she had been gently lifted, shaken too fast to understand it had even occurred, and put down with all the substance of her transformed to something else by that movement. "*We wish to hear those voices used in joy, instead. Or sorrow. Anything but silence.*"

The Lady spoke one more phrase, and then she was gone and Silver collapsed over her mate, her new substance too newborn weak to hold her up. But the Lady was *not* entirely gone, not yet. Beneath her arms, still sleeping, Dare's wild self slid into place, fur ticklish against her skin.

And the Tooth's blades clattered to the floor, because his wild self could not hold them and Irina, and Grace Zoya, and indeed any Were Silver could see now had wild self uppermost, tangled in clothes as they were. After a frozen beat of shivering incomprehension, each brought their tame self back to the fore, by individual efforts that staggered the timing and served to underline how all had first shifted together.

And Dare grumble-growled in Silver's arms. On opening his eyes, he seemed to be frustrated by trying to see her with his wild self's eyes, so shifted back. "Silver. You're all right," he said distinctly, then let his head down to be pillowed on his arm. "Tired." And so, he slept again.

But not forever. Not for the last time. What might had been the last time had passed; he'd awakened and spoken to her. She gathered him into her arms. Both working arms. She would carry her mate just a little farther, to safety.

Tatiana could see Silver needed no help with Andrew—nor would have accepted any, if she had—so she snatched up his wedding ring from the floor one last time as she followed her mother and Silver outside. If only those crowded there were as stunned by the Lady's miracle as those inside, they might have a chance of slipping away.

As stunned as Tatiana was herself. She couldn't remember exactly what she'd seen, even so soon, but she remembered that she'd seen the Lady, that was incontrovertible, Her light so very bright directly behind Silver.

Far from assisting their escape, Tatiana's mother blocked

their way, and as Tatiana fetched up behind her, she realized why. The cabin's doorway must have formed a barrier both to sight and to the unexpected shift, as the Teeth ranged before them here were angry still. Shock washed amongst them as a visible ripple as those few Teeth who had seen gasped out explanations to those at the edges.

"Do not hinder those with the Lady's blessing!" Irina stood tall, Silver beside her with Andrew in her arms. Silver might have looked incongruous, even to eyes calibrated for Were strength, as even with all the strength in the world, a taller person made an unwieldy load. But no one so recently filled with the Lady, still glowing with the force of Her—and her own— love for her mate, could ever look incongruous.

Grace Zoya slipped by Tatiana to reach Irina's side. She spoke softly, but the kind of soft that carried, as all hushed and strained to catch it. "Truly, the Lady has given Her blessing also to our former alpha's successor." Tears stood out in her eyes as she placed both hands on Irina's shoulders as for a blessing, but did not sully that of the Goddess with a mortal one. Instead, she kissed Irina's hair, then stepped around to stand before her. In a smooth movement, braid curling at her side, she knelt— no, prostrated herself, ending with her forehead at the grass.

So too did everyone who had seen, who had shifted, and the other pack members massed beyond the Teeth took up the obeisance. Silver gave a little wavering gasp, half humor, perhaps, and whispered so only Tatiana and her mother could hear. "I remember this. Watch those who are last to give in, though they will not always be your worst trouble."

Tatiana's mother waited for all to kneel, and did watch and undoubtedly note those who had to look around first, be pushed upon by the pressure of the whole. Only then did she speak. "Those who have witnessed this miracle, tell it far and wide, that all might feel the brush of Her voice."

In the murmur that followed, growing rapidly louder and louder as those witnesses were interrogated before they could even begin to tell, Tatiana set her hand on Silver's back. Now was their time for slipping away.

She guided Silver to the cars, got the door open on the first in line, and helped Silver lay Andrew across the back seat. And of course she'd have to go with them, Silver couldn't drive. Tatiana didn't think beyond that, until her mother arrived as well, coming to a diffident stop about a meter away. Tatiana doubted it would last long, but this new, Lady-blessed alpha had a last space of privacy while the chaos was constrained to around the priestesses' cabin.

"I sent one of the children for your suitcases," her mother said. "Roanoke Silver mentioned trouble—I'm sure the Jaw will be mine. Those that didn't see Her will not be easily swayed out of their loyalty to Konstantin. I'll have to win them over gradually. If one or two decide to seek independent revenge—what I mean is, don't take the usual route to the airport. To set my mind at ease?"

"Of course." Tatiana rolled Andrew's ring against her opposite palm. "We'll be heading the other way to the coast, anyway. We have a different exit planned." When she looked up again, examined her mother, she was a little blank faced, probably due to delayed shock. Or it was settling in, the rough trail ahead to hang on to power. Tatiana knew she could, but no doubt it would take longer for her mother to believe it in the core of her voice.

One of them needed to move first, so Tatiana crossed the distance between them to close an embrace. "Perhaps a blessing is an interpretation, but it is incontrovertible, that the Lady chose you to see Her, not—" The word tasted wrong, but she needed to get used to it eventually. "Father."

Her mother gave a sob of breath. "You're right. I'll remember that." She clung very tight for a moment. "Say the word, you could be alpha, instead of me."

Tatiana had to pull back, a little jerkily, to see if her mother was being serious. Apparently she was. "I'm no alpha."

"That's what Silver said." Her mother smoothed her hair, clearly wishing she were in wolf to have a much better sweep available for such an endeavor. "Promise me on the Lady you'll visit."

"I'll come back!" The counter was instinctive. Such a strange feeling, to know in her voice once more that she *could*.

Her mother gave her a lopsided smile. "To visit," she appended, with finality.

And she was right, Tatiana admitted to herself. The truth of it seeped into the space the Lady's presence had opened up in her, where she'd been clenched so close to protect her voice from all the harms of the world and also the love in it. "Her name's Allison," she offered, because it seemed the right thing to say.

Her mother drew her close for a last time, until her visit. "Don't leave without saying goodbye to Alexei as well. I have to speak briefly to Roanoke Silver yet, myself." A pause, a sob of a breath. "And you, puppy: speak—" Or live; the word in Old Were had shades of both. "Not loudly, but richly." The Lady's blessing, delivered through Silver.

And spoken in Old Were, though Silver knew not a word of the language.

23

Andrew woke to breathing in ocean, while he and everything around him moved with a gentle rock. Which was an improvement on how he'd woken for nearly a week if not more. He seemed to come up more gently than he had for some time either, giving his mind time to assemble scattered impressions and present them as a full understanding. They were on Hugh's sailboat. He'd killed—Russia had abdicated. Silver's work, not his. And then things got very blurry. He must have come at least half awake before now, to use the facilities and eat, given that he didn't feel ready to storm into a galley somewhere and start tearing open packages with his teeth.

That did prompt a better survey of his surroundings, however. He was on a bed minimally wide enough for two in what must be the bow, as the walls narrowed in around it. He pushed to his feet, hand on one of the ubiquitous wood cupboards that covered every wall, or perhaps this piece was paneling instead, with boat parts on the other side. Somewhere was an engine, after all. He couldn't hear it at the moment, but he could smell the diesel. That, and Hugh *everywhere*. About all that was keeping his Were instincts in check at the moment was the fact that Silver had left traces around the little cabin. Probably on purpose, bless her. It wasn't a matter of dominance between the two of them, it was that this was Hugh's personal space, and he didn't particularly like the man.

Which should probably change, considering how he'd come through for them. Andrew ducked through a doorway, both low and narrow, into a larger area of the cabin, though large was strictly comparative. It had seating around a table bolted into the floor, and the galley Andrew had been thinking about earlier. He could see a second bed through another doorway, also dubiously double, and one of the closed doors would lead to the bathroom—or head, or whatever, Andrew didn't much care—and presumably some kind of engine access. His curiosity petered out, and he took a seat on of the bench-couches around the table.

"Ah, the sleeper awakes. I have strict orders to push food on you." Hugh himself came down the ladder from the deck, facing outward despite the lack of handholds past ceiling level. He looked wind ruffled and utterly himself in a way Andrew hadn't realized he hadn't looked, at the wedding. He banged around cupboards and in a small fridge, assembling ingredients including a carton of eggs and bacon and setting the resulting omelet to cook on the stove. "I'm taking us along hugging the coast. Makes for a gentler ride, and means we can stop for supplies more often. So we're a week or more out from Seattle yet. Having seen you when my daughter carried you aboard, I didn't think you'd mind the time to recover before anyone besides your annoying father-in-law sees you."

Silver carried—but that was physically impossible. Hugh must mean metaphorically. "Silver's all right—" It wasn't quite a question. If she was scent-marking around the cabin for him, she was clearly healthy enough to be up and about, but he couldn't make his instincts believe it.

"Silver is *fine*. You're the one worrying everyone." Hugh gave Andrew a rather sharp look as he carved up the omelet sufficiently to stack it on a plate and set it in front of him. "I hear you have the Lady's protection, and you rather *needed* it."

Andrew had no answer for that, and Hugh didn't seem to expect one. "Help yourself to whatever you can find in the cupboards once you finish that," he invited, and then disappeared back up on deck.

Once Andrew had inhaled the omelet, he opened doors until he found a bathroom with its tiny mirror. He remembered times when he'd felt considerably worse—like that time when he'd had to heal a broken back—but he had to admit he felt more tired throughout his entire body than any of those times. He also felt deeply unwashed, though his nose had turned off to any of the other signs of that. Rather than try to figure out if his face looked drawn, he set about an abbreviated wash instead.

When he lifted his face from scrubbing that, black dye trickled down between his fingers. He was wary of wasting too much water, but he wet his fingers anew and combed through his hair properly, more of the white streaks revealed at each temple with each swipe.

"You always were more hers than mine," Death said, visible behind Andrew in the mirror. The constrained dimensions of the space reflected oddly for Andrew, since he wasn't used to them, but Death seemed to break the reality of the small cabin even further, silhouette and especially his great, proud ruff and ears standing stark against the wood. No fading into shadows today.

"I sent you a lot of voices for one who isn't yours." Andrew clenched his hands on the edge of the basin as the weight of that truly settled onto his shoulders.

Death bared his teeth in a smile that held more humor than threat—barely. "And don't you forget them. I, however, know you won't, and thus I have no wish to hear you whine about your guilt. Don't be sorry, be better."

It was a familiar weight, at least, increased only slightly in degree, not kind. As he told Tatiana, he had his kills before now. And he wouldn't forget them.

But there was more than that, that he needed to say to Death. "I hope..." Andrew didn't have the words for what he felt, which was not strange, given he didn't know what he felt. "That I did you justice. That you're happy with what I said in your name."

"I," Death said, and laughed low enough to shake the world, "have the good fortune to care nothing for what anyone says of me, or does in my name. And you're getting soft, caring what a figment of your imagination thinks."

And there it was, the central knot of what Andrew no longer knew. "I'm still seeing you. I can't possibly have much wolfsbane left in my system—Lady knows I'm familiar with how it feels, now. And I saw you before the wolfsbane anyway." Hands still braced on the sink, he watched Death through the mirror instead of directly, because he needed that buffer right now.

"Proof of the divine just means you've abdicated your own reasoning." Death gave his teeth an exasperated snap. Andrew jumped. "Because it's not actually proof. Examine your memories point by point, and you'll discover no time when I told you more than you could already have known, or guessed. There is no *proof* I am more than a part of your own mind."

"And no proof you aren't." And that was—reassuring, though Andrew was not sure why. The world was as it always had been, and had not shifted beneath his feet. If he moved his position in reference to the world, it would be a choice he made.

"Good boy," Death murmured. He dipped a canine bow over his front legs. "And here is a further gift. I promise that when I am gone, you will see me but one more time in your life."

And when Andrew turned away from the mirror, he was alone in the cabin.

The boat—she'd worked hard to grasp and keep that word, then gave up on all the others her father tried to teach her about boat parts—was small enough Silver couldn't help but hear Dare was awake and talking to her father, but if she stood against the railing in the greatest flow of wind, she could avoid making out the words. She'd go down when her father came up, as there was no need to press three Were of their complicated relationships into such a small space. Three in a combination of friends or lovers, yes. Not a couple and father-in-law who still bore some slight burden of guilt Silver could smell, but couldn't quite figure out the basis of.

Her father came up and paused on his way past her for more of his round of boat adjustments. Tatiana sometimes got told to hang on to things for those, but Silver was excused on account of not seeing what she was working with. "I was thinking," he said, wind whipping up his short hair and making Silver simultaneously glad hers was long enough to fasten back and disappointed because she couldn't let it free because it would simply blind her rather than ruffling. "You two never got a honeymoon."

Silver shook her head. They'd had their wedding night, which was honestly more than she'd expected. Though even that seemed impossibly far back in her memories now. "When we get home—"

"If you really needed to be getting home fast, I should be dropping you off to travel some other way. Alaska can probably even send someone to pick you up from the dock." He laughed, seeing Silver's face. "Okay, not asking Alaska for anything at the moment. That's fair. But your husband needs to heal and you two haven't had a honeymoon. Why not enjoy the journey?" He held his arms wide, to water and sky with the proper gray of home and bluffs rumpled and spiked with green trees to their side.

"You realize you're inviting us to play chase in your house." Silver raised her brows at her father. She couldn't smell if he felt awkward, in this wind, but he certainly grinned like he didn't at all.

"Cabin," he corrected, and Silver let the word slide off. "And that's a sacrifice I'm prepared to make, for the sake of my daughter's happiness."

He was making something of a sacrifice already, him and Tatiana both as there was only one other bed, even if it had room for two who were friendly. He and Tatiana had worked something out privately, which involved one or the other of them spending the night in wolf, and might mean one slept on the floor, but Silver stayed out of it. "All right. I'll consider it permission if the mood is right," Silver finally allowed, laughing to dispel her own awkwardness as much as she could. Dare was healing yet, in any case. It didn't matter that Silver's mind had gone back to that wedding night now, all the power of the relief of still being alive coalescing around the memory of this caress or that, giving them a shivery electricity even in memory.

Her father moved off, looking pleased with himself. Silver went to the top of the ladder to the house, where she heard Dare washing up now. But she wanted to stuff her current mood back down again so he didn't smell it on her and feel pressured, so she turned aside for the moment. Tatiana had a position at the railing on the other side of the house, facing into the wind so her golden hair could stream free. She looked like an icon of someone dreaming of flying, her eyes closed and chin tilted up.

"I told my mother I was staying in North America, and only then thought about how I hadn't actually asked you two." Tatiana grounded herself in the mundanity of gathering up the last few mischievous tendrils of hair to fasten it back and allow her to face Silver on the railing beside her.

"We need a Russian liaison to cement our relationship with the Russian pack, once the new alpha has solidified her hold," Silver murmured. She'd have expected it to be a wrench, but thoughts of packs and business grounded her in the familiar as well. She did not think Irina's next few months would be smooth, but her pack was large, and within that would be a substantial number of Were to cling to routine once they could find it again. That, as she and Andrew had found, formed a good buffer against troublemakers. "As there is no competition for territory, there's no reason not to maintain cordial ties with the new alpha. And there will be translation needed sometimes, of course."

Tatiana cast Silver a look, sharpness layered over dawning hope. "Where would a liaison be in the pack hierarchy?"

"Answering to the alphas, of course. As for the sub-alphas—" Silver wavered her hand. "They prod and snap amongst themselves over precedence when they get bored and mostly we let them if it doesn't go too far. Stay out of that, and I think there shouldn't be an issue." Silver frowned, running through Were in her mind. "Don't wade into whatever pissing match Sacramento has with Reno at the moment—if there is one. But there nearly always is. She and Portland obviously have an amicable border."

"That's—" Tatiana shook her head after a moment. "Very generous. I can only thank you for it, Roanoke. I might end up living with you, though, if I can't make it work with Allison."

Silver put her hand to Tatiana's back, where her Mark no longer was. "We don't waste good talent, in Roanoke." None of her business, but she'd ask gently, and retreat if rebuffed. "You're going to try to make it work, then?"

Tatiana lifted her chin again. "Try *properly* this time. Now I'm in possession of all of my own secrets, maybe I can share them a bit more easily."

"I think that will make her very happy. Lady guide your trail in this, but I think you two are quite likely to find your balance now," Silver murmured. Now she couldn't wait a moment longer to check on Dare. With a nod of farewell to Tatiana, she let herself down the ladder into the house, holding on carefully at both sides.

Death watched her from the top, making no move to follow. The constrained space hadn't bothered him before, so she paused and gave him a questioning look. He laughed. "You'll arrive at chasing sooner or later, whatever you may think. I'm staying out of the way."

Dare was there when she reached the bottom, stepping into her so she fetched up against his chest. "Silver, your arm," he murmured in amazement. "Irina said that's what they'd been trying to do, but I guess it didn't really register. I must have seen you in the hall, but I don't remember. I was pretty out of my mind." He grimaced. "Not that that's an excuse for anything else I did."

Silver turned into him and lifted her formerly bad hand upward between them, letting him manipulate it however he wanted, testing her reactions. She'd moved her wedding ring to that hand, to match his, and he touched that too. "Irina wanted me to convey a message about that. She said, to be mercenary about it, you've done her a favor. The Teeth have always been so much the former alpha's creatures, isolated from everyone else…you've made her job easier. She plans to say that with you under the influence of the wolfsbane, your actions were practically the Lady's will, and she plans to repeat it loudly and often."

"Whatever its influence, I chose to take the wolfsbane." Andrew let a long breath trickle free. "What's done is done. And you're all right. Better, maybe."

She freed her hand from his and tried to touch each fingertip to thumb, not entirely successfully, but she opened and closed it several times to show she had a general grip at least. "I don't see any differently," she said carefully. She couldn't imagine Dare would object to that, but something in her wished, maybe a little, that her wild self would have been there to greet her on waking, not just the repaired muscles.

"I'm sorry," Dare offered, like he wasn't sure if she wanted him to be or not. She didn't know either. Whether they were sorry or not, it was true. He laid her hand, still palm up, over his, and rolled her sleeve up to where nothing remained now, no sign of her injuries after the borrowed blood, except in her mind and his memories.

"I put it to good use, carrying you." She laughed, seeing his face. "Ask Tatiana, if you don't believe me." She stepped into him now, taking her arm back, and feeling along the small of his back. "Tatiana also said she cut out the scars on your back for you." The touch might have edged into something more than that, but Dare didn't seem to read her interest properly. He turned, tugged up the hem of his shirt, clinical.

He'd gained those scars after meeting her, but not long after, and she'd never been skin to skin with him without them, the white, twisted runnels stretching in a bar from hip to hip. Now, smooth skin.

Both of their scars had hidden down somewhere deeper. Or perhaps it was better to say, both of their scars had healed to something lighter, as was the process sometimes in life.

"Silver, I need to talk to you." He took her hands—both her hands, though he still tugged rather more on the injured one, used to holding its weight for her—and pulled her with him as he sat on his bed. Their bed, as she'd shared with him each night since they'd been swimming, because there was too little space and because she needed the comfort though he'd been sleeping too deeply to notice her. "I need to apologize."

There was her answer, for why he hadn't reacted to her touch, Silver realized. He was wound much too tight, undoubtedly rehearsing the perfect words in his mind. She should perhaps have been rehearsing her perfect reply, because she found herself suddenly worried. What if he truly didn't understand, even now? She'd forgiven him already, yet it didn't seem fair to him or her to deny him the chance to say all he'd rehearsed.

She sat beside him, and kept hold of one of his hands. "Okay."

"I should have told you I saw Death. You were absolutely right, when you said that I was afraid you'd ask me how I could continue not to believe. And being an atheist was such a huge part of how I made it through life—I should have faced up to that squarely, questioned it if it needed to be questioned, but instead I took the coward's way out, and hurt you. It may have made it seem like I was putting up with your weakness, but I think it's been more than proved, in Russia, that you're putting up with *mine*, which I don't deserve, and never will. How you see the world is your strength, and I love you for it."

He paused in the rush of words, and Silver could see in his face that he would keep stumbling on for as long as she asked it of him, and she could turn the hurt the other way by doing so. She clenched her bad hand tight as she could around his. "To go to Russia, that was not a decision only for myself, but for you, and for our pack. I shouldn't have made it alone. Don't make me into a paragon in this." She laughed, unevenly. "I just escaped that."

"Promise," Dare said. He lifted her hand and kissed the knuckles, twitched as if waiting for some sound, some interruption that never came. "And now I'm not entirely used to him being gone. He said he'd only see me once more in my life—at the *end* of my life, I presume."

Silver bit her lip. Now Dare was sounding much more like he had with all the wolfsbane in his blood than the man she'd thought she knew. She didn't know what question to ask to figure that out, though, so she tried stating something instead, to see how he'd react. "Dare...you weren't aware at the time, but the Lady—She was *there*, when the Teeth were coming after you. She spoke through me, in Old Were, then made you and everyone in sight shift. Tatiana was there, she shifted too."

Dare nodded. Silver couldn't tell if it was in agreement with the Lady's literal presence, or only her experience of it. "With what you've said about feeling separated from Her, how do you feel now?"

Yes. That was the *right* question, Silver could feel it. Bless him. "I feel—" She closed eyes, the better to focus on it. "So much more balanced. To know She's there, there's no barrier at all, simply that She dims her light so as not to hurt me… and now I know what it is to have Her speak through me, and thus to *not* have her do so. Others may still not understand the difference, but I will."

"Good," Dare said, and brushed an errant white hair from her cheek with the side of his thumb.

But Silver was still worried, because she couldn't tell what he thought of it. "Tatiana also said the phrase in Old Were the Lady used—it's a common blessing, I could have heard it anywhere around the settlement, and not realized I remembered it. And I suppose if everyone *thought* the Lady was there, they could have shifted themselves…" Silver didn't really know how Dare's explanations for himself went, just that he always had them.

Dare searched her face, then his cleared with understanding. "Oh, love. I didn't mean to worry you. The wolfsbane is gone. But you want to know where I am now, with the Lady?"

"Please," Silver begged, and they both of them fell into laughter because they'd been too tightly wound not to fall apart a little with the relief of it when worries released.

Dare looked just past her, at nothing in particular, as he spoke. "I've spent a significant portion of my life, by now, working so *hard* at being an atheist. I needed that, then, but now I'm not sure it's worth the effort. Death himself told me there would never be proof either way, but that's not entirely true. There will be, at the end. Then, I'll find out for sure. Until that time, it's a matter of…patience, I think. Patience and the confidence to live with doubt. I think the closest human concept would be being agnostic."

"Well said," Silver could imagine Death saying, if he hadn't absented himself. It occurred to her that he might also have been giving them both space for this conversation as well as any chasing—which still seemed decidedly off the menu. "That sounds like a very good way to be happy, love," she told him, for herself, and his smile lit up his whole face.

Well. She could at least ask, Silver decided, when Dare moved to tuck his shirt back in. She pretended to help, slid her hand down to grab his ass instead. "You know, my father tells me I'm supposed to think of this as a honeymoon," she teased. Lightly. The answer might still be no.

"At least that way we know he's going to be making every effort not to hear," Dare said, and flopped back, trapping her hand underneath him. She didn't have to see how wicked his smile had turned, or smell his dawning arousal to recognize the first move in a chasing game suited to a small space.

He'd pretend surrender, she'd gloat—Silver straddled and leaned over him, braced high to withhold a kiss, then dart down to close it. A memory came to her suddenly, of the first time they'd ever played chase, when she hadn't had two arms to hold herself up, to spare one to lace the fingers into the white lock at his temple. Dare might have been remembering it too, as he curled a hand up her bad arm, feeling the shape of her engaged muscles.

Then he surged up, to "capture" her in turn. Laughing, Silver made it to the edge of the bed and to her feet, but Dare claimed one of her wrists and leaned back with all his weight against it. She braced her feet against the bottom of the bed, but only to delay, making him reel her in, hand over hand up her arm. She could feel his strength so viscerally with each movement, so familiar and so reassuring. When he drew her in close enough to set a hand to the back of her neck and hold her in for a kiss full of delicious promise of things to come, her hips arched into him of their own accord. *That* was the way to win the game. For both of them.

ACKNOWLEDGMENTS

When I was going to college in Bellingham, Washington, my friends and I got word of a special advance screening of the Firefly movie, Serenity. Seattle was sold out, so together we drove all the way down to Portland instead (five hours!). Before the movie began, they played a clip of Joss Whedon saying that Serenity owed its existence entirely to the fans: together, we were mighty.

I tell this story because the SILVER series is finishing entirely due to the fans. At the point when my original publisher dropped the series, Book 4 was already written—bringing it out myself was a pretty easy decision. Writing Book 5, of which only a few chapters already existed, was a much harder one. As I wavered, questions from fans came in: would there be a final book in the series? Or perhaps they were really asking: what was going to happen to their favorite characters? And I realized that though I knew in abstract how I planned to tie up those characters' stories, I also wanted the closure of writing an ending for the characters I'd spent a whole series with. So here it is, for all of us together, who are mighty.

My astoundingly amazing critique group, Corry L. Lee, Erin M. Evans, Kate Marshall, Monte Cook, Shanna Germain, and Susan Morris, offered keen suggestions on not just the manuscript but the outline and even the cover copy, as well as wise advice in general. Andrea Howe provided copy editing, and Kate Marshall cover design and formatting. Duane Wilkins at the University Bookstore and Peter Honigstock at Powell's have generously supported me and many other Pacific Northwest authors over the years. My agent, Cameron McClure, and

Katie Shea Boutillier assisted with making the audiobooks for this and the others series books a reality, through Anji Cornette and the amazing folks at Graphic Audio.

Other supporters are, as ever, too numerous to name, among my family and the local communities of speculative fiction writers, archaeologists, and choristers. Thank you all!

Read on for a sneak peek of Rhiannon Held's urban
fantasy in an exciting new world.

Mirror Bound

When Verity and Dakota approached the small park, Verity spotted three mantas immediately. To Verity's eyes, as a creature of the mirror realm herself, the mantas looked like spun glass, shimmering like liquid in the middle and refracting into rainbows at the edges. One manta spotted them and left the floating group to bank in their direction. It swerved off at the last moment, the tips of its long, flat wings rippling in a way that evoked the ocean-going animal it had been nicknamed for.

"Three," Verity called after Dakota as the woman jogged for the edge of the park where lawn met sidewalk along the road. They'd found a good location for this hunt: a patch of tall, urban forest abutted the park on two sides, and the back of a library formed the third, leaving only the sidewalk for Dakota to block off with an illusion.

The lazy orange cast to the sunlight, this late in the day, made Dakota look especially golden. It wasn't just the tint of her hair, but the confidence of her movements as she lifted one hand in acknowledgment of Verity's count. She paced along the concrete, dragging the glow of an illusion spell behind her. It would show caution tape, or something similar, Verity assumed, to keep people out as well as hiding the coming light show.

Verity planted herself on the lawn near the library and did a quick scan for innocent bystanders as Dakota worked. No one so far, after the library's closing time and in the middle of the dinner hour on a chill fall day. Good. Mantas could kill a human, in theory, if they caught one sufficiently unaware. The mantas who made it through to this realm tended to only bumble around, disoriented, and Dakota was paid to hunt them mostly to prevent panic from people encountering invisible monsters, but it never hurt to be careful.

The group of three mantas roiled as three more zipped in from the trees to join them. Six? There couldn't possibly be that many. In the mirror realm, the mantas traveled in flocks of up to ten, but only a few could slip through the boundary between realms at any time. Before tonight, the most Dakota had ever fought at once had been three. The anxious movement of the flock kept increasing until one broke free and buzzed right for Dakota's head as she returned from setting the illusion.

Her reactions were good enough that she sensed something was wrong and ducked what was to her an invisible presence before Verity finished shouting her warning. Dakota jerked out her modified paintball pistol as the manta swerved off. She settled into a looser stance, paintball pistol up, ready to burst into motion at the right moment.

When the manta curved back around toward her, she shot, missing it by only a narrow margin. The creature's dodge dipped it into a beam of the day's last sunlight that lanced between the shadows of two great evergreens. The light caught the manta, refracting into a flash visible even to human eyes. Dakota nailed the creature with a blue splotch square on the centerline of its body. The electricity spell bound to the paintball exploded with an audible pop and a singed smell. The manta dropped. One down.

Verity tucked her hands into the pockets of her hand-me-down fleece jacket and returned to her regular hunt role, keeping half an eye on the mantas, and another half out for approaching bystanders. Maybe she could convince Dakota to let her teleport them home after this hunt. It would save time, after all. None of the new team members Dakota had been accumulating lately could offer anything like it, either.

And the binding spell that kept her human, kept her under Dakota's control—however reluctant that control was—would shred just a tiny bit more in the act of teleporting. Verity glanced sideways at the library building. With the sun so low, one of the windows might provide the flawless reflection she needed.

She shouldn't let herself get distracted, though. Verity refocused on the mantas, which were twisting in an even tighter knot. Not only were there too many, but they were behaving strangely. They should have been floating in lazy arcs, senses disrupted by being outside the mirror realm. They'd adjust eventually, but the process took days for less intelligent monsters. These ones seemed riled up. Frightened?

Dakota brought an explosion spell into being in her hand. She tossed it up, and the bodies of the three closest mantas exploded briefly with bluish light, like shining a bright beam into a faceted crystal. Dakota squeezed off shots as fast as she could, trying to tag each one with paint even if she couldn't get the electricity burst central enough to drop them. Three went down in succession, and Verity called out to confirm the kills.

Shimmering movement in the trees caught Verity's attention. She shifted her position to try to get a better angle on it.

Had she lost track of one of the mantas? No, four on the ground, two in the air. But there *was* something there.

Verity broke into a run toward the trees. A jogging path revealed itself fully between two bushes as she approached it straight on. A woman, dressed in the blinding colors of fashionable athletic-wear, folded silently to the ground. A manta was spread across her face and upper body, another at her side, fouling whatever instinctive defense she might have attempted with her arms.

"No—" Verity wasn't sure why she shouted. The human couldn't hear her. The woman's brain was dark, the manta having eaten her living electricity even if she could have come back from the suffocation. But that wasn't *right*. In the mirror realm, mantas were a danger to those of her people who slept outdoors without precautions, but if one attacked you while you were aware, you could generally fight it off.

Then again, attacked by an invisible monster she didn't know existed, the human wouldn't have been very aware, Verity realized with a sick feeling.

Dakota whirled when Verity yelled and arrived a few steps behind her. The manta on the human's side took to the air, but Dakota shot the manta on the woman's face before it could rise off its prey, twice, three times. She fell to her knees and hauled the limp corpse off, pounded the woman's chest in a motion Verity vaguely recognized from television. Something to do with the heart, but of course the heart wasn't the problem. "Dakota, she's dead, you have to—"

Dakota gasped something inarticulately negative. Verity hauled at Dakota's shoulder, but the woman was apparently too much in shock to hear her. She kept pounding.

Verity fumbled out her own paintball gun from the back of